A CHRISTMAS KISS

"I apologize, Miss DiMarco," Richard said. "But when I saw Max kissing you, I thought—"

"You thought what?" demanded Alexandra. "That I had been encouraging him? Oh, but that is unjust, my lord! Unjust, and infamous, and vile."

Richard shook his head. "Now *you* are being unjust, Miss DiMarco," he said. "My thought was of something quite different, I assure you."

"Then what was it?" said Alexandra, looking up at him. He returned her gaze steadily, with an expression which she could not understand.

"You truly want to know?" he said at last. "Well, why not? I thought— I thought that I would like to kiss you myself, Miss DiMarco."

"Oh!" Alexandra exclaimed. She gazed at Richard blankly. He took a deliberate step toward her, laying his hands on her shoulders. A tremor went through her body, but she did not make any protest. She only went on gazing up at him with wide, dark-fringed eyes. Their beauty acted on Richard like a powerful intoxicant. Gathering her in his arms, he lowered his lips to hers.

A thousand thoughts went through Alexandra's head in that instant. She reflected that the whole situation, which had been like a nightmare a short while ago, now seemed like a dream—an impossibly lovely dream from which she feared she might awake at any moment.

Books by Joy Reed

AN INCONVENIENT ENGAGEMENT
TWELFTH NIGHT
THE SEDUCTION OF LADY CARROLL
MIDSUMMER MOON
LORD WYLAND TAKES A WIFE
THE DUKE AND MISS DENNY
A HOME FOR THE HOLIDAYS

Published by Zebra Books

A HOME FOR THE HOLIDAYS

JOY REED

Zebra Books
Kensington Publishing Corp.
http://www.zebrabooks.com

For Angela

ZEBRA BOOKS are published by

Kensington Publishing Corp.
850 Third Avenue
New York, NY 10022

Zebra and the Z logo Reg. U.S. Pat. & TM Off.

First Printing: December, 1998
10 9 8 7 6 5 4 3 2 1

Printed in the United States of America

ONE

From the moment of her birth, Alexandra Elizabeth Manning DiMarco was accustomed to the best of everything.

She had not, it is true, a mother. Contessa DiMarco, born Miss Elizabeth Manning of Mannington, Wiltshire, had unfortunately possessed a most sickly constitution and had capped a lifelong series of indispositions by dying shortly after giving birth to her daughter. Nor did Alexandra have a father, for that gentleman, a youthful sprig of Italian nobility, had in the twenty-third year of his life managed to get himself killed in an argument over a card game, predeceasing his wife by several months and perhaps contributing to her early demise.

Given these sad occurrences, the orphaned Alexandra was fortunate in possessing a great-aunt and -uncle such as Mr. and Mrs. Frederick Manning. The Mannings, having raised her mother from a child, were disposed to regard Alexandra as their own grandchild, and they were in a rather better position to provide for her than her natural parents.

There were no lengths to which these two fond people would not go to see their grandniece happy, healthy, and well provided for. A cradle of the latest hygienic design graced the spacious and airy apartment that served as her nursery. Woolen blankets and linen sheets were determined to be insufficiently fine for the infant Alexandra. Only silk would do, and then only silk of the best quality. Her wet nurse was no common country lass, but rather a lady of refinement and breeding. Alexandra's great-uncle had strong opinions about the rearing of children, and one of his strongest opinions was that more was received from mother's milk than mere nourishment. Therefore Alexandra's wet nurse was a young matron of aristocratic family who, owing to the exigencies of an improvident husband, was only too willing to suckle Alexandra along with her own offspring.

As Alexandra grew older, her great-aunt and -uncle were careful to see that the development of her mind received as much attention as the development of her body. She was attended by a French maid, so that her baby lips might early learn to lisp with the true Parisian pronunciation. She had a German nanny to instruct her in the intricacies of that language and to provide her with the discipline which her great-uncle (himself a man of German ancestry) believed no other race could so well supply.

From an early age she had also Italian masters whose duty it was to tutor her in music, dancing, and the Italian tongue. Her great-aunt and -uncle were naturally preju- diced against Italians, considering (quite fairly) that Alex- andra's father had been responsible for stealing their cherished niece away from them. Rather less fairly, they tended to visit the late Conte DiMarco's sins upon all per- sons of Italian nationality. But even so, they were unwilling to deprive their niece's daughter of any part of the edu- cation which a lady ought to possess. Alexandra was there- fore schooled in Italian, in addition to French, German, the rudiments of Greek and Latin, and an ambitious cur- riculum that included Philosophy, Geography, Mathemat- ics, and History.

Lest too much study take a toll on her constitution, Al- exandra's lessons were carefully interspersed with sessions of physical activity. "One must exercise the body as well as the mind, my dear," was one of her great-uncle's frequent exhortations. "A brisk walk in the park after breakfast—a ride in the afternoon before you change for dinner—and perhaps a session with the dumbbells or India-clubs on the days you have no dancing lessons. That is the regimen I recommend to keep you bursting with health."

It could not be denied that this regimen had done a good deal to keep Alexandra "bursting with health" throughout her childhood and adolescence. A good deal more was owed to Trudy, the German nurse who was Alexandra's chief caretaker. Trudy had ideas as decided as Mr. Manning's upon the subject of rearing children, and quite a bit more practical experience. She took it upon herself to moderate Mr Manning's orders whenever she judged them harmful or excessive, and she quietly disposed of the quantities of patent medicine which Alexandra's great-aunt anxiously pressed upon her, under the delusion that her health needed bolstering up.

"For myself, I think there is harm in taking much medicine," Trudy would explain to Alexandra, as she emptied a bottle of Dr. Davis's Exceptional Elixir or Professor Peterson's Patent Pills into the slop bucket. "Fresh air, and good food, and exercise in plenty—those to me are the best medicines. Your aunt, she means well, I know, so we will not distress her by refusing her gift, *ja?* We will merely dispose of him, so—and then nobody need suffer. Do you now go down to the Music Room, Miss Alexandra. Signor Richetti will be waiting to give you your voice lesson."

Of all the various lessons and activities that filled Alexandra's busy days, it was her music lessons that she enjoyed most. She had a natural love and aptitude for music, perhaps inherited from her Italian father. This aptitude she tended to hide from her great-aunt and -uncle, for reasons that had partly to do with a certain diffidence about performing for others and even more to do with the kind of reception her performances invariably received. Alexandra had often, as a child, played for her great-aunt and -uncle some hard-learned piece, only to have it greeted by a tepid, "That was not ill-done, my dear. But I think—correct me if I am wrong, Frederick—I think perhaps the fingering was just a *little* off toward the end." Or, even more frustratingly, her great-uncle would chime in with a condescending, "Very nice, I'm sure, my dear. I have no doubt you will play excellently someday if only you apply yourself a little harder."

It was not that she minded criticism, as Alexandra assured herself. She endured frequent and voluble criticism from Signor Richetti, who was apt to become quite emotional when a piece was ill-rendered in his hearing. But his criticisms, however vituperative, were always justified, while her great-aunt and -uncle's were not. The plain fact was that they knew little about music and cared even less. So Alexandra began to make excuses when they asked her to sing or play for them, and to do most of her performing and practicing in private. The fact that her great-aunt and -uncle never seemed to miss her musical performances only added to her determination henceforth to perform for no one but Signor Richetti.

It was indeed this lack of musical appreciation that first made Alexandra see Mr. and Mrs. Manning as something other than the infallible creatures she had imagined them as a child. As time went on, she began to perceive other failings in her near relations. Her great-uncle was prone to reject any opinion not his own, without first considering whether or not it might possess merits. Her great-aunt was too much inclined to put her faith in quacks, plausible clergymen, and her husband's opinions. And both her great-aunt and -uncle were fond of espousing principles they did not actually practice.

This tendency was particularly pronounced at mealtimes. "Alexandra, you are not eating. Take a little soup, I pray you," her great-uncle would say. Overruling Alexandra's protests that she wanted no soup, her uncle would proceed to fill a generous plateful and hand it to his butler. "Rogers, give Miss Alexandra her soup," he would say, and the butler, with a sympathetic glance at Alexandra, would obediently set the soup-plate in front of her.

"You must eat your soup, Alexandra," her great-uncle would then tell her, as she stared rebelliously at her unwanted plate. "Soup is a very healthful food. You know your aunt and I make no demands upon you which are not for your own good. There is nothing better for the health than a well-made clear soup, and I do not believe in catering to children's whims in the matter of diet. Therefore, before you leave the table, I must insist that you eat every drop of your soup."

Yet Alexandra learned early on that such statements need not be taken at face value. She had only to toy with the contents of her soup plate for a few minutes, and before long her great-aunt or -uncle would grow concerned, order her plate to be removed, and attempt to entice her with some more palatable dish.

There were many such contradictions in Alexandra's upbringing. She was petted and indulged on one hand, yet expected to excel at a course of study as demanding as any university student's. She was continually being urged to develop qualities of independence and self-discipline, only to find, when she tried to exert such qualities, that her great-aunt and -uncle invariably found some way to thwart her.

The effects of such an upbringing might have been ruinous indeed, had it not been for two factors. One was the devoted Trudy, whose affection for Alexandra did not prevent her from administering a much more evenhanded discipline than that practiced by Mr. and Mrs. Manning. The other factor was Alexandra's own native intelligence.

As the years went by, and her mind expanded under the influence of education, she came to see that her relatives were lacking both in common sense and proportion. This made her love them nonetheless, of course, but as time went on, her love came more and more to be tempered with irritation.

Most irritating of all, without doubt, was the constant, anxious surveillance that her great-aunt and -uncle kept on her. Part of this was prompted by simple concern for her health. Alexandra supposed such concern was natural enough, given their experience with her mother's sickly constitution, but it was exasperating to a child who had always enjoyed perfect health.

And anxiety about their niece's health was not the sole motive for the Mannings' surveillance. As Alexandra grew older, it began to dawn upon her what a cloistered life she led in comparison with other girls her age. Her great-aunt and -uncle rarely socialized, and then only with people their own age. They did not even go to church, preferring the expense of keeping a private chaplain in their household. They disliked Alexandra to go out riding or walking beyond the bounds of their own property, and when she did, they always questioned her closely about what persons she had met and what conversation she had had with them.

The reason for this, as Alexandra soon realized, again had its roots in the Mannings' experience with her mother. Having had one adopted daughter stolen away from them, they were determined to see that no repetition of the incident should occur. Alexandra would have no opportunity to meet and marry a handsome scoundrel, as her mother had done. The Mannings' resentment toward the late Giovanni Baptista Alessandro DiMarco remained fresh as ever, even after Alexandra had reached the age of putting up her hair and letting down her skirts. By her relatives' wish she was known as Miss Manning instead of Miss Di-Marco, and it was only a scrupulous respect for her mother's dying wish that had impelled them to call her after the Christian name of the man they despised so heartily.

Alexandra could understand such feelings, but they were aggravating to her nonetheless. No child liked feeling spied upon, and an adolescent was apt to rebel outright against such treatment. Alexandra's rebellion took a more subtle form. She could not escape outwardly from the watch that was kept on her, so she escaped inwardly: through her music, which she continued to love and practice diligently, and through reading. Her great-uncle possessed, among other assets, an extensive library containing many thousands of volumes. By the time she had reached her majority, Alexandra had read and digested an impressive amount of history, biography, poetry, and philosophy, not to mention dozens of more or less well-written novels.

The result was that Alexandra Manning, at the age of twenty-one, was a most formidably educated young woman. Her solitary reading, in combination with her rigorous formal education, had given her a knowledge of the world both extensive and diverse. The problem was that almost all of her knowledge was theoretical. Alexandra herself was vaguely aware of the deficiencies of her education, and this awareness manifested itself in a growing sense of restlessness and discontent as she grew older. She began to alarm her great-aunt and -uncle by talking about traveling: perhaps going to Scotland and the Lake District, or even farther afield, to France, Italy, and Switzerland.

"I don't see why we shouldn't take a trip this autumn," said Alexandra at dinner one evening, broaching the subject for perhaps the fiftieth time that week. She and her great-aunt and -uncle were seated at the dinner table, and Alexandra had been extolling the beauty of the Lake District as described by Gilpin and Wordsworth. She refused an offer of fish tendered by one of the footmen, then resumed her address to her great-aunt and -uncle. "It's a lovely time of year for traveling—past the heat of summer, but not yet really cold. And I doubt we would be more than a day on the road."

"Travel all the way to Cumberland in a single day!" said Mrs. Manning with an eloquent shudder. "My dear child, I am sure such a journey would knock me up completely! And I am sure it would be very bad for you, too. You know what delicate health you enjoy. She had much better not think of such a thing, hadn't she, Frederick?"

Alexandra's great-uncle did not immediately reply to this speech, being occupied in recalling the footman with the platter of fish and instructing him to serve his grand-niece from its contents. He then gave his attention to his wife's question.

"Bad for her? Yes, to be sure, such a journey would be very bad for her. It would be very bad for us all, if it comes to that. The idea is not to be thought of, Alexandra. Why should we want to rattle ourselves to pieces in a carriage all the way to Cumberland and then run the risk of picking up an illness in some badly aired inn room? Much better we should stop comfortably here at home."

"I don't want to stop comfortably at home," said Alexandra, poking resentfully at her unwanted fish. "I want to see the Lakes. And even more, I would like to see France and Italy and Switzerland. And I don't in the least see why we shouldn't see them. You spoke of buying me a set of sapphires like the ones Aunt and I admired in last month's *La Belle Assemblée*. If you were to take the money instead and use it for a journey—"

"Out of the question, my dear." Her great-uncle spoke with finality. "There will be no journeying for any of us this fall, or indeed anytime in the near future." With a smile intended to soften the severity of his refusal, he continued: "Children have these whims, I know, but I assure you that you will do much better in resigning yourself to stay at home, Alexandra. Your health is still in a very delicate state, and of course you have your studies to attend to. When you are older, you will see the wisdom in what I am saying."

As a clincher to these arguments, or perhaps merely as a bribe to secure Alexandra's submission, her great-uncle presented her with the promised sapphires the following day. Alexandra naturally was pleased with this gift, but as she stood in her bedchamber that evening, regarding her sapphire-adorned reflection in the looking glass, she told herself that she would much rather have seen the Lakes, or France, Italy, and Switzerland.

"Quelle belle toilette! You look very lovely, miss," exclaimed Marie, the French maid who had attended Alexandra since she was a child. She began to take down her mistress's hair, shaking her head with professional regret all the while. "It is a pity there is no one but Monsieur and Madame Manning to admire you. In Paris or London no doubt you would cause a great sensation—but alas, I know Monsieur and Madame's prejudices too well."

Alexandra nodded sadly. She, too, knew Mr. and Mrs. Manning's prejudices only too well. As Marie put away the comb and brushes and went to pour water in the wash-stand, Alexandra turned again to survey her reflection in the glass. What she saw was a slender girl, slightly over medium height, dressed in a robe of cerulean blue taffeta worn over a white satin petticoat. A necklace and earrings of diamond-encircled sapphires glinted around the girl's neck and in her ears. White satin sandals adorned her feet, and long white gloves completed the toilette.

As for the rest of the girl's reflection, Alexandra spared it hardly a glance. Her own face was too well known to her to be of much interest, and in fact she had been brought up to think modestly of her looks. Her great-aunt and -uncle frequently praised her in her own hearing as a pretty girl, but since they invariably added a remark to the effect that she could never hold a candle to her mother's beauty, Alexandra was in no danger of becoming vain through such praise. Indeed, knowing how partial was her relatives' judgment—and knowing, too, their tendency to criticize what was good and praise what was faulty—she was more inclined to discount their compliments altogether and think of her looks as passing at best.

This was a palpable injustice. Marie had spoken no more than the truth when she had praised her mistress's beauty. Alexandra had inherited her English mother's honey-colored hair and deep-blue eyes, but she also had her Italian father's dark brows and long lashes, which served to make the blue of her eyes appear yet more vivid. From her father also she had inherited a certain un-English richness of complexion and a faint, exotic cast of feature that was as difficult to define as it was attractive. Her appearance overall might not be so conventionally beautiful as her mother's had been, but it was a good deal more striking and unusual.

Marie, as she helped her mistress remove her dress and jewels, reflected once again what a waste it was that so much loveliness should "blush unseen on the desert air." It seemed to her Gallic nature almost a crime that Alexandra should have no suitors to admire her. She could only wonder at her young mistress's stoical acceptance of her solitary state.

Had she but known it, Alexandra at that moment was feeling far from stoical. She was not repining her lack of suitors exactly, but it did seem strange to her that at the age of twenty-one she was kept immured in the schoolroom as though she were still a child. Obviously her greataunt and -uncle still thought her a child—but she was not a child, Alexandra told herself defiantly, looking at her reflection in the mirror. She was fully of age now, and it was time she set about gaining some firsthand acquaintance with the world, instead of learning about it secondhand through books.

As Alexandra changed into her nightdress and made her preparations for bed, she continued to brood about the iniquities of her position. For a while she played with the idea of escape. If she only had the nerve, she might leave this very night and be miles away by the time her great-aunt and -uncle discovered her absence. She had some money of her own, she knew—indeed, from the Mannings she had gathered that she was a considerable heiress, but she was uncertain if her inheritance was derived from her parents' estates or from the Mannings' own fortune. If from the latter, then of course she could not count on it as a means of dependence. But in her current mood, Alexandra felt she would prefer to be penniless and independent rather than continue in her present luxurious servitude.

Such reflections were only a diversion, however. Much as she longed to escape, Alexandra knew in her heart that she could never abandon her great-aunt and -uncle. They had not yet recovered from her mother's abandonment, and that had taken place more than twenty-two years ago. At their present age, Alexandra feared that another such blow might very well prove fatal. "And I love Uncle Frederick and Aunt Elizabeth," Alexandra told herself, as she lay in bed that night, meditating on her difficulties. It was only that she longed for something more than the unvarying routine of her present existence.

Sighing, Alexandra turned on her side and closed her eyes. As she composed herself for sleep, she addressed a last, silent plea to the powers above. "Dear God, let something happen," she prayed. "Something—anything—I don't care what it is. Only let something different happen for a change. A little change, dear Lord, that's all I ask . . . just a little change." And having conscientiously added a postscript that the change should not affect in any way her great-aunt and -uncle's health and happiness, she fell asleep.

TWO

Alexandra's prayer was answered with astonishing rapidity. When Marie brought in her chocolate the next morning, she brought also a piece of news as unexpected as it was alarming.

"Madame Manning is ill," announced Marie, as she set the tray with the chocolate across Alexandra's knees. "The apothecary has already called twice, and Monsieur Manning has sent for Dr. Trent. Poor Madame, she is quite unwell, they say. Hortense and Annie were up with her all night."

"My aunt, ill?" said Alexandra. Her mind flew guiltily to the prayer she had made last night. Here was change, to be sure, but change in a most unwelcome form. She had never meant to bring suffering upon her great-aunt, she assured herself unhappily, stirring her unwanted chocolate. Setting it and the tray aside, she got out of bed.

"Never mind the chocolate, Marie. I must go to my aunt."

Marie, however, opposed this idea with determination. She was supported by Trudy, who had come into the room in time to hear the last part of the argument. "Go to your aunt? No, indeed, Miss Alexandra. Your aunt has given very specific orders that you are to go nowhere near her. The doctor thinks it is the influenza, you see, and both your great-aunt and -uncle are determined that you should not take it, too. If you do not intend to drink your chocolate, then let Marie help you with your dress, and you can go down to breakfast with your uncle."

At breakfast, Alexandra received a further shock. Her uncle was there, attended as usual by his chaplain and steward, but his normally ruddy face was wan and heavy-eyed. He tried to pass this off as merely the effects of sleeplessness. "To be sure, your aunt is very ill, Alexandra, but the doctor and I are certain that she will recover completely with time and proper nursing. This need not affect you and your studies at all. I myself am not ill, fortunately—"

Here Mr. Manning fell into a prolonged fit of coughing. When it was over, however, he went on again with ponderous determination: "I myself am not ill, and I am determined that this illness of your aunt's should not affect the routine of the household more than it must. Discipline and self-control are the cornerstones to all success and happiness in life, as you must know, Alexandra. Of course your aunt's constitution is delicate, like all women's, but I myself have always made it a point never to allow myself to succumb to illness in any form. Therefore, I plan to supervise your studies just as I always do. You may come to the library after you have your morning walk, and I will hear you read your lessons in Philosophy, History, and Mathematics."

But before the morning was over, Mr. Manning was forced to abandon this plan. He, like his wife, took to his bed, and the doctor, upon being hastily sent for, confirmed that Frederick, too, had the influenza.

Alexandra, now seriously alarmed, refused to heed Trudy and Marie's earnest pleas that she not expose herself to illness. Late that afternoon, she presented herself in her great-aunt's bedchamber to see if there was anything she might do herself to relieve her aunt's sufferings. She found her great-aunt lying in bed, a most elegant lace cap adorning her silver curls, but her face touchingly drawn and pale. Her aunt's maid, Hortense, was busily burning pastilles, while another maidservant was bustling about attending to the fire and making tea on the hob.

The wan expression on Mrs. Manning's face changed to one of lively horror as soon as she saw Alexandra. "No, no!" she shrieked, sitting up in bed and signing frantically for Alexandra to come no nearer. "Alexandra dear, stay just where you are, I beg of you. Hortense, bring those pastilles over here—just waft the smoke in Miss Alexandra's direction, if you please. Thank you, that will do very well. Alexandra dear, you ought not to be here. I gave very particular orders that you were not to be admitted under any circumstances. Not that I am not very glad to see you, my dear, but you must know that my only concern is for your health. I would never forgive myself if you were to take this nasty infection and become ill, too."

"I don't care a penny for that," said Alexandra stubbornly. "And I doubt I will become ill in any case. Despite what you and my uncle like to believe, I am healthy as a horse. And if there is anything I can do to make you more comfortable—"

"No, indeed, my dear. Hortense and Annie can tend me perfectly well. There is no need for you to come anywhere near. Indeed, I would very much rather you did not." Mrs. Manning accepted a draught from the solicitous Hortense, drank it, then turned watery but determined eyes on her grand-niece. "I have been thinking, Alexandra dear. You know your uncle and I would never forgive ourselves if we were the cause of undermining your health. I believe the best thing to do, under the circumstances, is to send you to my sister in Tunbridge Wells for a month or two."

"You mean to send me to Aunt Emily?" said Alexandra in astonishment.

"I believe it would be best, Alexandra dear. I know Emily

would take every precaution for your health, just as we would. Of course, I do not like the idea of sending you alone on such a long journey." Mrs. Manning surveyed her grand-niece dubiously. "You are very young to be traveling without a chaperone, but of course Marie and Trudy would accompany you to Wells and see that you were no charge on Emily's servants. And with our dear old William to drive you, I am sure you would come to no harm. William is so steady! I would trust him a hundred times rather than one of these younger men."

Alexandra opened her mouth, then closed it again. She knew for a fact that at that moment William lay groaning on his sickbed, a victim to the same illness that had stricken his master and mistress. Yet she thought it better not to distress Mrs. Manning with this detail. In truth, she was so overcome by the plan her great-aunt had so matter-of-factly outlined to her, that she could scarcely speak at all.

She, to go to Tunbridge Wells! And to go alone, too, or as good as alone, with only Trudy and Marie to bear her company! In all her twenty-one years, Alexandra had never been farther afield than Mannington-on-the Marsh, the village that lay just beyond the gates of her great-aunt and -uncle's property. The prospect of a carriage journey of a hundred miles, with stops at inns and a stay of some months, perhaps, in the new and unknown town of Tunbridge Wells, was as exciting as her great-aunt blandly proposing that she visit the Sandwich Islands.

To be sure, the idea of staying with her great-aunt Emily was a less exciting prospect. Aunt Emily had not been a frequent visitor at Mannington through the years, but she had been there often enough to imbue Alexandra with a strong dislike for her character. Aunt Emily was as fussy about her own health as the Mannings were about Alexandra's, and with almost as little reason. She was never too sick to do what she wished to do. The only time illness intervened was when she was called on to perform some action she found uncongenial. Her disposition was nervous and fretful; she was an incessant complainer and finder of fault; and such affections as she possessed appeared to be lavished wholly upon her fat, wheezy pug dog, whose disposition bore a strong resemblance to her own.

But all these disadvantages seemed of little moment to Alexandra when compared to the prospect of travel, freedom, and adventure. That the travel would be brief, the freedom only comparative, and the adventure of the very mildest sort did not matter. Her soul rose up rejoicing when she thought of escaping the tedium of existence at Mannington. Indeed, she was so rejoiced, that she began to feel guilty for obtaining pleasure at the cost of her greataunt and -uncle's health. Overcome by self-reproach, she went to the doctor and begged him to let her stay and help nurse the invalids back to health.

This the doctor refused to do, however: "I'm sure your feelings do you great credit, Miss Manning," he said, looking at her kindly over his spectacles, "but you must know that your staying here would do your great-aunt and -uncle more harm than good. They would only fret about your taking the illness, and perhaps make themselves sicker in the process. Much better you should humor them by taking this trip they speak of. I promise I'll let you know if their illness should take a turn for the worse. But I don't anticipate it. For their age, they are both in very fair health."

With this promise Alexandra had to be content. The doctor smiled and patted her shoulder. "You're a sensible girl, I know, and so you won't let yourself feel injured about being shut out of the sickroom," he told her. "Bless you, if your great-aunt and -uncle didn't care so much about you, they wouldn't be frantic to send you away. Just you go off to Wells and have a nice time for a month or two. Try drinking the waters—go dancing at the local assemblies—and don't worry yourself about what's passing here. That's my prescription for *you,* Miss Manning, and I advise you to take it." The doctor laughed heartily at his own joke.

Alexandra smiled politely. She was still dubious about the propriety of enjoying herself while her great-aunt and -uncle lay ill, but the worst of her qualms were set to rest by the doctor's words. He clearly felt that she would do more harm than good by staying, and so there seemed nothing wrong about trying his jocular prescription for the next month or two. Remembering her great-aunt Emily's disposition, however, she doubted that she would be attending many assemblies during her stay in Tunbridge Wells. Aunt Emily's ideas of suitable evening entertainment were probably a good deal more sedate.

But at the very worst they could hardly be more sedate than those prevailing at Mannington; even if she never attended a single assembly, she would still have the pleasure of seeing new places and people and gaining some firsthand experience of the world. Alexandra's heart leaped at the thought of trying her wings for the first time away from her great-aunt and -uncle's anxious surveillance. She hurried back to her own rooms to tell Trudy and Marie the great news.

A flurry of activity followed this announcement. A footman was dispatched to Tunbridge Wells on a fast horse to inform Aunt Emily of her grandniece's imminent arrival. Marie and Trudy devoted themselves to packing up Alexandra's belongings, quarreling amiably as to what she would find necessary during her stay with her great-aunt. Neither of them judged her sapphires or her blue taffeta evening dress necessary, but at the last minute Alexandra packed them herself, reflecting that her great-aunt might—just might—plan on attending a formal party during the next few weeks. If so, she reasoned, it would do well to be ready for it, instead of trusting to a local dress-maker!

By eight o'clock the next morning, all was ready. In Alexandra's reticule were fifty pounds in gold her uncle had given her, via his steward, for travel expenses. He had sent an affectionate message along with the money, bidding her to be a good girl and instructing her to draw on his banker for any additional funds she might need during her stay with Aunt Emily. Alexandra's fur-trimmed pelisse of gray-blue velvet was buttoned over her matching merino carriage dress, and her hat (a neat chinchilla toque warranted not to show the dust) was precisely centered atop her carefully dressed curls. All that remained was for Trudy and Marie to appear with their own personal baggage, and then they would be ready to leave.

Alexandra settled down to wait amid her assembled bags and boxes. She was in a happy and not-at-all-impatient mood. Her mind was already on the road to Tunbridge Wells, trying to imagine the adventures that awaited her there. So busy was she with these imaginings that when Trudy finally put in a belated appearance, it took Alexandra several minutes to realize something was wrong.

"There you are, Trudy," she exclaimed happily. "What an age you have been! The carriage has been waiting these twenty minutes. Is Marie already downstairs?" Alexandra got to her feet as she was speaking and began to gather up her hand luggage.

Trudy, however, put out a hand to restrain her. "No, child, I am afraid Marie is not downstairs," she said soberly. "The sad fact is— Ach, I can hardly say it! . . . The sad fact is that Marie, too, has fallen ill with this wretched influenza. I have come this minute from putting her in her bed, and I much doubt whether she will be fit to leave it anytime this fortnight."

"Oh no, poor Marie!" exclaimed Alexandra with concern. "What a dreadful thing, Trudy! She won't be able to go with us to Wells, then?"

Trudy shook her head mutely. Alexandra, looking at her closely, perceived that her face was flushed and her eyes unnaturally bright. "Trudy, you look quite feverish," she said with alarm. "I believe you are ill yourself!"

"*Gott in Himmel,* I very much fear it," said Trudy, and burst into tears.

This was a disconcerting phenomenon to Alexandra. She had never seen her nurse cry before, not in all the twenty years Trudy had attended her. Neither had she known the German woman to admit to the smallest indisposition. Now, it was almost as though their roles were reversed. Alexandra hardly felt competent to enact the role of nurse and comforter, but she attempted to take Trudy's arm. The German woman shook her off fiercely, however, and backed away, her face tearful but resolute.

"No, no, you must not, *liebling,*" she said earnestly. "You must not to me come near. It would be best if you left for Tunbridge Wells this minute, before you fall ill yourself. But how you are to go, when half the servants in the house are ill, is more than I can see."

Alexandra looked blank. She had not yet considered the effect her attendants' illness might have on her plans. Making a heroic effort at self-renunciation, she smiled at Trudy. "Of course I cannot go now, Trudy. I must stay and help nurse you all back to health. And indeed, you ought to be in your bed, like Marie, instead of standing here talking to me."

Trudy, however, was having none of this. She might be ill, but she knew what was fitting and what was not, and it was definitely not fitting that her mistress should involve herself in nursing. She shook her head vigorously. "No, indeed, Miss Alexandra. You to your great-aunt must go, even if Marie and I cannot accompany you. Mr. and Mrs.

Manning have to me entrusted your care, and of my bed I must not think until you are well embarked on your journey."

Alexandra, looking at Trudy's determined face, saw there was no use in arguing. Sick or not, Trudy was quite capable of remaining on her feet and making a martyr of herself in the cause of Alexandra's well-being.

"Very well," said Alexandra at last. "I shall go to Aunt Emily's alone, then. If I have Edward drive straight through, I won't have to worry about staying on the road overnight—and if I don't stay at any inns, I don't suppose it much matters if I have a maid to accompany me. By leaving now, we ought to be able to get to Tunbridge Wells late tonight."

Trudy could not like this plan, but lacking any better one, she was eventually forced to assent. Alexandra's baggage was loaded into the carriage, and with Edward the undercoachman to drive her, and only a couple of junior footmen to accompany her, Alexandra set off for Tunbridge Wells.

Alexandra spent the first part of her journey prey to guilt and self-reproach. It seemed to her that by leaving Mannington at such a time, she was indulging her own selfish desires instead of following the line duty clearly indicated. She ought to be at home nursing her relatives and devoted servants instead of dashing off to Wells in search of gaiety!

Gradually, however, her guilty mood gave way to a more rational state of mind. Even if she had stayed at Mannington, she never would have been allowed to take a hand at nursing as long as her patients had an ounce of strength to oppose her. Indeed, their illnesses probably would have been prolonged worrying about her taking the infection, as the doctor had said. It seemed that in this case, duty and inclination really were in perfect accord; and, that being the case, there was no reason why she should not go to Tunbridge Wells and enjoy herself.

So Alexandra settled back to make the most of her first long carriage journey. Her route took her through the counties of Hampshire and Surrey—both were completely unknown to her and were, in consequence, fascinating as any foreign country. Gazing at fields of new-sown wheat, and at cherry and apple orchards now turning to russet and gold, she could imagine with what verdant glory they must shine forth in spring.

She was also fascinated by the technicalities of travel. Toll-gates and posting houses were things she had only read and heard about, and now she was seeing and experiencing them for herself. Every carriage or horseman that passed her on the road was a fresh source of interest and speculation; every village, cottage, or farmhouse a novelty to be stared at until it had passed out of sight. She almost wished she were not obliged to travel with such speed. Edward, mindful of his mistress's need to reach Tunbridge that night, did not spare his horses, and it was only early afternoon when they arrived in the village of Wanworth, some miles from the Kentish border.

Alexandra was not yet weary of traveling, but she was beginning to feel hungry and cramped after sitting so long. She was therefore much relieved when Edward pulled into the innyard of the Rose and Crown, a small but prosperous-looking hostelry that served as a posting house. "I think I shall go in and get something to eat while the horses are being changed," she told Edward and the footmen. Gathering up her muff and reticule, she stepped down from the chaise and began to make her way across the yard.

Near the door of the inn stood a young man in livery, who had just dismounted from a winded-looking horse. Both the man and the livery had a familiar look to Alexandra. Surveying them more closely, she was astonished to recognize the man as one of her great-uncle's footmen: the very same footman who had been dispatched with the message to her great-aunt Emily.

"Why, if it isn't Sam!" she exclaimed, pausing beside the door. "This is a coincidence, isn't it?" She smiled at the young man. "I suppose you must be on your way back from Tunbridge Wells."

Sam, who had turned in surprise at this address, looked as astonished to see Alexandra as she had been to see him. But his look of astonishment changed swiftly to one of relief. "Oh, miss, it's quite providential that I should have run up against you like this," he cried. "I knew you must have already left for Tunbridge, and what you'd do when you got there and found the house closed up, I couldn't think."

"Closed up?" echoed Alexandra. She was conscious of a sudden constriction in her throat. "Whatever do you mean, Sam?" she managed to say with difficulty. "Whose house did you find closed up?"

"Miss Emily Abbott's house," answered Sam without hesitation. "When I got there, I found the knocker off the door and nobody there but an old beldame who told me Miss Emily'd gone to visit friends in Devon. They don't expect her back in Tunbridge till sometime after Christmas."

This news struck Alexandra like a thunderbolt. She could only stare at Sam incredulously. "I knew you'd find yourself in a fix when you got there and found the house shut up, so I headed straight back to warn you," continued Sam. His face was solemn but his voice betrayed a certain enjoyment in being the bearer of bad news. "I nearly killed a horse getting here, upon my word, miss. And there's no saying how many more I'd have killed if I hadn't run across you so providential-like. What'll you do now, miss? Will you go back to Mannington, or go on to Wells?"

Alexandra thought of Mannington, and the consternation her great-aunt and -uncle would feel to have her once more within the range of infection. Clearly she could not return there—and in fact she had little desire to do so, being all too happy to have escaped Mannington's confines for a time. But equally clearly, there was no point in going on to Tunbridge Wells. "I hardly know, Sam," she said slowly. "Perhaps I ought to discuss it with Edward and the others."

When Edward and the other footmen were informed of the situation, however, their reaction was not particularly helpful. They were full of sympathy, to be sure, but instead of offering their young mistress counsel, they merely stood looking at her with expectant faces, waiting for orders. This was a novel experience for Alexandra, and in other circumstances she might have enjoyed it, but at the moment she found it rather unnerving to be the person in authority.

"I shall have to think this situation over carefully before making any decision," she said finally. "I believe I'll go on into the inn and have something to eat, as I originally intended. Why don't all of you go inside and take some refreshment, too? I should be finished eating in—well, let us say in an hour's time. I'll let you know then what my decision will be."

This decision found unanimous favor with the footmen and undercoachman. Alexandra, feeling slightly nervous but elated at her first exercise of authority, went into the inn to order her meal.

THREE

Having no experience of inns, Alexandra boldly entered the nearest door, which proved to be the entrance to the taproom. There was no one in the taproom apart from a pair of rustics drinking beer at the bar. They subjected Alexandra to a brief, searching scrutiny, then returned their attention to their tankards. A moment later, a stout, balding gentleman in an apron came bustling into the room. His eyes widened slightly when he saw Alexandra. "What can I do for ye, miss?" he inquired, looking her up and down in a manner that made her slightly uncomfortable.

"I should like some tea, if you please," said Alexandra in her politest voice. "Also some sandwiches or cakes if you have any. Is there a private parlor where I might sit?" Trudy had been at pains to impress on her the importance of dining in privacy while she was traveling, and the landlord's manner made Alexandra more anxious than ever to show herself attuned to the niceties of polite behavior. Innocent as she was, she could not help seeing that he suspected her of being a very dubious and undesirable character.

Her voice alone seemed sufficient to set the landlord's suspicions to rest, however. His manner underwent an immediate change, becoming at once more friendly and respectful. "To be sure I can bring you some tea, miss," he

told Alexandra with a smile. "There's sandwiches, too, and
I daresay my wife can put her hand on some cakes for you.
But I'm afraid we haven't such a thing as a private parlor.
Every room we have is full up. There isn't so much as a
spare bedchamber where you might sit."

Alexandra's face was expressive of the dismay she felt at
this news. "Oh dear," she said. "I suppose I must not stay,
then. I can hardly sit in one of your public rooms, especially since I have not my maid with me. Perhaps you can
make up a packet of sandwiches for me to take with me?"

The landlord thumbed his lower lip. "I daresay I could.
But I tell you what, miss. There's nary a soul in the coffee
room at the moment but for one lady—a young lady like
yourself, miss, and a quiet, genteel lass if I ever saw one.
If you didn't mind sharing the room with her, you might
sit there and have your bite and sup in comfort."

Alexandra reflected. She could see no harm in sharing
a room with another lady, and the suggestion was infinitely
more appealing than trying to eat her tea and sandwiches
while being jounced over the road at the pace Edward had
been affecting. Besides, she had been looking forward to
a period of reflection in which to make her decision. So
she acceded graciously to the landlord's suggestion and
was duly conducted to the coffee room, an admirably clean
and spacious chamber with whitewashed walls, small dia-
mond-paned windows, and a massive fireplace wherein
burned a cheerful fire.

At first, in spite of the landlord's warning, Alexandra
thought herself the room's only occupant. Then she spied
the other traveler of whom he had spoken, a young lady
dressed in black who was seated in the corner looking out
the window.

The young lady looked around quickly at Alexandra's
entrance. Alexandra, surveying her with interest, saw that
she was very young indeed: no more than eighteen or nine-
teen, with smoothly braided dark hair and a pale, pretty

face. At the moment, however, her face wore a look of deepest anxiety. Alexandra smiled at her in a friendly way, and after an instant's hesitation the girl returned her smile, but it was clear she was engrossed in some private concern. She turned back to the window and continued to gaze out with an anxious and abstracted expression.

Alexandra, having her own private concerns to think about, was perfectly willing to give the girl the solitude she seemed to desire. When the landlord brought in the refreshments she had ordered, however, Alexandra thought it no more than polite to offer the girl a share of them.

"Thank you," said the girl, her voice melancholy but bearing the unmistakable stamp of education and refinement. "You are very kind. But I want nothing—nothing but a cup of tea, perhaps."

Alexandra gave the girl a cup of tea, then settled down to enjoy the sandwiches and fresh-baked cakes the landlord had brought her. As she ate, she tried to think what was best to be done about her situation. Ought she simply return home to Mannington? Or ought she go on to her great-aunt's house in Tunbridge Wells, on the chance that the servants left in charge there might be willing to let her stay until a letter could be sent to her great-aunt in Devon explaining her plight? Or—more daringly still—ought she herself to go to Devon and trust to the good nature of her great-aunt's friends to take her in?

Alexandra found it impossible to choose between these three alternatives. There were glaring objections to all of them, and the matter was made worse by her own uncertain state of mind. She was, moreover, distracted by the increasingly disturbing behavior of her companion in the coffee room. Several times Alexandra saw the girl take her handkerchief from her reticule and apply it to her eyes, and once a small but audible sob escaped her.

That sob was too much for Alexandra. Pushing away her

teacup and plate, she rose and went over to where the girl sat by the window. "My dear, is something the matter?" she asked gently, laying her hand on the girl's shoulder. "I don't wish to intrude, but if there is anything I can do . . . ?"

The girl shook her head, trying to smile. "No one can do anything," she said, then buried her face in her handkerchief. A series of wracking sobs shook her slender figure. Alexandra surveyed her with alarm and perplexity; then, remembering the various remedies which her great-aunt always insisted she carry, she fumbled in her reticule and brought out her vinaigrette.

"Here," she said, presenting it to the girl. "I've got sal volatile here, too, and some blue pills. And I rather think there's a flask of hartshorn and water out in my chaise."

The girl laughed shakily as she accepted the vinaigrette. "My goodness, do you always travel with a complete pharmacopoeia?" she asked.

Alexandra smiled back at her. "Truth to tell, I've never traveled before," she confessed. "But my great-aunt has a nervous disposition, and just now she is convinced I am on the verge of contracting influenza. So she made sure I was supplied with every conceivable remedy before I left home."

The girl, having refreshed herself with several sniffs from the vinaigrette, returned it to Alexandra. "Thank you," she said. "You are very good. Thank you very much for your kindness. I didn't mean to behave so foolishly. But you see, I have had some rather disturbing news and— and I haven't quite recovered from it." Here the girl's voice broke, and she buried her face in her handkerchief once more.

"I'm so sorry," said Alexandra softly. She had no wish to intrude on what she could see was a very private grief. After a minute, however, the girl went on, her voice calm but dejected.

"It's my mother," she said. "I just learned today that she is very ill. She must have an operation if she is to live, and the doctor says it will be a question whether she lives even then. And I have just accepted a new position, so I won't even be at home when she has the operation. And I am so afraid—so dreadfully afraid—that by the time I can return to visit her, she will be gone." Once again the girl's voice was suspended by tears.

"That *is* sad news," agreed Alexandra in a voice of sympathy. "It seems too bad that you cannot be with your mother at such a time. Would not your employer be willing to give you a leave of absence for a week or two?"

The girl shook her head sadly. "I don't dare ask him," she said. "It's a new position, you see, and a very good one. Indeed, I am lucky to have obtained it at all. And I'm afraid that if I ask for a leave of absence now, before I've even taken up my duties, my employer will simply find someone else for the position. And then I will be out of a job—and with this illness of Mother's, we need the money worse than ever. You can see I simply don't dare take the chance."

Alexandra nodded, pondering this dilemma. It occurred to her in passing that her own difficulties were very minor compared to this girl's. "What kind of a position is it that you are going to take?" she asked.

"A governess's. I have just graduated from Miss Evanston's Academy in London." The girl's voice betrayed a hint of pride as she pronounced these words. "It's a very fine school, and Miss Evanston said I was one of the best pupils she has ever taught. And so when the Earl of Brentwood and Barstock wrote to her, asking her to find a governess for his daughter, she wrote back recommending me. And he engaged me on Miss Evanston's recommendation without even seeing me."

"That is a great compliment," said Alexandra admiringly. The girl nodded, looking pleased, but the next moment her face clouded again.

"Yes, but I do wish I wasn't going to the Earl's for another month or two. Even a week's delay would be a godsend. I am sure Mother would be more likely to recover if I could be there with her. As it is, though, it's out of the question." The girl sighed deeply, then forced a smile to her lips. "But there, I don't mean to burden you with my problems. You've been an angel to listen so sympathetically, but I must not trespass on your good nature any longer. I am sure I must be keeping you from your journey."

"No, indeed," Alexandra assured her. "There is nowhere I must go at this particular moment, and no one who is expecting me. I can stay as long as I please."

"Can you? But I cannot," said the girl, drawing another sigh. "The Earl's carriage will be along at any moment to collect me."

Alexandra looked at the girl and thought what a pity it was that she should be obliged to go where she did not want to go, all for the sake of a little money. It seemed a very unfair business. She, Alexandra, had plenty of money and nowhere on earth that she was obliged to go, for the next month or two, at least. She could not return to Mannington while any risk of infection remained; she could not go on to Tunbridge Wells or Devon without giving inconvenience to any number of people. At the moment there was no one who needed or wanted or even expected her.

Just then an idea was born in Alexandra's brain. It was an idea so daring and at the same time so breathtaking in its simplicity that she could only stare at the girl with wide eyes. "What is it?" said the girl, regarding her with surprise.

Alexandra grasped the girl's wrist. "I have an idea," she said. "A way for you to stay with your mother and yet keep your position. And I think—I am almost sure—that it would work."

The girl looked hopeful but skeptical. "I have thought and thought until my head ached, and yet I cannot see my way clear to doing both those things," she told Alexandra. "Of course I should be glad to hear your idea, but you must realize that I can run no risk of losing my position."

Alexandra nodded, her eyes dancing. "You won't have to risk it. I will go to the Earl and act as governess to his daughter while you are nursing your mother. Then, whenever you are ready, you can come and claim your position, and I will leave."

The girl did not look much impressed by this plan. "You say *you* will act as a governess?" she said, and the incredulity in her voice was hardly flattering. Fortunately, Alexandra was too taken with her idea to register any insult.

"I'm sure I could teach," she told the girl. "I have not attended Miss Evanston's Academy, but I have had a very fine education. And, indeed, I would enjoy it, Miss . . . Miss— I don't believe I know your name."

"Miss Harcourt," said the girl automatically. "But I don't think—"

"Oh, but I do. I am sure the Earl would not mind my substituting for a month or two, if I explain the circumstances. I am Miss Manning, by the way." Alexandra extended her hand, and the girl took it and shook it, still with an automatic air. Her brow was wrinkled in thought.

"Yes, but look here, Miss Manning. Even if you can convince the Earl to accept you as a substitute, I still cannot like the idea of putting you to so much trouble. What I mean to say is—you hardly look as though you needed to work for a living." Miss Harcourt's eyes rested on Alexandra's fur-and-velvet costume with a dubious expression.

"It's true I have never had to earn my living up till now," said Alexandra. "But I have had to work hard nonetheless. I cannot believe teaching could be any more demanding. And I would quite enjoy it as a change from my regular routine. What's more, I would welcome a chance to help you and your mother, Miss Harcourt. Won't you please let me do this for you?"

Miss Harcourt, visibly wavering, said that she could not like to accept such a favor from a perfect stranger. Alexandra scoffed at this objection. Producing a pencil and tiny tablet from her reticule, she instructed Miss Harcourt to write out her name and home direction.

"That way, if any difficulty arises—if for some reason the Earl refuses to accept me as a substitute, for instance—I can communicate with you immediately," she told Miss Harcourt. "And I will write out my name and home direction for you. When you write to me at the Earl's, however, I think you had better address me as Miss DiMarco. That is my real name. I only use Manning because the relatives whom I live with prefer it."

It had occurred to Alexandra that the name of her great-aunt and -uncle conceivably might be known to the Earl, and that questions might arise as to why the heiress of the house of Manning should be earning her living as a governess. The name DiMarco, she reasoned, was by contrast an obscure one in England and ought to pass without remark.

Miss Harcourt was too grateful at having found a solution to her difficulties to make further objections. She consented docilely to be conveyed home in Alexandra's carriage and even consented, after a brief argument, to take the ten pounds Alexandra pressed upon her at parting.

"After all, I shall be collecting your salary for the next month or two," Alexandra told her with a merry smile. "I owe you at least that much for putting this position in my way. It's just as if I were buying a commission in the army!"

Brushing aside Miss Harcourt's protestations of eternal gratitude, Alexandra then led her out to the innyard and introduced her to Edward, Tom, and the other servants.

These worthies were naturally surprised to hear Alexandra
intended to stay at the inn while they conveyed an unknown young lady to her dwelling place some thirty miles
away, but Alexandra explained that there had been a
change of plans and that she would write her great-aunt
and -uncle later fully explaining the circumstances. Then,
having seen her own baggage unloaded and Miss Harcourt's put up in the boot, she waved good-bye to her grateful protégée and walked back into the inn to await the
arrival of the Earl's servants.

Along with her own name and direction, Miss Harcourt
had also written those of her future employer. Alexandra
studied the slip of paper curiously. *The Earl of Brentwood
and Barstock,* she read. *Residence, Brentwood. Wanworth, Sus-
sex.*

Alexandra had never encountered an earl before. The
Mannings, though an old and aristocratic family, had never
been members of the nobility, and tended to be proud
rather than otherwise of the fact. Her father's family had
been of the nobility, to be sure, but that had been Italian
nobility, and Alexandra had been raised to think Italian
nobility a very inferior thing. She wondered what an English earl would be like. Earls in books tended to be
haughty creatures, and often exceedingly licentious as
well. That was in books, however, and Alexandra suspected
that an earl in real life might be quite a different thing.
She hoped so, at any rate. Seating herself in the chair Miss
Harcourt had vacated, she sat down to watch for the arrival
of the Earl's carriage.

Only a few minutes later, a carriage bearing a nobleman's coat-of-arms pulled up before the inn. A manservant
in livery dismounted and entered the coffee room where
Alexandra sat. His eyes rested briefly on Alexandra, then
as quickly dismissed her. He looked about the room as
though searching for someone else. Alexandra rose to her

feet. "You are looking for me, I think," she said. "Are you here from the Earl of Brentwood and Barstock?"

The servant's eyes rested on Alexandra again, this time with an expression of astonishment. "Are you Miss Harcourt?" he asked, looking her up and down.

"Oh, no," said Alexandra blithely. "But I am a friend of hers, and she has engaged me to come in her place. Her mother is ill, you see, and I am to perform her duties at Brentwood until she is ready to come there herself."

"I see," said the servant, who very obviously did not see at all. Once more he surveyed Alexandra, his eyes taking in every detail of her appearance from the dashing little toque atop her honey-colored hair to the neat kidskin boots peeping beneath the flounce of her dress. "You are a governess?" he said in a voice struggling with incredulity.

Alexandra raised her chin. "Yes, I am," she said. It was not a lie, as she assured herself. She was as much a governess as Miss Harcourt, who by her own testimony had never held a governess's position before. It was the position itself that conferred the title of governess upon a lady, not any special formal training. "I am Miss DiMarco," she said firmly. "Will you please take me to his lordship's carriage? I am eager to reach Brentwood as soon as possible."

The servant acquiesced to this speech, still with an air of incredulity. His incredulity grew greater when he saw the style and quantity of Alexandra's baggage. Alexandra perceived that there might be some incongruity in a governess possessing so many trunks, bags, and bandboxes, but it was too late to rid herself of any of them now.

"I thought it well to bring a good many of my own books with me, in case his lordship's library should prove insufficient," she told the manservant, hoping in this way to explain away the superfluity of her baggage. This statement, like her previous one, was not exactly a lie. There were indeed some dozen of her favorite books from Mannington packed in one of her smaller bags. Still, as the

Earl's servants sweated and struggled to load her trunks atop the carriage, she could not help feeling slightly self-conscious.

She continued to feel self-conscious during the drive to Brentwood. A sixth sense told her that her excuses to the Earl's servants had not met with universal acceptance, and that even now she was an object of discussion on the box outside. Clearly she had somehow failed to conform to their stereotyped notions of what a governess should be. Miss Harcourt, too, somehow had had the idea that she was a frivolous, featherheaded creature, but she had succeeded in convincing Miss Harcourt otherwise, and she felt confident that she would eventually convince these others of their mistake, too.

It was not the Earl's servants so much as the Earl himself that Alexandra was worried about at that moment. Unless she could convince him of her competence as a governess, the whole scheme would necessarily fall through. And then poor Miss Harcourt would have to leave her mother—and very likely her mother would die as a result. And the fault for this tragedy would be at least partly hers, Alexandra's. It was a grave responsibility that rested upon her shoulders. Alexandra squared her shoulders and vowed to do her utmost to fulfill the charge laid upon her. If only the Earl could be convinced to accept her, all would yet be well.

Of her ability to teach she had no doubts. She knew herself to be fluent in French, German, and Italian, and competent at Greek and Latin. She had studied the higher branches of mathematics and the globes both celestial and terrestrial. She had read most of the principal philosophers and had a good understanding of their writings.

In addition to this useful knowledge, she also possessed the accomplishments of a lady. She could dance and ride, sketch and paint, sew, darn, and embroider. She could also sing and play upon the harp and pianoforte, although here Alexandra was a little uncertain as to the extent of her

abilities. Signor Richetti had occasionally condescended
to tell her that she was a fine musician, but since he inevitably added the words "for an Englishwoman"—and his
opinion of the English was not much higher than the Mannings' opinion of Italians—Alexandra did not feel this to
be unduly high praise. But perhaps the Earl would not
demand a very high standard where music was concerned.
His daughter might not be musical, or perhaps she would
have a separate master for music. Alexandra fervently
hoped this was the case.

Meanwhile, the Earl's carriage was pursuing a leisurely
course down a tree-lined country lane. Presently it slowed
to negotiate a turn between a pair of narrow iron gates
set in an ivy-covered stone gatehouse. Alexandra, looking
out the window, could see a cluster of towers looming
above the trees. *This must be Brentwood,* she thought, and
her heart beat a little faster.

Like the gate, the drive was rather narrow. The trees on
either side masked the approach until, quite suddenly, the
drive turned into an open court before the house. Alexandra found herself face-to-face with Brentwood for the
first time.

Her first thought was that it looked a very old place,
quite ancient, in fact. She was to learn later that the original structure dated back to the fifteenth century, although
there had been numerous additions and renovations since
then. Built of creamy limestone ashlar, the main body of
the house was rectangular in shape with towers here and
there punctuating its battlemented roofline.

Alexandra, surveying it critically, thought it looked a
very suitable nobleman's residence. She was surprised,
however, to see that it was no larger or finer than it was.
Mannington, her great-uncle and -aunt's home, was at least
as large and (she thought) quite a good deal finer. Though
not exactly shabby, the facade of Brentwood showed signs
of age and wear. But the ivy sprawling over its walls and

towers gave it a picturesque appearance, and Alexandra, in an expansive mood, decided she liked it. She began to gather up her muff and reticule in preparation of quitting the carriage.

The carriage came to a stop beside the house, and one of the Earl's footmen opened the door for her. The same manservant who had taken charge of her at the inn led her to a side door opening into a wide, stone-flagged hall. From here, he conducted her up a flight of shallow stone steps that twisted and turned in an oddly aimless fashion. *I should soon be quite lost if I were to try to find my way about alone in this house,* Alexandra told herself, as she trudged after the manservant. At last, just as she was beginning to think they would never get anywhere at all, the staircase ended and they entered another hall as wide and a good deal more lofty than the one below.

There were several doors opening into this hall. The manservant led Alexandra to the nearest one and opened the door for her to pass through. "You will find his lordship in here, miss," he told Alexandra.

There were two men in the room. Both turned to look as Alexandra came in. One was a tall, square-built gentleman with graying hair. A quizzing glass dangled between his fingers, and he was dressed with an elegance that made Alexandra blink. The other gentleman was even taller than the other but a good deal younger, no more than twenty-nine or thirty, Alexandra judged. He had a rangy, loose-limbed figure, a rough-hewn, handsome face, and wavy dark hair worn long over his collar. Alexandra observed him with interest, but addressed herself instead to the other man, whom she had decided must be the Earl. "Good day, sir. Do I have the pleasure of addressing the Earl of Brentwood and Barstock?"

The gentleman burst out in loud guffaws of laughter. "There's one up on you, Brentwood," he told the dark-haired gentleman. "By Jove, I've half a mind to claim the title and let you go scratch for yourself!"

The dark-haired gentleman smiled absently, but his eyes were on Alexandra, whom he was surveying with interest and some curiosity. "Dear ma'am, never mind my brother-in-law," he told her in a pleasant deep voice. "His sense of humor is not of the first order, I'm afraid. I am the Earl of Brentwood and Barstock. Now, what can I do for you?"

FOUR

Richard, Earl of Brentwood and Barstock, and his brother-in-law, Mr. Charles Taft, had been in the midst of an acrimonious discussion when Alexandra arrived.

"Damn it all, man, you've been a widower for a year and a half now," expostulated Mr. Taft. He and Richard were standing at the window of Richard's library, looking out across the expanse of the south lawn where sheep were grazing peacefully. "High time you was thinking of getting buckled again," continued Mr. Taft in a persuasive voice. "You've got to think of the succession, y'know. And then there's that daughter of yours. She'd be the better for having a stepmother, somebody to look after her and see she's kept out of trouble. If you'll take my advice, you'll quit moping over what happened between you and Aurelia and have a second go at marriage."

Richard turned away from him with an impatient gesture. "I suppose Eleanor put you up to this," he said over his shoulder. "She never will learn that I prefer to manage my own affairs in my own way. You may tell her so, with my compliments."

Mr. Taft shuffled his feet uneasily. "Fact of the matter is, Eleanor did just mention the subject," he admitted. "But she didn't ask me to say anything to you about it. The thing is, you've said yourself you're worried about Margaret running wild since her mother died. Seems to

me you'd be better off finding her a stepmother than depending on a lot of poor fish of governesses."

Richard ran his fingers through his hair. "Possibly," he
said. "But there are other factors to consider, Charles. Call
me a romantic if you will, but I cannot reconcile myself to
marrying again merely to provide Margaret with a stepmother. And I think any woman with an ounce of proper
feeling would be insulted by an offer of marriage given
for such a reason alone."

Mr. Taft let out one of his loud guffaws. "If that's what
you think, then you don't know much about women," he
told Richard. "You're a good-looking fellow with a title
and a fortune—"

"Not so much fortune as I possessed before I married
Aurelia," said Richard bitterly. "In that respect, at least, I
may be said to know all there is to know about women!"

Mr. Taft disregarded this interruption and went on dog-
gedly. "You're a good-looking fellow with a title, Richard,
and even with all Aurelia's extravagance you're not wanting for brass. Why, I daresay nine out of ten women'd snap
you up in a minute and never ask or care why you proposed
to 'em."

"Very likely," said Richard. "But it is just possible that
such a woman as you describe might not fulfill my own
idea of what a wife should be."

Mr. Taft looked at him and shook his head in a marvel-
ing way. "You're a funny fellow, Richard. Cynical as the
devil on one hand, and yet you've still got a lot of romantic
notions in your head about love and marriage. I would
think after Aurelia you'd be willing enough to let love
alone."

Again Richard turned away. "You may well say so," he
said over his shoulder. "And that is why I have chosen not
to marry again, Charles, even despite Margaret and the
succession and all the other excellent reasons you adduce."

He spoke with finality, but Mr. Taft, after surveying his back for a moment or two, could not resist making one final attempt. "Still, there *is* Margaret," he pointed out. "You've got to do something with that girl, Richard. You were saying so yourself a few weeks ago, after she sent that poor old Frenchwoman to the rightabout."

"Her new governess should be here shortly," said Richard, glancing at the clock on the wall. "I have great hopes of this girl. She came highly recommended—and she is a younger lady, which might be more congenial to Margaret. At any rate, we seem not to have had much success with older ladies."

Remembering some of the more outrageous pranks Lady Margaret had played on her last governess, Mr. Taft let out a loud guffaw. Fearing this might injure his brother-in-law's feelings, however, he changed it into a cough. "She's a deal of spirit, Lady Margaret," he remarked in a considering way. "Shows her breeding, I suppose. A regular thoroughbred filly, with no touch of the commoner about her."

Richard merely sighed deeply. Mr. Taft, supposing he was reflecting on the beautiful, highbred but singularly ungovernable lady on whom he had sired this particular filly, fell tactfully silent. There was no conversation between the two men for some minutes. It came as a relief to Mr. Taft when he heard a bustle and sound of voices belowstairs. "Sounds as though your new governess might have arrived," he told Richard. "Wonder what she'll be like."

Richard roused himself from his reflections and looked toward the door. It was opened a moment later by his head footman. The footman's face wore a peculiar expression, and he made no announcement of the visitor's name, as would have been the usual way. He merely ushered her inside, bowed, and withdrew with a reluctant air, as though he would rather have lingered to observe the coming interview.

Richard transferred his gaze to the lady who stood on the library threshold.

His first thought was that she was the most dazzling creature he had ever beheld in his life.

She was tall and slim with honey-colored hair and vivid blue eyes thickly fringed with dark lashes. There was grace and elegance in her bearing, while her gray-blue merino dress and matching fur-trimmed pelisse had been chosen with a nice taste to accentuate her considerable beauty. But it was not so much these external things as the force of her personality that took Richard's breath away. From the moment she stepped into the room, he was aware of it, like a tangible force emanating from her person. Those dazzling dark-fringed eyes met his, rested on him a moment in a considering way, then passed on to Mr. Taft. "Good day, sir. Have I the honor of addressing the Earl of Brentwood and Barstock?" she asked Mr. Taft politely.

Richard was irritated when his brother-in-law laughed. He also found himself irrationally irritated by the girl's quick dismissal of him. She had thought Mr. Taft an earl, but not him! "Dear ma'am, never mind my brother-in-law," he told her. "His sense of humor is not of the first order, I'm afraid. I am the Earl of Brentwood and Barstock. Now what can I do for you?"

The girl's eyes returned to him, doubt and astonishment in their depths. The next moment she had recovered herself, however, and advanced on him with a smile, holding out a slender hand sheathed in a neat gray kid glove. "Then you are my employer," she said. "Forgive me, but you know we have never met. I am Alexandra DiMarco, and I am here as governess to your daughter."

Of all the possible explanations for the girl's presence in his library, this one had not occurred to Richard. Once more he found himself struck dumb. The girl looked at him as though expecting some reply, but receiving none, she went on, speaking rapidly and looking at him with a certain anxiety in her expression.

"I daresay you are surprised because I am not Miss Harcourt. The fact is that Miss Harcourt was unable to come, my lord. Her mother is very ill, and she will not be able to leave her for some weeks, perhaps as much as a month or two. So as I am a friend of hers, we arranged that I should come instead and teach your daughter until Miss Harcourt is able to come herself."

Still Richard gazed at the girl, unable to speak. It was Mr. Taft who put his thoughts into words. "You are a governess, ma'am?" he asked the girl incredulously.

She raised her chin in a manner that struck Richard as slightly defiant. "Yes, I am," she said. "I assure you I am very well educated, sir. I am qualified to teach history, geography, mathematics, philosophy, music, dancing, drawing, and most of the modern and ancient languages."

"Are you indeed!" exclaimed Mr. Taft in an unbelieving voice. Taking up his quizzing glass, he looked the girl over, his expression appreciative but markedly skeptical. "I never would have believed it. You don't look a bit blue, 'pon my word, ma'am."

Richard, who was by now recovering himself, shot his brother-in-law a withering look. "Do you speak French, Miss DiMarco?" he asked the girl in French.

"Yes, I had a French maid as a child, and I have been told I speak it quite passably," she replied in perfect French. With a smile, she added, "You speak French rather well yourself, my lord."

"By Jove, don't she rattle it off quicklike, though," exclaimed Mr. Taft in an enraptured voice. "Try her in something else, Brentwood, old man."

This Richard did, quizzing her haltingly in German, asking her to perform a couple of Latin declensions and conjugations, and posing a few random questions in geography, mathematics, and philosophy. Her replies convinced him that she had spoken no more than the truth concerning her scholastic abilities.

"You can see that I am qualified to teach," she said, looking at him anxiously. "And so I hope you have no objection to my taking Miss Harcourt's place for a month or two? I assure you, I will do my very best for your daughter, my lord. And both Miss Harcourt and I would take it as a great personal favor if you would allow it." She fastened her eyes on him with a pleading expression.

Richard hesitated. He had been so overwhelmed by what he had seen and heard of Miss DiMarco thus far that he felt at that moment incapable of refusing her anything. This was the more true because she really did seem qualified for the position she desired. Yet it was impossible to think of a lady of such style and elegance as a governess.

"I am afraid the work will be too much for you," he said, looking at her doubtingly.

"Oh, I am very strong," she said earnestly. "I don't in the least mind working hard. Indeed, I am used to it."

"Indeed," said Richard, still more doubtingly.

"Oh, yes," she assured him. "I am sure I can do the necessary work, my lord. And in any case, it will only be for a month or two, just till Miss Harcourt's mother is well again."

Again Richard hesitated. He felt he was being seduced into Miss DiMarco's proposition against his better judgment. Yet it would have been unfair to call her manner seductive. It was more like a force of nature: potent, determined, and well-nigh irresistible. "All this is most irregular," he said helplessly.

"Yes, it is," she agreed readily enough. "And that is why I thought I had better come along and explain it to you in person, my lord, instead of writing to you. I hope you will allow me to at least make a trial. Of course, if you find me unsatisfactory, you need not keep me on, but I think—I am sure—that I can do the job." Once more she fixed her dazzling dark-fringed eyes on his.

Richard felt his resistance slipping. He let it go without a murmur. There was within him a growing desire to see what this odd, unexpected, and wholly charming girl would do or say next. She did seem to be a qualified governess, too, which served to quiet any qualms of conscience he might have felt. As it happened, however, he felt very few of those.

"Very well, Miss DiMarco, you have convinced me," he said with a smile. "The position is yours."

Alexandra felt a dizzying wave of relief at these words. Every fiber of her physical, emotional, and intellectual being had been strained to the utmost in her anxiety to carry Miss Harcourt's case. She returned Richard's smile joyfully. "I am so glad, my lord," she exclaimed. "You shall not be sorry—indeed you shall not. I will work my fingers to the bone for your daughter."

This onslaught of gratitude—and the smile that accompanied it—served to further dazzle Richard. Clearing his throat, he made an effort to be conscientiously business-like.

"We have not settled the matter of your salary yet, Miss DiMarco," he said. "What amount do you usually command?"

Alexandra was unprepared for this question. She had supposed, if she had reflected on the matter at all, that the amount of the salary to be paid had already been fixed between him and Miss Harcourt. She had no idea what pay a governess usually commanded. Her great-uncle had always taken care of paying the various masters brought in to tend to her education, and he had never seen fit to inform her as to the expense involved. "A hundred pounds a quarter?" she hazarded. It seemed to her that no genteel person could possibly subsist on less than this modest sum.

She could tell at once from the dumbfounded expressions on Richard and his brother-in-law's faces that her guess had been on the high side. Instantly Alexandra sought to recover herself. "How foolish of me," she said, with a little laugh. "Did I say a hundred pounds a quarter? Of course I meant a hundred pounds a year!"

The dumbfounded expressions on her listeners' faces did not noticeably lessen. Alexandra was daunted, but she felt she had committed herself now and could not back down without loss of face. She raised her chin slightly. "Of course my charges are slightly higher than most governesses, but that is because I pride myself on the quality of my teaching," she told Richard. "If a hundred pounds a year seems too high to you, you may pay me what you usually pay your governesses to begin with. Then you can make it up afterward if you find I am worth it."

There was an odd little smile on her employer's face as she finished this speech. Alexandra observed it dubiously, wondering what it portended. However, all he said was, "Your terms do seem to me rather high, Miss DiMarco, but I have no doubt your teaching is all you say it is. I shall expect great things of a lady demanding such a princely salary."

"But, Brentwood! A hundred pounds a year!" sputtered Mr. Taft.

Richard turned to smile at him. "You think a hundred a year a large sum? Yet I daresay you've dropped more than that at Watier's of an evening."

"A deuce of a lot more than that," said Mr. Taft frankly. "But to pay that much for a governess!"

"You must excuse Mr. Taft," Richard told Alexandra. "Education is not one of the priorities in his life. It is one of mine, however." He looked at her searchingly. "My daughter is just turned six. Lady Margaret is, I believe, an intelligent child, but unfortunately the circumstances of her early life have not encouraged her to acquire the habits of discipline and self-control. I am afraid you will have to teach her those before any other learning can take place."

Alexandra could hardly repress a smile to hear her great-uncle's two favorite watchwords brought forward in this way. "Indeed, I believe I am exactly the governess you need, my lord," she told Richard. "I was myself raised to believe that discipline and self-control are the cornerstones of all success and happiness in life. I trust I may be able to impart the same belief to Lady Margaret."

"I hope so," said Richard soberly. "But I tell you frankly that your predecessors have not enjoyed much success in that direction. I have tried several governesses during the past year and a half, but all have proven unsatisfactory in one way or another. Either they were what I considered unnecessarily harsh in their dealings with Margaret, or else they went to the opposite extreme and allowed her to ride over them roughshod. I do not object to your disciplining Lady Margaret, you understand, but I would rather the discipline were tempered with kindness."

Again he looked searchingly at Alexandra. "You look as though you possess the quality of understanding, Miss Di-Marco. I hope you will be able to teach Lady Margaret—and if possible, that you will be able to make her happy, too. She has not had much happiness in her life thus far, I fear. It would be a great comfort to me if you could do something toward remedying that."

"I will try," said Alexandra. Inwardly, however, she was alarmed by Richard's words. The change in his manner, too, had given her a vague sense of alarm. A minute ago he had been smiling and cheerful, but as soon as he had begun to speak of his daughter, his manner had sobered. For the first time since beginning her adventure, Alexandra began to wonder whether she was equal to the task she had taken on. Here she was, engaged to teach a young child who by all accounts lacked discipline and self-control—and she was expected to succeed where other, more experienced governesses had failed! It was a daunting prospect altogether.

Richard, meanwhile, had excused himself to his brother-in-law and moved toward the library door. "I will take you up to the nursery now, Miss DiMarco," he said. "You will no doubt be wanting to meet your pupil."

Rather apprehensively, Alexandra followed him down the hall and up a flight of stairs to the nursery. This proved to be a spacious room decorated with a painted frieze depicting the animals of Noah's ark. The floor was covered with a Wilton carpet, whose pattern was nearly obscured by the impressive array of toys that littered its surface. Adjoining the nursery on one side was the schoolroom, and on the other was the night nursery containing Lady Margaret's little crib-bed. Of Lady Margaret herself, however, there was no sign. The only occupant of the rooms appeared to be a harassed-looking maidservant, who was addressing a closed cabinet in the corner of the nursery.

"Now, do come out of there, Lady Margaret, do. It's been nigh on an hour since you shut yourself in there, and I'm sure I've nearly lost patience with you. Your supper's nearly ready, and if you don't come out so I can get you cleaned up—"

"That will do, Rachel," said Richard, interrupting this soliloquy. "Go on downstairs, and I'll speak to Lady Margaret." Addressing himself to the cabinet in turn, he said sternly, "Margaret, this is your father. I thought we had agreed that you were not to shut yourself up when Rachel came to tidy you for meals?"

"Yes," came a sulky reply from within the cabinet's depths. Changing to a plaintive tone, the voice added, "But Rachel pulls my hair when she combs it. And it hurts!"

"Well, never mind that now, Margaret. Rachel is gone, and there is someone I want to introduce you to. Your new governess is here, and if you do not want to give her a very odd idea of your manners, you will come out at once and greet her properly."

As Alexandra looked on with wonder, the cabinet opened and a small girl came out. She was quite a pretty little girl, although her cambric dress was streaked with dust and her hair looked as though it had not seen a comb or brush for days. From beneath a tangled mass of brunette curls, a pair of sharp dark eyes surveyed Alexandra curiously. "Is that my new governess?" she demanded, pointing at Alexandra.

"Yes, although you ought not to point, my dear. Miss DiMarco, this is Lady Margaret; Margaret, this is Miss Di-Marco, your new governess."

"I am very pleased to make your acquaintance, Lady Margaret," said Alexandra, smiling and holding out her hand.

Lady Margaret ignored the outstretched hand and went on staring at Alexandra. Finally, in a decided tone, she announced, "You look exactly like Méchante."

"Like who?" said Alexandra, at a loss to understand this strange address. "May Shaunt? Is that a friend of yours?"

"No, this is Méchante," said Lady Margaret, producing a large wax doll from behind her skirts with the air of a conjurer. The doll's hair and dress were as dusty and bedraggled as her mistress's, but where Lady Margaret's eyes and hair were dark, the doll had a tangle of honey-colored hair through which a pair of large, staring blue-glass eyes could be glimpsed.

Alexandra looked at her employer. He was obviously biting back a smile. "Her doll's name is Méchante?" she said incredulously. "But that is . . . surely *méchante* is the French word for 'naughty'?"

Richard nodded, biting his lip. "You must understand that Lady Margaret's last governess was a French lady," he told Alexandra. "And you must understand also that my daughter is accustomed to blame her misdeeds on her doll." He cast a rueful look at Lady Margaret. "And so mam'selle frequently used to shake her head and exclaim, 'Ah, but that child is *méchante*'—and my daughter took the word as a proper name for her doll instead of an adjective for herself.''

He was smiling as he spoke, and Alexandra could not help smiling also. "I see," she said. Stooping down, she took one of the doll's hands in hers and shook it gravely. "I am very pleased to make your acquaintance, Madame Méchante," she told the doll. "And I am flattered to be compared to a beauty of your distinction. I am also pleased to make the acquaintance of Lady Margaret, your distinguished mistress."

Again she extended her hand to Lady Margaret, and this time Lady Margaret consented to take it in her own for a brief instant. "You don't look in the least like a governess," she told Alexandra, her shrewd eyes still scrutinizing Alexandra's face.

"That is because I am wearing my traveling clothes," said Alexandra cheerfully. "When I have changed and tidied my hair, I expect I will look much more the thing. Can you show me to my room?"

"Yes," said Lady Margaret. Her small face became suddenly animated. "Your room is just through the schoolroom here. You've got a mirror and a washstand and a cupboard to put your things in." Transferring Méchante to one hand, she grasped Alexandra's hand in her other and began to pull her toward the schoolroom door.

"I shall take leave of you now, my lord," said Alexandra, addressing Richard over her shoulder. "Lady Margaret can assist me in finding my way about, I am sure."

"I am sure she can," he responded faintly. There was a bemused look on his face as he watched them disappear through the schoolroom door.

FIVE

The servants had brought up Alexandra's bags while she was making the acquaintance of her employer and his daughter. When she and Lady Margaret reached the small chamber which was set apart for the governess's use, they found it so crammed with trunks, bags, and boxes that Alexandra could scarcely make her way to the bed.

"My, but you have a lot of things," said Lady Margaret, gazing around the room with round eyes. "I'm sure mam'selle and my other governesses had not half this many."

Alexandra looked around the room in a helpless manner. Once again she felt inadequate to the situation. If Trudy and Marie had been there, they would have seen to the unpacking of her bags. They would have assisted her in changing her dress, too, and soon made her at home in her new quarters. But she was on her own now, and it was up to her to do all these things without the assistance of servants.

"Here is my dressing case," she said aloud. "That should have my brushes and combs in it." Gingerly picking her way through trunks and boxes, she placed the dressing case atop a trunk that stood beside the washstand. This made a useful dressing table, she noted, and was pleased with her first arrangement. "Now I must find a dress to change into. I wonder in which trunk Marie packed my morning dresses?"

"Who's Marie?" asked Lady Margaret, investigating the contents of a bandbox. "Ooh, what a pretty hat!"

"Marie is my maid," said Alexandra, busy with the locks of her trunks. "She's French and very clever. It was she who taught me to speak French as a child."

Lady Margaret accepted without question the incongruity of a governess possessing a personal maid. "I know some French, too," she said proudly. "Mam'selle was teaching me before she had to leave. *Chapeau,*" she enunciated with great care, pointing to Alexandra's hat. "And that's a *miroir,*" she added, pointing to the looking glass above the washstand.

"Very good," said Alexandra approvingly. She saw the opportunity to give her pupil a painless lesson in French while accomplishing her unpacking. While she removed from her trunks those things she judged most useful to her new position and arranged her remaining bags and boxes as best she could within the small space allotted to her, she asked Lady Margaret in French the names of various objects situated around the room. Lady Margaret proved to know a surprising number of them already, and Alexandra mentally praised the late mam'selle's efforts.

"Now if only I can stack this *malle* atop the other, I think I will be able to get to my bed tonight," she told Lady Margaret, gasping a little as she attempted to lift one large trunk atop another. Lady Margaret obligingly lent her assistance to the effort, and soon the room was as neat as circumstances allowed.

Alexandra looked around her with satisfaction. The cupboard was filled with her most utilitarian dresses, and one trunk was actually empty, ready to be removed to some place of storage. Two other trunks, containing the more frivolous items in her wardrobe, were placed against the wall with her jewel case buried in the bottom one. The bandboxes containing her hats were piled atop one another in a stack that reached nearly to the ceiling. Her miscellaneous bags and boxes stood jumbled in the corner where she might draw upon their contents as needed. She had already removed her books from the one and arranged them on the shelf above her bed along with her traveling clock. Her brushes and other toiletries were neatly laid out atop the trunk beside the washstand.

"I think that will do very nicely," she said. "Now I must wash, change my dress, and tidy my hair."

Lady Margaret, perched atop a large packing case, was an interested spectator to this process. Indeed, she soon became an active participant, for when Alexandra went to put on the neat French gray morning dress which she had judged the most suitable attire for a governess, she found herself quite incapable of fastening the tiny buttons that closed it down the back.

"Thank you very much," Alexandra told Lady Margaret with a smile, when the child's small fingers had completed this task. Lady Margaret smiled shyly back at her from beneath her tangle of hair. As Alexandra took up her brushes to tidy her own hair, she cast a speculative glance at her pupil. Lady Margaret's appearance at the moment did not exactly do her credit. Was there perhaps some way she might effect a positive improvement in the child's appearance before supper? "Now my hair is all tidy," she said aloud, surveying her appearance in the glass. "Shall I brush out yours for you while I am at it, Lady Margaret?"

Lady Margaret shook her head violently and began to back away. Alexandra, fearing a repetition of the cupboard incident, cast around in her mind for a different approach to the problem. "At least let me brush Méchante's hair," she suggested. "It is not fitting that such a grand lady should go about in such a disheveled state."

Lady Margaret looked interested by this suggestion. "All right," she said, proffering the doll to Alexandra. Alexandra took it and carefully brushed out its tangled locks, then tied them back with a ribbon from one of her boxes. "There," she said, showing the doll to Lady Margaret. "Does she not look much better?"

"Yes," agreed Lady Margaret, surveying her doll with admiration. "She looks beautiful."

"I could fix your hair the same way," said Alexandra in a wheedling voice. "See, here is a pretty red ribbon—or I have a green one if you prefer it."

"I don't want a red or green ribbon," said Lady Margaret, thrusting out her underlip. "I want a blue one like Méchante's."

Alexandra pretended to consider. "Well, you *could* wear a blue ribbon—but only if you change your dress first. The dress you are wearing is green, you know, and blue and green are commonly held to wash each other out."

There was a long moment of silence while Lady Margaret considered. Alexandra held her breath. "All right," said Lady Margaret at last, in a voice of decision. "Come tell me which of my dresses would look best with a blue ribbon."

Disguising her joy, Alexandra went to Lady Margaret's room and helped her choose a clean dress of flowered blue muslin. She then brushed and combed out the child's tangled hair, being very mindful not to pull. "That didn't hurt at all," said Lady Margaret in surprise, as Alexandra smoothed her curls back from her face. "It always hurts when Rachel brushes my hair."

"It probably wouldn't if you let her brush it more often," said Alexandra, as she tied the coveted blue ribbon in her pupil's hair. "Now, then! You and Méchante are ready for supper."

As she spoke, the nursery door opened, and the maid-servant Rachel came in. She cast an appraising and rather scornful glance at Alexandra, but her expression changed to one of astonishment when she looked at Lady Margaret.

"Well, aren't you looking fine, my lady!" she exclaimed. "So you decided to let your hair be brushed after all?"

Alexandra deplored this tactless speech, but Lady Margaret was fortunately too pleased with her new finery to take offense. "Miss DiMarco did it," she said, proudly touching her ribbon. "She brushed Méchante's hair, too—see?"

"I see," said Rachel. She gave Alexandra a look of new respect. "Well, it looks as though the two of you are ready for supper. That reminds me, I've a message from his lordship. He sends his compliments to you, ma'am, and asks if you and Lady Margaret would dine downstairs tonight rather than take supper in the nursery?"

Alexandra looked at Lady Margaret. That young lady's lower lip protruded once more. "If we go downstairs, we won't be able to eat for hours and hours yet," she said. "And I'm hungry now."

"Perhaps it would be better if we took supper in the nursery this evening," Alexandra told Rachel. "I only just arrived today, after all. And I need to get acquainted with Lady Margaret before I do anything else." She smiled at her pupil as she spoke, but inwardly she was conscious of a sense of disappointment. She had conceived a strong interest in the man who was her employer, and she would not have minded furthering her acquaintance with him as well as his daughter. Nor would she have minded dining downstairs and seeing more of Brentwood's formal rooms instead of being confined to a nursery suite.

But of course, she reminded herself, she was a governess now, and her first duty was to her pupil. And in all likelihood there would be others at the table besides herself who would engage most of the Earl's attention. There would be Mr. Taft, for instance, the gentleman whom she had initially mistaken for the Earl and whom the Earl had referred to as his brother-in-law. Alexandra wondered now how she could have made such an error. The little she had heard of Mr. Taft's conversation had been sufficient to brand him as a fool in her mind—an amiable fool, perhaps, but a fool nonetheless. Alexandra knew little more of the Earl than she did of his brother-in-law, but she was already convinced that he was no fool.

So she damped down her disappointment and settled down to spend her evening in the nursery. Rachel presently brought up a tray containing bread, butter, cheese, and fruit, in addition to a pot of tea and a pitcher of milk. Having placed these things on the table by the fire, she turned to go. "Before you leave, Rachel, I wonder if you might help me with my trunk," said Alexandra with a friendly smile. "It is most dreadfully in the way in my room, and I don't know what I should do with it. Is there a boxroom in the attic where I can store it?"

"Sure there is, miss," said Rachel, neither returning Alexandra's smile nor slowing her progress toward the door. With a hint of contempt in her voice, she added, "I daresay one of the footmen would carry it there for you if you asked."

Alexandra regarded her with honest surprise. She was accustomed to look upon the servants in her great-aunt and -uncle's house as friends and allies. Insolence such as this was new to her. "Perhaps you will be so kind as to ask one of them for me?" she suggested politely.

Rachel made no reply, but merely threw Alexandra a look of dislike. Alexandra, alerted to trouble now but determined to carry her point, repeated her request in a louder voice. "I think you had better come with me to my room right now," she said, looking Rachel levelly in the eye. "I can show you which trunk it is, so you will be able to point it out to the footman who comes for it."

So saying, she led the way across the nursery. Rachel trailed sullenly behind her, but when they reached Alexandra's room, the maidservant's manner underwent a subtle change. "Is all this yours, miss?" she said, looking with

awe at the stacked heap of bandboxes and at the silver-
backed brushes laid out beside the washstand.

"Yes, unfortunately," said Alexandra, looking ruefully
around her. "As you can see, it's very crowded." She
pointed out the empty trunk to Rachel, who nodded and
promised to see it was carried away to the boxroom. Alexandra was pleased to see that the maidservant's manner
was more respectful than it had been before. It occurred
to her that probably Rachel had had sole care of Lady
Margaret since the last governess departed. She might well
be jealous of a newcomer usurping what she perceived to
be her role. Accordingly, Alexandra set out to try to soothe
Rachel's wounded feelings.

"I suppose you have been taking care of Lady Margaret
these last few weeks, Rachel? I would appreciate any advice
you can give me on how to deal with her. I'm sure you
probably know her and her ways better than anyone in the
house."

"Aye, that I do," said Rachel with emphasis. In a softer
voice, she added, "Not that I mean to speak ill of her, poor
mite. Minding her's no treat, but she ain't an out-and-out
wicked child, like some I've seen. It's her temper that
makes her hard to reckon with. Smart as a whip, she is,
but when she's in one of her moods there's no doing anything with her. Like the late mistress in that, she is," added
Rachel with an expressive grimace.

Alexandra had no wish to encourage servants' gossip,
but she had a strong curiosity to hear more on this subject.
"It is Lady Margaret's mother you are speaking of?" she
asked.

"Aye, and a rare Tartar she was. A handsome lady, mind
you, but bad-tempered as they come. None of us was sorry
when she went off, and it's my belief that his lordship was
more relieved than sorry, too. At any rate, he never lifted
a finger to bring her back. Made her have over half his
income, he did, and saw she had everything she needed,

but they lived separate-like until she died a year or two back."

Alexandra pondered these words. "So Lady Margaret was brought up away from her mother?" she said. "No wonder Lord Brentwood said she had lived an unhappy life."

Rachel laughed shortly. "No, you've got the wrong end of the stick there, miss. When her ladyship left Brentwood, she took Lady Margaret with her. 'Twas she who raised her from a babe, with his lordship never allowed to see her except it might be for an hour or two, when it suited her ladyship to run down to Brentwood and harangue his lordship about not giving her enough money. If you ask me, that's what did the mischief. His lordship's a kind, even-tempered gentleman with a deal of common sense, and if he'd had the raising of Lady Margaret she'd have been brought up judicious. By all I can understand, her ladyship used to let her sit up nights, and eat whatever she chose, and run wild as a savage day in and day out, until it's no wonder she won't brook discipline now."

"I see," said Alexandra. She felt a great pity for Lady Margaret, and an even greater pity for her father. No wonder he had looked somber in speaking of his daughter! "What a sad story," she mused aloud. "I am glad you told me all this, Rachel. It will help me to keep my patience if Lady Margaret should prove difficult at times."

Rachel laughed. "No, 'if' about that, miss, I should say! She's got a temper on her and no mistake." She surveyed Alexandra thoughtfully. "But then, you never know. It does look as though you've a way with her, miss. Perhaps you'll have more luck at teaching her than them others did." Again she looked curiously at Alexandra. "I'd give a deal to know what brings you here, miss. You're never a governess born—not with all this?" She nodded toward Alexandra's room with its luxurious appointments.

Alexandra felt a flush rise to her cheeks. "I don't suppose anyone is 'a governess born,' " she said lightly. "As far as I know, any lady can become one, assuming she has the proper qualifications."

"Aye, but there's not many ladies like you as would choose to," returned Rachel. She surveyed Alexandra curiously, her eyes lingering on the simple but stylish lines of her French gray morning dress. "Meaning no disrespect, miss, but you don't seem the type."

"Well, the truth is, I am only here in a temporary capacity," explained Alexandra. There seemed no reason to lie and so she gave a brief account of Miss Harcourt's predicament and of her own decision to come to Brentwood in her place. She omitted only the details of her own background and situation.

Rachel listened avidly. "Well, it's a queer start and no mistake," she said, at the end of Alexandra's speech. "I doubt not you've a kind heart, miss, to help out this Miss Harcourt like you've done. But it still seems queer, a lady like you being a governess." Having made two or three more remarks about the queerness of the situation, she finally took herself off, promising to see to the speedy removal of Alexandra's empty trunk. Alexandra thanked her and went to join her pupil for her long-delayed supper.

Rachel was good as her word and dutifully saw to the removal of Alexandra's trunk. She also relayed the news to her employer that Alexandra had decided to take supper in the nursery that evening instead of joining the family at the dinner table.

Richard received this news with outward calm but inward disappointment. What he had seen of Alexandra had intrigued him mightily, and he was eager to learn more of the young woman whom he had—perhaps foolishly—engaged as a substitute governess.

I must have been bewitched, he thought, as he reviewed the whole fantastic scenario in his mind. Remembering again Alexandra's vivid blue eyes and dazzling smile, he was inclined to think this indeed had been the case.

But there's no harm done, he assured himself. *If she proves incompetent, I'll simply discharge her as I did the others. I am under no obligation to retain her simply because she is holding the place for someone else. If worse comes to worst, Margaret can do without a governess until Miss Harcourt's mother recovers.*

He thought again of Alexandra, and of her assurances that she could teach his daughter. She was an unconventional governess, no doubt about it—an unconventional girl altogether, judging by the look of her. What was she, exactly? Her appearance was that of a lady of quality, yet no lady of quality he knew would have considered taking a governess's position unless compelled to by financial circumstances. This did not seem to be the case with Miss DiMarco. Richard smiled when he remembered how she had innocently suggested a hundred pounds a quarter as a reasonable salary for a governess. Her naiveté concerning such matters showed well enough that she had been brought up in surroundings where money was no object.

Yet despite her ignorance of money matters, she had shown herself to be a exceptionally well educated young woman. There was a slight, not unpleasing touch of pedantry in her speech that contrasted curiously with her modish exterior. *There's some mystery there, I'll wager,* thought Richard, and vowed to investigate the mystery more fully before the week was out.

Dinner that evening seemed to him a tiresomely protracted meal. His thoughts kept winging away toward the nursery suite, speculating about the mysterious character of the new governess he had hired. It was an effort to concentrate on the conversation at the table. His sister, Lady Eleanor, several times accused him of woolgathering.

Lady Eleanor and her husband Charles Taft had been staying at Brentwood for several weeks now, and it was Lady Eleanor's contention that something needed to be done to relieve the tedium of existence there.

"Not that the country is not very well in its place, Richard," Lady Eleanor told him, as she helped herself to curried fowl. She was a handsome dark-haired woman some years older than her brother and accustomed to taking an older sister's autocratic tone in her dealings with him. "There is no objection to your spending the greater part of your time on your estate, but to live as you do, in virtual isolation, cannot but be very bad for you. It makes you insular and stupid."

"Thank you," said Richard dryly. "You are always so flattering in your assessments, Eleanor."

"Of course I do not mean to call you stupid, Richard," she went on, smiling at him with a kindly air. "But it would be better if you went into society of some kind now and then. I cannot find you even attending the local assemblies at Wanworth."

"I don't care much for assemblies," said Richard shortly. "In any case, I am better off tending to my property. Brentwood has had some difficult years of late, and though I think the worst is behind us, still we're not out of the woods."

"Oh, Richard, are you still paying off Aurelia's debts?" said Lady Eleanor, opening her eyes wide. "I had not thought it was so bad as that."

Richard was irritated by this plain speaking, but he forced himself to speak calmly. "No, things are not quite that bad, Eleanor. The debts are all paid now, but some of the money that went to pay them by rights ought to have been used for other things—necessary things such as repairing fences and building barns, for instance. It's only these last few months I find myself in a way to take up some of the slack."

Lady Eleanor meditated. "That's very well, then," she announced at last, in a voice of finality. "You can certainly stand the expense of a house party at Christmas. And if you can't, then Charles and I will be happy to assist you."

"A house party at Christmas?" repeated Richard incredulously. "What nonsense is this, Eleanor?"

"No nonsense at all," said Lady Eleanor with spirit. "You are dull down here, Richard, and need something to liven you up. Mama and Papa always used to have wonderful parties at Brentwood at Christmastime—you must remember them from when we were children. I have a tentative guest list all made out. You need only give me the names of any additional people you wish to invite, and I'll send the invitations out this week. They ought to go out immediately, for Christmas is less than two months away."

Richard turned his eyes upon Mr. Taft. "What have you to say to this idea, Charles?" he demanded.

"Seems a good notion to me," said Mr. Taft judiciously. "Mean to say, it *is* pretty dull down here, Brentwood. A house party would be very good fun."

Richard eyed him a moment, then returned his gaze to his sister. "I have no objection to the idea of a house party, but I can't help but think you've an ulterior motive in wishing to give one here at this particular time, Eleanor," he told her. "There isn't some charming girl attending whom you think might make me a perfect second wife?"

"There will be lots of charming girls attending, Richard," said Lady Eleanor cheerfully. "I intend to invite every eligible female I know, so you may take your pick." In a more serious voice, she added, "I do wish you were not so set against the idea of marrying again, Richard. It has been nearly two years now since Aurelia died. It's absurd to cut yourself off from society merely because you have had one bad matrimonial experience."

Richard said nothing. Lady Eleanor apparently judged she had said enough on the subject, for her voice became cheerful and inconsequential once more. "However, I don't mean to try to bully you, Richard. You must do what you think is best, but I believe you will enjoy this party. I'll confer with your housekeeper after dinner, and together we will determine what needs to be done."

She went on to discuss various technical details pertaining to the party. Once more Richard found his thoughts wandering. Up in the nursery they would have already finished their evening meal. What would they be doing now? Would Miss DiMarco be able to control his daughter's vagaries, or would she prove to be a failure, too, like the series of governesses whom he had already been obliged to discharge? As he thought of Alexandra, it came as a shock to hear Mr. Taft speak her name aloud.

"DiMarco, that's what I think it was," he told his wife. "Miss DiMarco. DiMarco was the name of the gal you engaged this afternoon, wasn't it, Brentwood?" he said, appealing to Richard. "The new governess?"

"Er—yes. Yes, I believe so," said Richard, momentarily discomposed at having the subject of his thoughts brought into the conversation. "DiMarco was certainly the name she gave."

"DiMarco," said Lady Eleanor thoughtfully. "I was acquainted with a DiMarco once." A reminiscent smile played about her lips. "It was the first year that I was out. Conte DiMarco was his name—the most handsome, romantic creature you can imagine. All of us girls were desperately in love with him." She looked mischievously at her husband. "Fortunately, I decided to choose solid English worth over Italian romance! I married Charles here—and Conte DiMarco ended up eloping with Elizabeth Manning. I daresay this girl is no relation. She is an Englishwoman?"

"Aye, but she speaks half a dozen languages, easy as winking," said Mr. Taft with vicarious pride. "A pretty gal, too, didn't you think, Brentwood?"

"I suppose so," said Richard doubtfully. "Pretty" seemed somehow an inadequate word to describe Alexandra. *Beautiful* was more like it, yet when he attempted to summon her image to his mind, he could recall only a jumbled impression of blue eyes, honey-colored hair, and an incandescent smile. The overall effect had been so dazzling that it was difficult to particularize her features with any accuracy.

"Well, I hope this governess works out better for you than the others," said Lady Eleanor. Having dismissed the subject of Miss DiMarco with these words, she began to talk about the party again. Richard listened politely, but as soon as dinner was over he excused himself to his sister and Mr. Taft and went upstairs to the nursery.

SIX

When Richard reached the nursery, he found it deserted and dark. There was a light in the night nursery beyond, however, so he headed in that direction. Upon reaching the doorway of the night nursery, he paused, looking with surprise and appreciation at the scene within.

Lady Margaret, clad in her nightdress and with her hair neatly braided, was lying in her crib-bed with Méchante clasped in her arms. In a chair beside the crib sat Alexandra, reading aloud from a worn calf-bound book. As Richard watched, she closed the book and laid it upon a nearby table. "That's all for tonight," she told Lady Margaret. "I will read you some more tomorrow night if you like. But now you need to go to sleep."

"I'm not tired," protested Lady Margaret, opening her eyes wide in an effort to belie their drowsy state.

"Nevertheless, you need to go to sleep," said Alexandra with authority. "We have any number of things to do tomorrow, and you'll never be fit to do them all if you don't get your sleep tonight." She hesitated a moment, then bent and kissed Lady Margaret on the forehead. "Good night, my dear," she said.

"Good night," said Lady Margaret, regarding Alexandra with dark and inscrutable eyes. Turning her head, she caught sight of Richard standing in the doorway. "Papa!"

Richard, feeling slightly embarrassed, came forward. "I

came to see how you and Miss DiMarco were getting on," he said. "Time for bed, is it?"

"*She* says so," said Lady Margaret, throwing a reproachful look at Alexandra. In a more cheerful tone, she added, "She's been reading me a story. It's very interesting, although I don't understand all of it."

"It's *The Vicar of Wakefield,*" said Alexandra in an undertone, displaying the covers of the book to Richard. "I always loved it when I was a child. It's a bit advanced for her, perhaps, but there's no harm in it."

"No, certainly not," agreed Richard. He looked again at his daughter. "Well, I had better not keep you from your rest," he said. "Good night, Margaret." He, too, stooped and kissed her on the brow.

"Good night, Papa," said Lady Margaret, smiling up at him sleepily.

Alexandra rose, picked up the lamp, and carried it into the day nursery. Richard followed her, shutting the door of the night nursery carefully behind him. Immediately there came an indignant howl from within. "Don't shut the door, Papa! I want the door to be open."

"I beg your pardon," said Richard, opening the door again. He cast a rueful smile at Alexandra. She returned his smile as she set the lamp on the mantel.

"I believe a great many children are nervous of the dark," she said in a low voice. "If I leave the lamp here until I myself am ready to retire, she can see it and be comforted. And it is probably better that her door be open anyway, so I can hear her if she needs me in the night."

Richard nodded. He watched as Alexandra went about the nursery, picking up toys and putting them away. She had changed her fur-trimmed traveling costume for a simple gray gown with pleated trimmings. But even in this plain dress she managed to look both distinguished and disarmingly lovely. She was not, he decided, a classical beauty, but there was something very attractive about her slim figure, clear-cut features, and golden coloring. He was surveying her with pleasure when she turned around and caught his eye.

Alexandra, at that moment, was feeling weary but triumphant. Dealing with Lady Margaret had proven an enterprise requiring every ounce of tact and guile that she possessed. On the whole she had been successful in managing her refractory pupil, although there had been one or two skirmishes between them that evening. At one point Lady Margaret had even threatened to take to the corner cabinet again, but this threat had not been put into execution, and Alexandra felt that she had done a day's work such as had never fallen to her lot even under her great-uncle's rigorous regime.

She had been surprised and pleased when Richard had appeared in the nursery. Watching him kiss Lady Margaret good night, she had been moved by his evident love and concern for his daughter. And she was proud that he had found all in order when he came to check upon her. Still, it flustered her a little to have him here now. She was even more flustered when she turned around and found his eyes upon her. Was he perhaps waiting for a report on the day's progress?

"I am afraid I had very little time today for formal lessons, my lord," she said with a nervous smile. "Lady Margaret and I spent most of the afternoon and evening getting acquainted. We did manage to work in a short French lesson, but that is all. I promise to do much better tomorrow."

"I am surprised you did so much," returned Richard. "Merely to get my daughter into her bed at night sometimes requires three people and a protracted siege."

Alexandra smiled again, more easily. "She can be challenging to deal with," she acknowledged. "But your daughter seems to be a very intelligent child, quite precocious, in fact. To hear her talk sometimes, one would never suppose she were merely six years old."

She noticed these words brought a faint crease to Richard's brow. "I suppose some of that would be due her upbringing," he said, speaking rather heavily. "As I mentioned before, Margaret has led a difficult and unsettled existence up till this last year or two." He was silent a moment, then went on in a carefully restrained voice. "Margaret was brought up by my late wife mainly in adult society. She never came into contact with other children—never had companions her own age whom she could talk to and play with. That may well have made her precocious, as you say, but I am afraid it has also made her rather difficult in her temperament. No doubt you have already experienced the difficulty I am talking about."

"Lady Margaret is very young," said Alexandra diplomatically. "I have no doubt she will become easier to deal with as time goes on."

Richard smiled at her. "You are sanguine, Miss DiMarco," he said. "I only hope you are not setting yourself up for a disappointment."

"I don't believe I am," said Alexandra firmly. "Lady Margaret is intelligent, my lord, and that is a great advantage, you know. In fact, I believe it to be the most important advantage we have in this situation. If your daughter were a stupid child, very probably one could do nothing with her. But if we only show her where her behavior is in error—not merely *tell* her, mind you, but show her, so that she herself is satisfied that we are right and she is wrong—she ought to be moved to change her behavior for the better."

Alexandra paused. Richard was regarding her with an odd expression. "I never heard such theories propounded before, Miss DiMarco," he said. "Are these your own ideas or someone else's?"

Alexandra laughed. "Do you know, I think they must be

my own," she said, "although I have heard my great-uncle say similar things on occasion."

"Your great-uncle must be a very wise gentleman," commented Richard.

"In many ways he is," said Alexandra with a smile. "Certainly my great-aunt considers him the sagest of sages." Thinking of her relatives made her feel an unexpected pang of homesickness. Pushing it aside, she went on in a brisk voice. "In any case, I intend to do my best by Lady Margaret. I can sympathize with her predicament more than most people, perhaps, for I myself was raised in a wholly adult environment, away from other children."

"Oh yes?" said Richard encouragingly.

Alexandra had no wish to be drawn into a discussion of her own background. She ignored Richard's question and went on. "As regards Lady Margaret's regular lessons, I did not know exactly what you desired, my lord. She has already learned some French, I find. Do you want her instructed in other languages as well?"

Richard waved his hand. "If you can only teach her to apply herself, I don't think it matters much what else you do," he said. "Use your own judgment in that matter, Miss DiMarco. I think I can trust you to teach Margaret all she needs to know."

"Yes, of course," said Alexandra, blinking a little at this sweeping commendation. Glancing at Richard, she was struck by something in his expression. It was not anything negative; on the contrary, it was distinctly flattering. But still it made her a bit uncomfortable. Smiling, she held out her hand. "I am glad we had this talk, my lord. Now we know better how we stand and how we intend to go on." It occurred to her as she spoke that such talks were probably common between governesses and their employers. "Do you want me to report to you weekly concerning Lady Margaret's progress?" she asked.

"Daily," said Richard firmly. "I should prefer to speak to you about it daily."

"Very well," said Alexandra, surprised but pleased to learn that governesses were subject to such frequent consultation. In a thoughtful voice, she added, "I suppose daily reports *would* be better. That way, we can deal with problems as they arise and perhaps nip them in the bud."

"Exactly," said Richard mendaciously. He hesitated a moment. "Now that Margaret is in bed, perhaps you would like to join me and my sister and brother-in-law downstairs in the drawing room? You are certainly very welcome to do so if you like. One of the maids can come and sit in the nursery in case Margaret should need something."

Alexandra was tempted, but she could see several objections against such a plan. She shook her head. "Thank you, but I think it would be better if I stayed upstairs tonight, my lord," she said. "Perhaps another time."

"Of course," said Richard. Bowing slightly, he wished Alexandra good evening and left the nursery.

Alexandra retired to her room soon after this interview. It took a longer time than usual to make herself ready for bed, owing to the absence of Marie and Trudy, but she managed it at last, and after a certain amount of tossing and turning, she succeeded in falling asleep. She was awakened early the next morning by a small figure that catapulted itself onto her bed, jarring her out of a sound sleep. Alexandra sat up with a stifled shriek.

"It's me," came Lady Margaret's voice out of the darkness. "Aren't you going to get up, Miss DiMarco? I've been awake for hours and hours now, and I'm hungry."

Rubbing her eyes, Alexandra squinted at the clock on the shelf above her bed. It was six o'clock: early, but not much earlier than she had been accustomed to getting up at home. One of her great-uncle's favorite maxims was

"Sanat, sanctificat, et ditat, surgere mane"—which, as her uncle invariably reminded her, translated literally as: "He who would be healthy, happy, and wise, let him rise early."

"Very well, Lady Margaret," said Alexandra. "You must give me a few minutes to get ready." Getting out of bed, she began to make her preparations for the day.

Lady Margaret assisted her in her toilette as before, and by exercise of the bribery of another ribbon, Alexandra got Lady Margaret herself washed and brushed and into clean clothes. They breakfasted on tea, toast, and rolls in the nursery, then went into the schoolroom to begin the day's lessons.

Lady Margaret perched herself on a chair and looked expectantly at Alexandra. Alexandra looked back at her with a sense of rising panic. She began to realize just what she had gotten herself into. It had been easy enough to teach the impromptu French lesson yesterday, but now, with Lady Margaret seated formally in front of her and a whole long day to fill, Alexandra hardly knew where to begin.

"Well, I suppose we must get started," she said, in an artificially cheerful voice. "Why don't you show me what you were doing with your last governess?"

"All right," said Lady Margaret, and obediently fetched a much-blotted copybook from the schoolroom cupboard. Alexandra, turning over its leaves, was relieved to see it contained a number of suggestions helpful to her situation. Sums and spelling and penmanship were all good straightforward subjects which even a novice governess ought to be able to teach. She wrote out a page of sums, and while Lady Margaret was wrestling with these she made a hasty search of the schoolroom for other useful material. Her search revealed several battered textbooks including a beginning French grammar and Goldsmith's *History of England*. Alexandra's spirits began to rise. With these references, she felt she could put together a tolerably comprehensive curriculum. She settled down to her morning's work.

All went well that morning and into the afternoon. The mathematics lesson was succeeded by lessons in penmanship and spelling. When Lady Margaret began to grow fidgety and to complain of being bored, Alexandra adjourned lessons for an hour and took her for a walk out-of-doors. Lady Margaret ran on ahead, while Alexandra strolled behind, admiring Brentwood's grounds and formal gardens. Lady Margaret showed her a pond with swans in it which she spoke wistfully of having fed on a previous occasion, and Alexandra promised to beg some stale bread from the cook for this purpose before they went for a walk the following day. They then returned to the house for lessons in French and history.

A light nuncheon of cold meat, fruit, and bread was served in the schoolroom at noon. Alexandra then settled down to give a geography lesson, but at once she ran into difficulties. Lady Margaret would not concentrate on the globes, or on putting together the dissected map Alexandra had found on one of the nursery shelves. All she wanted to do was to go and feed the swans with the remains of her nuncheon bread and butter.

"When you have finished putting together your map, then perhaps we can take another walk down to the pond," said Alexandra pacifically. "But you have done no lessons at all this afternoon, Lady Margaret. I think it would be better if you did a little work before we went out again."

Lady Margaret's lower lip protruded, and a defiant gleam appeared in her dark eyes. "I won't," she said, looking at Alexandra challengingly. "I won't do my geography lesson. I want to feed the swans now."

Alexandra saw that they had reached a point of crisis. So far Lady Margaret had obeyed her reasonably well, but only because it suited her to do so. It remained to be seen if Alexandra could influence her to obey when it ran contrary to her own whims.

"I cannot make you learn, Lady Margaret," she said, looking the child in the eye. "But I can keep you in the schoolroom until you either do so or grow too old to have a governess. You will not feed the swans until you have completed your lessons this afternoon."

An angry outburst followed. Lady Margaret stormed, sobbed, and threatened Alexandra with the most dire punishments. "I want to feed the swans," she wept. "I want to feed the swans now!"

"And so you shall, as soon as you complete your lessons," said Alexandra encouragingly. "You must see, Lady Margaret, that by behaving as you are doing, you are only delaying the time until you do feed them." Lady Margaret was deaf to this reasoning, however. With an angry sob, she began to run toward the corner cabinet.

Then Alexandra had an idea. "Lady Margaret, you are behaving badly," she said in her sternest voice. "Go shut yourself in the corner cabinet this minute!"

Lady Margaret came to a sudden stop. With a defiant look at Alexandra, she ran instead to the night nursery and slammed the door shut behind her.

"Lady Margaret, go to the night nursery this minute," commanded Alexandra, raising her voice to be heard inside the next room. "And stay there until I tell you to come out!"

The door to the night nursery instantly flew open, and Lady Margaret came running out. As she made for the corner cabinet once more, Alexandra commanded, "Lady Margaret, shut yourself in the corner cabinet!" Lady Margaret, giggling now, reversed directions and headed back toward the night nursery. "Go to the night nursery!" said Alexandra. Lady Margaret, overcome with laughter, collapsed in a giggling heap on the nursery floor.

"Miss DiMarco, you are silly!" she said, smiling up at Alexandra.

"If so, I don't think I'm the only one," said Alexandra, smiling back at her. "Do you realize what you just did?" Lady Margaret shook her head. "You just allowed yourself to be manipulated, Lady Margaret. Do you know what that word means?"

Again Lady Margaret shook her head. "To manipulate someone means to make them do something they don't necessarily want to do themselves," explained Alexandra. "You went to the corner cabinet because you thought I would not like it. Then when it appeared I did like it, you went to the night nursery instead. Does not that seem silly? Because you really did not want to go to either place. What you really wanted to do was to feed the swans."

The smile vanished from Lady Margaret's face. "I want to feed the swans," she said, looking at Alexandra piteously.

"Well then, why do you not complete your geography lesson? That is by far the quickest way to do it," said Alexandra. "I know you are angry at me for not letting you do what you like, and you think the way to punish me is not to do your lessons. But in fact not doing your lessons does not really hurt me, Lady Margaret. Teaching is hard work, and my life would be easier by far if I did nothing but take you to feed the swans all day. The only person hurt by not doing your lessons is you—and perhaps your father."

Lady Margaret looked interested. "How does it hurt me not to do lessons?" she asked.

"It hurts you because without lessons you will grow up ignorant and undisciplined," explained Alexandra. "And though I suppose it's possible for a person to be ignorant and undisciplined and happy, too, I can't imagine it myself. To my mind, both education and discipline are necessary to a person's happiness."

Lady Margaret mulled this over for a moment or two. "What about Papa?" she asked. "You said it would hurt Papa, too, if I didn't do my lessons. How would it hurt him?"

"It would hurt him because he loves you and wants you to be happy," said Alexandra. "And he believes, like I do, that your best chance of being happy is to grow up to be an intelligent, educated, and well-mannered woman."

"But I'm not happy now," complained Lady Margaret. "If you and Papa want me to be happy, why do you not let me do what I want to do? When I lived with Mama, I got to do whatever I wanted."

Alexandra had no idea how to counter such an argument as this. She ventured a shot in the dark. "And were you very happy, living with your mother?" she said gently.

A cloud passed over Lady Margaret's small face. "No," she said in a low voice.

Alexandra observed that her lower lip was trembling. She had no wish to press the lesson too far, but she thought it vital to make her point. "Perhaps when you were younger you were able to do as you pleased most of the time," she said, feeling her way carefully. "Children of four or five years of age are only a step removed from babies. They don't have to do any work, and they aren't responsible for their own behavior, because it's the duty of their mother or father or governess to discipline them if they need it. But you are growing up now, and it is time you begin to work and to learn to discipline yourself. It's a hard fact, but nobody grown-up gets to do what they want all the time."

"Don't they?" said Lady Margaret, looking skeptical. "What about Papa? He is a lord and very rich. At least, Mama always said he was rich, although he wouldn't give her but barely enough to live on. She was always complaining about it when I lived with her."

Alexandra was shocked by this speech, but contrived not

to show it. "I am sure your father is well-off, Lady Margaret, but the fact is that even people with money have to work," she said. "Owning a property this size must be a great care and responsibility for your father. And of course he has you to worry about, too."

Lady Margaret pondered this. "What about you?" she said. "You're all grown-up. Don't you get to do what you want to do?"

Alexandra could not repress a smile. "Hardly," she said. "I have always been obliged to work, from the time when I was younger than you."

Lady Margaret looked impressed. "Have you been a governess since you were five?"

Alexandra laughed. "No, I was merely learning to be one! It has taken me all this time to learn enough to teach you. If indeed I have learned enough," she added ruefully. "But there is one thing I *have* learned, and that is that there is a satisfaction in work well done. Even if it's work you don't much want to do—and even if no one much appreciates it when it's done."

Again Lady Margaret pondered. Alexandra went on in her most persuasive voice. "Fortunately, none of us have to work all the time. So if you will hurry and finish your geography lesson, Lady Margaret, we can still go and feed the swans this afternoon."

There was a long pause. Alexandra waited in suspense, hardly daring to breathe. "All right," said Lady Margaret at last. "I'll do it." She went over to the dissected map. With a look half affectionate and half rebellious, she added, "I don't *want* to do it. I would much rather feed the swans now. But I'll do it because you want me to, Miss DiMarco."

Alexandra was touched by this avowal, but she felt she could not allow it to pass without correction. "No, you must not do it for me, Lady Margaret," she told the child gently. "I will not always be here, you know, and it is not for me that you should be working in any case. I would rather you did it for yourself. You are growing old enough to take responsibility for your own actions, and if you are to become the woman your father and I hope you will become, you must learn to discipline yourself."

Lady Margaret nodded, her face solemnly impressed. "I will try, Miss DiMarco," she said, and bent to her task with an energy that boded well for its speedy completion.

SEVEN

Alexandra felt weary after her skirmish with Lady Margaret, as though she had been engaged in real warfare rather than merely a battle of wills. When the geography lesson had been successfully completed and the two of them went out to the pond again, Alexandra was happy to sink down on a convenient bench while Lady Margaret cavorted along the water's edge, throwing bread to the swans and shrieking with laughter and delight when they ate it.

All the same, Alexandra managed to gain several more valuable insights into her pupil during their time at the pond.

Having fed the swans all the bread, Lady Margaret came dancing over to Alexandra in an ecstatic mood. "Oh, Miss DiMarco, did you see how that big black swan chased after me?" she shouted. "I thought he was going to eat me and not the bread! And he took the whole slice right out of my hand!"

"Yes, I did see," said Alexandra. With a smile, she added, "But you know you need not shout, Lady Margaret. I can hear you perfectly well without, and it is one of the rules of good behavior that ladies—and gentlemen, too—should use a moderate voice at all times, unless of course it is a real matter of emergency. If that swan really had eaten you, now, you would be quite justified in shouting!"

Lady Margaret laughed at this, but the next instant her face grew thoughtful. "Sometimes ladies shout," she said. "Mama used to shout all the time. She shouted at her maid, and at the cook and footmen. And sometimes she threw things, too, when she was really angry."

Alexandra blinked at this exposition of the late Countess's character. "Of course, without knowing the situation, I cannot say whether your mother was justified in her behavior," she said carefully. "But I cannot think it was very pleasant for the maid and cook and footmen to be shouted at, do you? I don't like to be shouted at myself, so I try not to shout at other people. It stands to reason that they don't like it any better than I do."

Lady Margaret nodded solemnly. "I don't like being shouted at, either," she confided. "Mama shouted at me once because I spilled a box of powder all over her dressing room floor." Her lower lip trembled. "It was an accident, but she said I was a clumsy little ape, and that I could never come into her dressing room again."

There were tears in Lady Margaret's eyes now. Alexandra's heart went out to the child in her misery. She knelt and put her arms around Lady Margaret's shoulders.

"Of course your mother did not mean what she said," she said warmly. "We all lose our tempers now and then, and say things we do not mean." She hesitated a moment, then went on, looking at Lady Margaret earnestly. "That's another reason why it's so important that we practice self-discipline, Lady Margaret. I am sure your mother was sorry afterward that she had spoken so harshly to you. And I am equally sure—as sure as I can be of anything—that if she were here with us right now, she would tell you so."

"Do you think so?" said Lady Margaret wistfully.

"I am sure of it," said Alexandra firmly. "If I were you, I would try not to think of it anymore, Lady Margaret. Or if you do think of it, try to look on it as a lesson about the importance of thinking before you speak. Once words are spoken, you know, we can never take them back, and so they go on hurting and hurting and causing more damage. By practicing self-discipline in what we say and do, we can avoid hurting people and causing problems for ourselves."

Lady Margaret nodded. "I don't think Mama had much self-discipline," she said dolefully.

Alexandra felt privately assured that this was the case, but she saw no reason to say so. Instead, she gave Lady Margaret a hug. "It's a hard business sometimes, but learning self-discipline is like learning anything else," she told the child. "You will find it gets easier with practice. Now let's go on back to the house, and I will see about giving you a music lesson. Do you play the pianoforte at all?"

Lady Margaret nodded, looking quite restored to her former spirits. "Oh, yes, I can play very well," she said boastfully. "I can play three tunes, and I don't even need the music."

"Well, you can play your three tunes for me, and then we'll see where to go from there. And on the way back to the house, perhaps we can practice naming things in French, so that we get an extra lesson in that today."

Lady Margaret happily assented to this plan and named trees, clouds, grass, and other outdoor objects in French until presently they arrived back at the house.

Once inside the house, Lady Margaret led Alexandra into a room adjoining the drawing room on the house's ground floor. "This is the music room," she said. "The pianoforte is here, and we've a harp-si-core, too."

"Harpsichord," corrected Alexandra absently. She was surveying the handsome grand pianoforte that occupied the center of the music room. Drawing back the cover, she ran a hand experimentally along the keys.

"That was pretty," said Lady Margaret with interest. "Play that again, please, Miss DiMarco."

Alexandra laughed. "That's only a scale, child," she said, but obligingly repeated the exercise. Lady Margaret, charmed, begged her to play something else. Alexandra obediently played a couple of short songs, to which Lady Margaret listened with intense delight.

"You play *much* better than mam'selle and my other governesses," she said, looking at Alexandra with admiration. "Play something else."

Alexandra, having never before experienced such an appreciative audience, was not loath to comply. She played a sonata and several shorter pieces, until finally awakened by the sound of the clock striking the hour in the drawing room next door. She looked at Lady Margaret in dismay.

"It is five o'clock, and I haven't let you play a note yet! How could you let me go on and on like that?"

Lady Margaret laughed delightedly. "I didn't mind! I would rather hear you play than do it myself. Will you play some more for me?"

"Not now, at least. It is time for you to be cleaned up so you will be ready for your supper. Perhaps later this evening I will play for you—or if not this evening, tomorrow. But you will have to play for me first, and let me teach you something, so I can do the job I was hired to do."

With a rebellious look, Lady Margaret started to speak. Then, with a visible effort, she checked herself. "I would like to hear you play again," she said, quite mildly. "But I would like you to teach me, too. That way, perhaps I could play like you do someday."

Alexandra reached out and hugged her. "I have no doubt you will, my dear," she told Lady Margaret. "You have already taken the first step today. Now let's go upstairs and get ready for supper."

Lady Margaret fell in readily with this suggestion. She behaved well throughout that evening and made such praiseworthy efforts to keep her temper in check that Alexandra was both amazed and touched.

"Of course it would be too much to expect all to go smoothly hereafter," she reflected to herself, watching

Lady Margaret quietly turning over the leaves of a picture book that evening. "I am sure that we will experience setbacks now and then, but this does definitely appear to be the right way to manage her. My, but it's hard work being a governess! One needs the wisdom of a Socrates, the diplomacy of a Talleyrand, and the strength of a draft horse to get through the day."

Tired though she was that evening, Alexandra had the energy to smooth her dress and tidy her hair before her conference with Richard. She had worn her hair that day in a simple braid pinned over her head, partly because she had been in a hurry that morning to make her toilette and partly because she found it impossible to achieve any more elaborate arrangement without Marie's help. When Richard came softly into the nursery that evening, he found her once again reading from *The Vicar of Wakefield*.

"Good evening," he said with smile.

Richard had found the day an extremely long one. Although he was not consciously counting the hours until his evening conference with Alexandra, he had nonetheless found his usual daytime activities less absorbing than usual. Half a dozen times he had repressed an urge to go upstairs and see what was transpiring in the nursery. But even without going upstairs, he had managed to see something of Alexandra's activities. His study commanded a view of the pond, and he had been standing at the window that afternoon when Alexandra and Lady Margaret had come out the second time to feed the swans.

It had been a struggle not to go down and join them. But Richard had been reluctant to intrude himself on their party, as well as curious to see exactly how the two of them were getting along. Of course, he had been unable to hear what they said to each other at that distance, but he had seen enough to know when Lady Margaret grew upset and how Alexandra had gone about comforting her. And when he had seen his daughter skip away afterward, apparently restored to spirits, he had felt as though a burden had been lifted from his heart.

"I believe she'll do," he said aloud, and went back to his work with a renewed zest.

He had taken great pains dressing for dinner that evening, choosing to wear his best blue Bath-cloth topcoat and a pair of fawn-colored trousers. His hair and neckcloth he arranged with unusual care, and he was dissatisfied enough with the polish on his boots to ask his valet to give them an extra shine. If asked, he would have firmly denied that the governess upstairs had anything to do with these preparations. But he was conscious all during dinner that he was to see and speak with Alexandra later that evening. As during the previous night's dinner, he found himself impatient to be done with the seemingly interminable meal, and as soon as he could, he abandoned Mr. Taft and his sister and went upstairs to the nursery.

Alexandra was pleased to see him. She, too, had been looking forward to the interview, though she told herself it was only because she was eager to report on Lady Margaret's progress. But she found herself thinking how handsome Richard looked in his blue coat, close-fitting trousers, and shining Hessians. She wished she were wearing something more attractive than a dark green morning dress as she rose and greeted him.

"Good evening, my lord. You find us once more amid the residents of Wakefield Parish," she said with a smile.

"Then don't let me interrupt you, Miss DiMarco," said Richard. "I can wait until you're done before speaking to you." He seated himself on the end of Lady Margaret's bed.

"Hullo, Papa," said Lady Margaret, smiling sleepily and holding out her hand to him. Richard took it in his and held it, stroking it between his fingers, as Alexandra reopened the book and began to read once more.

As she read, Richard studied her covertly. He admired

the sweet, serious cast of her profile and the honey-colored hair that gleamed like gold in the lamplight. He admired the smooth, musical voice in which she read, and the way in which the characters seemed to come alive in her narrative. Familiar as the story was to him, he actually found himself growing interested in it as she read and was quite as disappointed as Lady Margaret when Alexandra stopped and closed the book. "That is all for tonight, Lady Margaret," she said. "We shall read some more tomorrow."

Lady Margaret, looking mutinous, opened her mouth. Then, abruptly, she closed it again. "All right," she said. Richard, who had been expecting a tantrum, was surprised. He was even more surprised to see Lady Margaret throw both arms around Alexandra and kiss her, when Alexandra bent to kiss her good night. "Good night, Miss DiMarco," she said, and added something in a whisper which Richard could not hear. Alexandra's reply was quite audible, however.

"Well, and I love you, too, Lady Margaret," she said, smiling down at the child. "You have done well today, and I am very proud of you. Good night, my dear, and I will see you in the morning."

Richard, amazed at these proceedings, silently bent to kiss his daughter in his turn. Lady Margaret held out her arms to him, too, and kissed him back resoundingly instead of passively accepting his kiss as she usually did. "Good night, Papa," she told him. "I'll try not to be a worry to you."

Richard, confused, murmured something to the effect that she was no worry to him, but on the contrary a great comfort. She smiled at him sweetly, then shut her eyes, clasped Méchante more firmly in her arms, and settled herself to go to sleep.

Richard followed Alexandra out of the night nursery, being careful this time to leave the door ajar behind him.

Once in the day nursery, he looked at Alexandra with amazement. "Are you an enchantress?" he asked.

Alexandra laughed. "Oh, no, my lord," she said. "I did speak to your daughter about one or two things today—but if she had not seen fit to act upon my words, most assuredly nothing would have been accomplished. This change is her own doing, not mine."

"That may be," said Richard. "But I can assure you that one or two people previous to now have also spoken to Margaret, including myself. And as far as I could see, it had no effect on her behavior at all."

Alexandra was pleased but embarrassed by this praise. "Indeed, I know not whether this change will be permanent, my lord," she said earnestly. "We must not count on its being so. But I do think I have found the proper way to approach Lady Margaret about her behavior. She really is an intelligent child, capable of understanding quite adult concepts and of putting them into practice, too."

Richard shook his head, a smile on his lips. "Perhaps so, Miss DiMarco," he said. "But I am still inclined to the theory that you have something of the enchantress in you."

Alexandra, brushing this aside with a blush, went on to give a brief report of the day's progress. "I am afraid we did not manage to work in any music lesson," she said regretfully. "However, Lady Margaret does appear to love music, and according to what she has told me, she already has some acquaintance with the pianoforte. I am looking forward to instructing her in that, too."

Richard impulsively reached out and took Alexandra's hand. Alexandra was a trifle surprised by this action but said nothing, merely looking at him inquiringly. "Thank you, Miss DiMarco," he said, and raised her hand to his lips.

Alexandra felt herself flush once again, but it was a flush of pleasure. There was a glow in her heart even warmer than the one which flamed her cheeks. She smiled at Richard. "You need not thank me, my lord," she said. "I am only doing the job you are paying me for, after all."

He shook his head. "That may be. But I don't think anyone else could do the job you are doing, Miss DiMarco. Thank you, once again."

Alexandra found herself recalling Richard's words many times in the days that followed. They were extremely busy days, for it proved no easy matter to teach lessons in a dozen different subjects while supervising Lady Margaret's dress, play, and meals. But during her occasional unoccupied moment—when Lady Margaret was playing by herself, for instance, or after she had gone to bed in the evening—Alexandra had time to reflect with pleasure on her employer's words of praise.

She had other things to gratify her, too. The change in Lady Margaret's behavior appeared to be both permanent and profound. The words Alexandra had addressed to her that day in the nursery appeared to have made a deep impression on the little girl—so deep that Alexandra sometimes feared she had unwittingly touched some sensitive area within the child's psyche. Instead of having to chastise Lady Margaret, she now found herself having to comfort her when, as still happened on occasion, Lady Margaret committed some fault of conduct. She seemed to feel these failures so deeply and to grieve over them so sincerely that Alexandra had hard work sometimes to convince her that "to err is human."

"You have no self-discipline, Méchante," Alexandra overheard her telling her doll one day. "Undisciplined people are unhappy themselves, and they make the people around them unhappy, too. You must try to control yourself, my dear, and then you will be a woman I can be proud of."

Alexandra could not help smiling at this conversation, but it left her deeply thoughtful. Also thought-provoking was Lady Margaret's growing attachment to herself. From the date of the lecture on self-discipline, Lady Margaret had conceived a violent fondness for Alexandra that made her follow Alexandra about during the day and fret anytime she was absent from the house.

Alexandra was flattered by this devotion, but disturbed by it also. She began to grow rather worried when she reflected that she must leave Brentwood within a month or two. Her departure might even be sooner if Miss Harcourt's mother made a quick recovery. She tried to prepare Lady Margaret for the idea of her leaving, but Lady Margaret refused to hear of it or to consider her place ever being filled by Miss Harcourt. Alexandra could only hope that when the time came, the substitution could be effected with less upheaval than presently appeared likely.

She had written Miss Harcourt soon after her arrival, describing her successful interview with Richard and assuring Miss Harcourt that she could stay with her mother as long as necessary. After much deliberation, she had also written the following letter to her great-aunt and -uncle:

Dear Uncle Frederick and Aunt Elizabeth,

I trust you are both feeling better now and will soon be completely recovered from your illness. You will be happy to know I have thus far been perfectly well; thanks to your efforts it appears I have escaped taking the influenza. I did hate to leave Mannington while you were both unwell, but I understand that your insistence on my leaving was motivated only by concern for my health.

No doubt you have already heard from Edward and the other servants that I was forced to change my travel plans when we reached Wanworth. It developed that Aunt Emily was not in Tunbridge Wells, as we supposed, but staying at the home of friends.

Perhaps you will think I did wrong, but it seemed to me that any friends of Aunt Emily's might be willing to befriend me, too. I knew you would not want me to return to Mannington, except as a last resort. Having considered the matter at length, I finally elected to seek refuge at Brentwood (the home of the Earl of Brentwood and Barstock, as perhaps you know) and trusted to the Earl's hospitality to take me in. I may say that my trust was not misplaced. The Earl and his family have made me welcome in the kindest way, and I feel this arrangement to be quite as satisfactory as our original one. Brentwood is a lovely estate, and when I have not been enjoying myself among its grounds and gardens, I have been amusing myself giving lessons in French, music, et cetera, to the Earl's daughter Lady Margaret, a most lovely and amiable girl.

Since the Earl and his family seem eager to keep me here as long as possible, I have agreed to extend my stay, perhaps even through the Christmas holidays. I hope this will not conflict with any other plans you may have made for me. But knowing your concern for my health and your anxiety to err on the side of safety in such matters, I was fairly sure you would prefer me to stay away from Mannington until then anyway. Please believe I miss you both very much, and look forward to seeing you both sometime in the New Year.

> Your affectionate niece,
> Alexandra Manning

P.S. You may write me here in care of the Earl's daughter, Lady Margaret Brentwood.

Alexandra was pleased with this letter, which she felt to be a fairly accurate résumé of her situation. It was, after all, quite true to say that she had initially considered whether Aunt Emily's friends might be willing to take her in. It was also true that she had eventually taken refuge with the Earl of Brentwood. If her great-aunt and -uncle chose to take these two separate, individually truthful statements and assume they were related, that could not really be counted a lie, Alexandra told herself. She was satisfied that her letter must allay any anxiety her great-aunt and -uncle might be feeling on her account, and that it would also prepare them for a possible extension of her stay at Brentwood if such a thing became necessary.

It did worry her a little that her aunt and uncle would inevitably address their letters to Miss Manning if and when they wrote to Brentwood. But assuming the letters were addressed in care of Lady Margaret, she reasoned she ought to be able to obtain them easily enough no matter how they were addressed. She could always make some excuse to Lady Margaret and the servants for the difference in name. Indeed, it might even be that she could give them the true reason, for they were unlikely to know or care if she were half a Manning. In all the household it was only the Earl, his sister, and his brother-in-law from whom she needed to conceal her identity.

But it was fated that ere long one of these three was to learn the truth, in a manner unforeseen by Alexandra.

EIGHT

Lady Eleanor, sister to the Earl of Brentwood and Bar-stock, was a lady who prided herself upon her social acumen. During the London Season she enjoyed the reputation of a clever and hospitable hostess, one who could effortlessly bring together the compatible personalities in a gathering while separating those likely to clash. She was likewise in demand as a guest, for her mere presence was capable of infusing charm and liveliness into the dullest soirée. At the moment, all her thoughts and energies were bent on planning her holiday house party at Brentwood. But it gradually dawned on her, even in the midst of her preoccupation, that there was something a little odd about her brother's behavior.

"I have been thinking about this house party of ours, Richard," she told him one night at dinner. "And it seems to me that if we invite all these people to stay with us over the holidays, we are obliged to give at least one really grand party on their behalf. It would be a nice way to reacquaint ourselves with the neighbors, too. I thought perhaps a ball, on Christmas Day?"

Lady Eleanor put this suggestion forward perfunctorily, not really expecting a positive response. By asking for a ball, she reckoned she would eventually be haggled down to an assembly or rout-party, either of which she considered a satisfactory compromise. She was therefore much surprised when her brother replied, "A ball? I suppose it *has* been some time since we had a ball here at Brentwood. Why not, after all?"

Lady Eleanor looked at him in amazement. He was gazing off into space with a half smile on his lips, as though he saw there an extremely agreeable image. Lady Eleanor's interest was piqued. She began to pay closer attention to her brother throughout the rest of the meal, observing his absence of manner and the faint, self-conscious smile which returned to his lips from time to time.

It was not the house party he was thinking about. Lady Eleanor felt positive of that. Although she had done her best to interest him with glowing descriptions of Lady Rosalie, Miss Spence, and the other marriageable young ladies she was inviting, she could not flatter herself that she had been successful. It was clearly something else that was engaging his thoughts. Yet looking at him closely, it struck Lady Eleanor that his expression did look suspiciously like that of a man smitten by Cupid's arrow. Lady Eleanor determined to investigate the matter further.

She watched and listened closely throughout the rest of the meal, but obtained no further clue. There was, however, one illuminating remark made, just as she was quitting the table after the conclusion of dessert.

"Richard, I hope you will not take long over your port," she told him. "If we are to give a ball on Christmas Day, we need to sit down this evening and settle some of the details."

Her brother shifted in his chair. "I cannot come directly to the drawing room, Eleanor," he said. "I must run upstairs and attend to some business first. After that, I will be at your disposal."

"Got to talk to the governess, eh?" said Mr. Taft sapiently.

"Yes," said Richard. He spoke in a matter-of-fact voice,

but Lady Eleanor, looking at him attentively, thought there was a hint of a color in his face.

Mr. Taft rattled on, all unawares. "Seems to me you spend a lot of time in the nursery since Miss DiMarco came, Brentwood," he told Richard. "You'll hardly believe it, Eleanor, but he's left me to drink my port alone six nights out of the seven while he hobnobs upstairs with the governess."

Lady Eleanor returned a light answer, but she had seen and heard enough to enlighten her. She had hard work to conceal her perturbation. Her brother was being taken in by some scheming cat of a governess! Clearly it behooved her to do something about it, but what? Lady Eleanor knew better than to barge ahead in such a delicate matter without due reflection. Accordingly, she reflected all that evening, watching with inward vexation as her brother, arriving fresh from his interview with the governess, proceeded to cheerfully approve all her most lavish schemes. He was obviously smitten with this Miss DiMarco if he could be brought to agree to a hired orchestra, a seated supper, and unlimited champagne!

The next day, Lady Eleanor laid her plans carefully. She waited until late afternoon, when the sounds of the pianoforte came drifting out of the music room. She had heard such sounds regularly since the new governess's arrival, but since she was not particularly musical herself, she had never felt any interest in auditing Lady Margaret's pianoforte lessons. Now, however, she made for the music room with a purposeful step.

Entering the room silently, she was astonished to see she was not the only auditor to the lesson. Her brother was lounging on the sofa beside the fireplace, gazing at the pair seated at the pianoforte. Lady Eleanor looked, too, and blinked in surprise. Was this a governess? Her eyes appraised Alexandra's purple silk gown with its scalloped flounce and lace trimming; the glossy honey-gold hair braided atop her head; the lovely, vivid face bent over the keyboard. Lady Eleanor looked and looked again. Both Alexandra and Lady Margaret were so intent on the lesson that they did not notice her presence. But her brother presently caught sight of her standing in the doorway and rose to his feet with an expression of mingled guilt and dismay.

"Eleanor!"

Alexandra looked up from the pianoforte. She saw a handsome middle-aged lady standing in the doorway, regarding her with a searching expression. She saw also that Richard seemed to be discomposed by the lady's presence. "I'm sorry, did you need me for something, Eleanor?" he asked. "I was just listening to Margaret's pianoforte lesson."

"Yes, I could see that," said Lady Eleanor in a faintly ironic voice. "So this is Miss DiMarco?" Once more her eyes appraised Alexandra curiously. "Won't you introduce us, Richard?"

Richard reluctantly murmured an introduction. "But I do not mean to keep you here, Eleanor," he added. "Indeed, I was just going myself. If there is something you need from me—"

"No, not a thing, Richard. Like you, I have merely come to listen." Lady Eleanor seated herself on the sofa and folded her hands in her lap. "You run along, and I will stay here and observe the music lesson."

Richard quit the room, not without many an uneasy backward glance. Alexandra wondered that his sister's presence seemed to cause him so much discomfiture. She wondered also at Lady Eleanor's insistence on staying and listening. But she soon forgot the other lady's presence in the interest of teaching Lady Margaret her day's lesson.

Lady Margaret, having run through all her exercises,

now began urging Alexandra to play for her. "That song you played yesterday, please, Miss DiMarco?" she begged. "You said if I worked hard you'd play it again for me today."

"Very well," acquiesced Alexandra with a smile. She played the desired piece through, to Lady Margaret's acclaim. She had by this time thoroughly forgotten Lady Eleanor's presence and so it came as a shock when that lady applauded her, too.

"Brava, Miss DiMarco! That was an amazing performance. An amazing performance," repeated Lady Eleanor, looking Alexandra over with an unreadable expression.

"Thank you," said Alexandra politely. Turning to Lady Margaret, she continued, "We had better go upstairs now and change your dress for supper. That encounter with a mud puddle you had when we were out walking didn't do your clothes any good!"

Lady Margaret laughed and agreed. Alexandra helped her down from the pianoforte bench and led her upstairs to the nursery. She was surprised to see Lady Eleanor trailing after them. "I thought I'd like to see the old nursery again," explained Lady Eleanor with an easy smile. "You know I was born at Brentwood, and so I spent the first ten or twelve years of my life in these rooms."

"Yes, of course," said Alexandra, smiling. "This would have been your nursery, too."

"Did you used to be a child, Aunt Eleanor?" inquired Lady Margaret with round eyes. Both women laughed. Alexandra went about, laying out fresh clothing for Lady Margaret and tidying up a few toys that were lying about. Lady Eleanor stood watching for a moment or two, then wandered off in the direction of the schoolroom. When Alexandra went to her own room a few minutes later to fetch a ribbon for Lady Margaret's hair, she found Lady Eleanor standing in the doorway.

"This is your room?" she demanded, looking around Alexandra's crowded chamber with an expression of disbelief.

"Yes," said Alexandra warily. Lady Eleanor turned and regarded her for a long moment.

"Miss DiMarco, I wish you would tell me what your game is," she said. "Who and what, exactly, are you?"

"Why, that you already know, Lady Eleanor," said Alexandra, pretending to misunderstand her. "My name is DiMarco—Alexandra DiMarco. And as to who I am—I am a governess. Lady Margaret's governess, to be exact."

Lady Eleanor continued to regard her speculatively. "I knew a DiMarco once," she remarked. "A Conte DiMarco—an Italian gentleman. Perhaps he was some relation of yours, Miss DiMarco?"

Alexandra sought desperately for a way to evade this question without lying. "It may be," she said at last, in a noncommittal voice. "But you see my father died before I was born, and so I was never acquainted with him or any of his family. I was brought up by my mother's family, who were English." Alexandra reflected with satisfaction that this statement was true enough, taken by itself. But Lady Eleanor merely went on looking at her with that queer, searching gaze.

"You have a great look of him," she said. "And I can see your resemblance to your mother, too. Elizabeth Manning was one of my closest friends."

"Was she?" said Alexandra involuntarily. Lady Eleanor nodded, a smile overspreading her face.

"Yes, she was. And a sweeter, softer-hearted creature never drew breath. You look to be a little tougher than she was, which is a mercy, I suppose, considering that you have your own way to make in the world. But still, I find it hard to believe anyone of your pedigree is reduced to earning her living as a governess. Did your mother's family quite cast her off when she eloped with your father?"

"Oh no," said Alexandra earnestly. "They were unhappy about her marrying as she did, of course, but I know they never cast her off. They continued to make her an allowance as long as she was living with my father, and then when my father was killed and she was left a widow, they took her back to Mannington so they could care for her. And then when she died a few months later giving birth to me, they adopted me and treated me as though I had been their own child. Indeed, they have behaved with the utmost kindness and generosity."

"But still they allowed you to go out governessing," observed Lady Eleanor.

"Well, they didn't precisely allow it." Faced with a choice between doing the Mannings an injustice and telling the truth, Alexandra thought it better to tell the truth and trust Lady Eleanor not to betray her. She gave a brief but full account of the circumstances that had brought her to Brentwood. Lady Eleanor laughed immoderately at her story. She seemed to find particular amusement in hearing about Alexandra's initial encounter with her brother.

"And so you convinced Richard to take you as a governess," she said, wiping her streaming eyes. "What fools men are! Any woman could have seen at a glance that you were no governess. Indeed you are far too pretty, my dear—and if that dress you're wearing isn't trimmed with real Brussels lace, then I'm a Belgian myself."

"Oh, but you must not think I am imposing on Lord Brentwood," said Alexandra anxiously. "I really am doing my best to teach Lady Margaret. And though I may not have any previous experience teaching children, still I think I'm doing a fairly good job at it." She turned to look at Lady Margaret, who was struggling to button up the back of her own frock with rather indifferent results.

Lady Margaret looked up at that moment and saw Alexandra. "Miss DiMarco, did you find that ribbon?" she asked. "You've been ages and ages getting it."

"Just a moment, my dear," called Alexandra. She fetched the ribbon from her box and hastened back to the nursery. Lady Eleanor followed, an expression of amusement still on her face.

"I must say, you do appear to be rather successful at managing our enfant terrible," she said, watching as Alexandra rebuttoned Lady Margaret's dress and tied her hair back with the ribbon. Lady Margaret, who understood quite enough French to translate this, flashed her a look of reproach.

"I'm not an enfant terrible," she said, her lower lip trembling. "I'm a good girl, aren't I, Miss DiMarco?"

"Of course you are," said Alexandra, also shooting Lady Eleanor a look of reproach. "Your aunt was talking about Méchante, I believe. Were you not, Lady Eleanor?"

"Of course," agreed Lady Eleanor good-naturedly. "It was your doll I meant, not you, Margaret."

Lady Margaret shook her head gravely. "Yes, Méchante is very naughty sometimes. She has not a great deal of self-discipline. But Miss DiMarco and I are trying to teach her some."

"Well, I wish you luck with that endeavor," said Lady Eleanor, laughing. She watched as Lady Margaret went off to play with a stack of blocks in the corner. "You certainly have accomplished miracles with that child," she told Alexandra. "When I came here six weeks ago, she was the most dreadful little hellion. I would have said it was impossible to live in the same house with her, let alone teach her."

Alexandra shook her head. "Not at all. She is as intelligent a child as you could wish for, and now we understand each other I do not find her difficult to deal with."

"Still, it cannot be very agreeable for you," said Lady Eleanor, eyeing Alexandra a trifle incredulously. "Don't tell me you *like* being a governess?"

Alexandra considered this question seriously. "Indeed,

I think I do," she said, with an air of surprise. "Of course the days do get rather long, and sometimes the repetition of the work is tedious, but I do like it. It is good to feel I'm doing something real for a change—something that matters. I like Lady Margaret, too. She has intelligence, and determination, and a great desire to please. And if she has a few faults of temper—well, I cannot feel the blame is entirely hers. Her early upbringing sounds as though it left a great deal to be desired."

Lady Eleanor nodded. "Her mother had the most dreadful temper," she told Alexandra. "Really, there were times when I wondered if she were quite sane. The smallest thing would set her off, and sometimes it took hours to get her calmed down again. She was a Ballinger, you know, and all that family are a little unbalanced. Mama and I begged Richard not to marry Aurelia, but of course that only made him the more determined to have her."

"I had gathered Lord Brentwood's marriage was not a great success," said Alexandra carefully. "Lady Margaret has let one or two things drop, you see."

Lady Eleanor nodded, her face gloomy. "It was a great tragedy," she said. "And I could kick myself for the part I played in it. If only Mama and I had let Richard alone! Nagging men only sets their backs up, I know that now. If Mama and I had said nothing against Aurelia, ten to one Richard never would have married her." She sighed, then smiled brightly at Alexandra. "But there's no use crying over spilt milk. Aurelia herself is gone now, poor creature, and it looks as though her daughter may not turn out so badly after all, with a clever girl like you to manage her. As for Richard himself, it's true I have been worried about him in the past, but I have reason to believe he is now in the way of recovering from his matrimonial misadventure."

"Oh yes?" said Alexandra, innocently oblivious to the innuendo in Lady Eleanor's voice. "I am very glad to hear

it, ma'am. But though I'm flattered by your opinion of my
abilities, you must know that I will not be taking care of
Lady Margaret for more than another month or two. When
Miss Harcourt's mother is recovered, I shall have to leave
and let her take over. That was our agreement."

Lady Eleanor laughed. "No doubt," she said. "But still
I hope we may find a way to keep you here at Brentwood,
Miss DiMarco. You are not really a governess, no matter
what you are pretending to my brother."

Alexandra gave only passing attention to the first part
of this speech. It was the second part that engaged her
attention. "You won't tell him, will you?" she said anxiously. "As long as I am able to do the work, it seems to
me I am doing no harm by taking Miss Harcourt's place.
It might worry Lord Brentwood if he thought I was not
qualified to teach his daughter. And though it might be
mere conceit on my part, I believe I am doing Lady Margaret good."

Lady Eleanor surveyed her with a curious smile. "I think
the same, Miss DiMarco. Indeed, I think you are doing
more good than you realize. That is why I am determined
not to tell my brother what you have told me. I have learned
a thing or two in the past ten years, you see." She laughed
as though amused by some inward reflection. "Your secret
is safe with me, Miss DiMarco. You shall have to tell Richard
yourself if you wish him to know the dark truth about your
parentage." Giving her hand to Alexandra and then to
Lady Margaret, she wished them a good evening and left
the nursery, still chuckling to herself.

NINE

Over the next few weeks, Alexandra began to settle into the routine of teaching.

Her days were busy ones, given up almost fully to teaching and caring for Lady Margaret. Her evenings tended to be busy, too, divided between letter-writing, preparing lessons, and making necessary repairs to her wardrobe. But she still had time to think, whenever her pupil was busy playing by herself or at work upon some lesson. And as often as not, she found her thoughts returning to what Lady Eleanor had said about her brother's marriage.

It was a great pity that Lord Brentwood should have been so unhappy in his late wife. He seemed like such a pleasant gentleman—so agreeable, and well mannered, and full of quiet humor once you got to know him. Alexandra felt she did know him, after his many visits to the nursery. He was handsome, too, although that was beside the point, of course. She grieved that his life should have been blighted by his late wife's temper, and rejoiced that his sister seemed to feel he was on the road to recovery.

She herself was less sure of this than Lady Eleanor had been. The Earl had certainly demonstrated signs of recovering spirits during her first two days at Brentwood, but after the evening on which he had kissed her hand, his manners had become markedly more formal. Alexandra had adapted her manner to his, so that their daily interviews together were brisk and businesslike. But he came around frequently nonetheless—to see Lady Margaret, no doubt. The afternoon Lady Eleanor had discovered him in the music room had not been the first time he had sat in on his daughter's pianoforte lessons. And when she and Lady Margaret took their daily exercise out-of-doors, they were quite likely to encounter him—entirely by chance, of course—and to end up with his joining them on their walk.

Alexandra wholly approved this behavior. She thought it good that Lady Margaret should be in her father's company as much as possible. It seemed to her that the worst thing the late Lady Brentwood had done was to make her daughter insecure about being loved. It was clear from Lady Margaret's occasional remarks that her mother had alternated between moments of extravagant affection and complete rejection. Alexandra, contrasting this to her own upbringing, began to appreciate as never before her great-aunt and -uncle's anxious care. She might often have been frustrated, irritated, or exasperated while living at Mannington, but she had never doubted for a moment that she was loved. She resolved that when she returned to Mannington, she would make it a point to express her gratitude to her great-aunt and -uncle for their unfailing love and solicitude.

At the moment, however, the prospects of returning to Mannington appeared rather distant. Alexandra had received several letters from Miss Harcourt during the past six weeks. In her latest letter, Miss Harcourt explained that though her mother had survived her operation, she was still in a much-weakened state and dependent on her daughter's care. Could Miss DiMarco possibly continue in her position for a few weeks more?

Of course she could, Alexandra wrote back warmly. She was not at all sorry to prolong her stay at Brentwood. She had grown as fond of Lady Margaret as Lady Margaret had of her—and Lord Brentwood, in his quiet way, had made

her feel as though he depended on her. It was dismaying
to reflect that she must one day leave them both and return to Mannington. Of course she would be happy to see
her great-aunt and -uncle again, but she did not relish the
thought of entering once again upon her life of seclusion
and constant surveillance. A governess might not have
much freedom, but she had infinitely more than Miss Manning had enjoyed.

As it was, Alexandra had at least part of her evenings
free and one half-day a week in which she might walk to
the village, read in her room, or dawdle about the grounds.
She usually chose to go to the village, because it made
more of a change from her usual routine. One day, early
in December, she was walking along the road toward the
village when she was overtaken by Richard in his curricle.

"Good day, Miss DiMarco," he said, raising his hat to
her. "May I offer you a ride?"

"If you are going to the village, I should be very glad
of a ride, my lord," said Alexandra with a shiver. "It is
colder than I knew when I set out, and I would be happy
to be spared part of a very chilly walk." She was surprised
to see Richard out and about at an hour when he was
usually busy with estate business. She could not know that
he had seen her set off toward the village, guessed her
purpose, and hurriedly had his horses harnessed merely
for the pleasure of taking her up beside him.

Richard turned the reins over to his groom and got
down to assist Alexandra into the curricle. She mounted
rather gingerly, having never had acquaintance with such
a high-sprung vehicle before. "This is lovely," she said,
looking around her with pleasure. "One can see so clearly!
I like it much better than a closed carriage."

"It is much colder, however," Richard warned her. "I
am afraid you will find it even chillier than walking." He
looked admiringly but doubtfully at Alexandra's plush

spencer and matching bonnet. "Ought I to take you back home so you can put on warmer clothing?"

"Oh, that is not necessary, my lord," she assured him. "I will not mind being cold for such a short time. But next time I go out walking I will assuredly have to wear my furs. I would have today, only I couldn't find out which trunk they were packed in," she added naively.

Richard looked at her, but said nothing. He touched up his horses, and the curricle began to roll once more toward the village.

Alexandra felt a bit self-conscious to be riding along at what seemed to her a giddy height, out in the open for all the world to see. She was also a bit self-conscious about being seated in such close proximity to Richard. The capes of his greatcoat brushed her sleeve now and then as he manipulated the whip and the reins, and his booted and pantalooned leg was only inches from her skirted one. She could not help noticing that it was a very well shaped leg, thoroughly masculine in its lineaments. There was, in fact, something very masculine and attractive about Richard's whole form, clad as it was in the dashing uniform of the Corinthian. Alexandra was aware of him as a man instead of merely her employer, and the awareness made her a little uncomfortable.

To be sure, they were not alone in the curricle. The silent groom perched up behind did very well as a chaperone, but still she felt uncomfortable. "Lady Margaret is making good progress in her studies," she offered, after a moment or two had gone by in silence. This was the subject on which she and Richard usually conversed, and she supposed he would welcome such conversation as he usually did.

True to form, his face brightened at the mention of his daughter. "Yes, I have been very pleased by her progress. But I tell you plainly, Miss DiMarco, that I have been even more pleased by the improvement in her deportment. The change is most striking. I can only look on and shake my head in wonder."

Alexandra nodded seriously. "I begin to believe the change may be lasting, too. I hope so at any rate." With a little shyness in her voice, she added, "You know, Lady Margaret thinks a great deal of you, my lord. I believe half her progress lately is simply due to the interest you are taking in her. When you go for a walk with her, or spend an hour playing with her in the nursery, it pleases her to no end and inspires her to try even harder. I don't think many fathers spend as much time with their children as you do."

Richard meditated as to what he ought to say in response to this speech. He decided on a policy of modified honesty. "It is good of you to praise me, Miss DiMarco, but in fact I spent very little time in the nursery before you came," he told Alexandra. "You may call me a coward if you like, but it was heartbreaking for me to see my daughter as she used to be. I did try to do my duty by her, but I avoided being around her as much as possible. Now it is a pleasure to be with her, and so I spend a good deal more time in her company—and that is all because of you, as far as I can see."

Alexandra looked distressed. "I hope not. Indeed, I am certain not, my lord. I may have gotten Lady Margaret started in the right direction, but I feel confident she will now continue aright, even after I am gone." She looked anxiously at Richard's profile. "And I hope you will continue to spend time with your daughter no matter what may happen in the future. She needs you, my lord—she needs the strength and stability you represent. No governess can possibly supply that."

"No," agreed Richard. He just glanced at Alexandra as he spoke, but something in his glance made her feel uncomfortable once again. Fortunately, they reached the village a few minutes later, and she quickly forgot her momentary discomposure.

"You may set me down here at the corner, my lord," she told him. "And I thank you very much for giving me a ride."

Richard assisted her in dismounting from the curricle, but to Alexandra's surprise he did not immediately remount and drive off again. "I have nothing special to do this afternoon, Miss DiMarco," he said, looking down at her. "And I have a great curiosity to see how a governess spends her half-day off. Would you mind my accompanying you?"

Although surprised, Alexandra was by no means displeased by this request. She shook her head with a smile. "Not at all, my lord. But I am not sure if my half-day will be representative of most governesses'. I had planned to spend mine at the village shop looking at lace and ribbons." Lowering her voice, she added, "I am making some new clothes for Lady Margaret's doll as a Christmas gift. Poor Méchante, she has grown sadly shabby wearing the same evening gown day in and day out."

"In that case, I shall certainly accompany you," said Richard with satisfaction. "Your errand concerns my daughter, and therefore it is my errand, too." Dismissing his curricle in care of the groom, he took Alexandra's arm.

They entered the shop together, and Alexandra went at once to the ribbon counter. Richard watched in amusement as she debated solemnly between twilled and plain ribbon and anxiously compared shades from a sample she had brought. She bought a few scraps of lace, too, and a short length of pink satin. When he took out his purse to pay for her purchases, however, she shook her head at him and produced a purse of her own. "This gift is from me, my lord," she said, looking him firmly in the eye. "If you want to buy a gift for Lady Margaret, then do so—but let it be your own gift."

Richard looked around the store. "What would you suggest, Miss DiMarco?" he said. "I'm rather out of my element here."

"She could use some new clothes," said Alexandra thoughtfully. "Indeed, your daughter's needs in that direction are almost as urgent as Méchante's, my lord! All her dresses are getting rather short on her. I am sure she has grown a full inch just in the time I have been here."

"I will buy whatever you direct me to," said Richard, taking out his purse again. "What will you have, Miss DiMarco? You choose the fabric, and I'll have the maidservants make the dresses up."

Alexandra looked around the store carefully, reflecting on what materials would be suitable for a six-year-old girl's wardrobe. At length she selected half a dozen assorted lengths of merino and printed cambric in hues she thought compatible with Lady Margaret's coloring. When these had been cut and wrapped, she lingered wistfully over the bolt of pink satin once again. "It's such pretty stuff, and it would look lovely with your daughter's dark hair and eyes," she told Richard. "But of course it would not be really suitable or practical for a child's dress. If Méchante has a dress of it, that will be enough."

Richard looked at Alexandra's face, then at the bolt of satin. "I don't know that we need be as practical as all that," he said, taking out his purse once more. "Why should the child not have one impractical dress? If you think she would like it, Miss DiMarco, then let us get it by all means. With the Christmas holidays coming up, I daresay there will be occasion to wear it," he added in a meditative voice.

"Oh, she will love it, my lord," said Alexandra joyfully. "She is always begging me to wear my light silks and satins, but I have told her they are not suitable for a governess."

Richard slanted a quizzical look at her, but Alexandra was unaware of it. She was examining with delight some

quaintly carved wooden animals which the shopkeeper
had displayed on a counter. Richard bought those, too,
and a set of gilt-edged storybooks that she also happened
to admire. When these purchases were concluded, Alexandra led him firmly out of the store.

"That was very extravagant of you, my lord," she
scolded. "I had no thought of your buying all those things
merely because I happened to admire them. Lady Margaret will love them, though," she added with satisfaction.
"And they will mean twice as much because they come
from you."

"Perhaps, but I doubt I would have chosen so well without your assistance," said Richard. He felt in an extravagant, expansive mood all at once. It was a mood such as
he had not experienced in several years. Indeed, casting
his mind backward, he was not sure he had ever experienced anything of that exact nature before. Looking into
the lovely face of his companion moved him to further
extravagance. "Should you like something to eat after all
your shopping labors, Miss DiMarco? There's a pastrycook's just down the street from here."

"That sounds lovely," agreed Alexandra. Richard es-
corted her to the pastrycook's shop and stood by, watching
in amusement as she made her selection. She took considerable time over this, exclaiming over the different buns
and pastries and then weighing the merits of each as solemnly as though her decision were a matter of immense
moment. When she had vacillated several minutes between
a card of gingerbread, a fruit bun, and a cream-filled cake,
Richard put an end to her dilemma by buying her all three.

"Now you are being extravagant again, my lord! I can't
possibly eat all this," exclaimed Alexandra, surveying her
largess with pleasure nonetheless. "You will have to help
me." She divided the three pastries carefully in two, then
poured herself and Richard some tea from the pot he had
ordered from the proprietor. "This is lovely," she said,

munching happily on gingerbread. "I'm sorry it took me so long to make up my mind, my lord, but you see I have never been in a pastrycook's shop before."

Richard expressed himself gravely surprised at these words, though he had already guessed at her inexperience. He watched with curiosity as Alexandra finished her gingerbread and embarked on the bun. "Where did you grow up if you never went into a pastrycook's?" he asked. "It must have been a very small village."

"Oh, it wasn't a village," said Alexandra. "To be sure, we did go into Mannington-on-the-Marsh sometimes, but there was only a baker's shop there. I don't think they sold delightful things like this." She looked affectionately at her cream-filled cake.

"I see," said Richard, storing this information away for later use. He ventured on to another question. "Who is the 'we' you mention? Did you have brothers and sisters?"

Alexandra shook her head. "No, there was only me. I would have liked a brother or sister," she added wistfully. "But my father died before I was born, and my mother died soon after, so I grew up alone."

"You astonish me, Miss DiMarco," said Richard gravely. "I never would have supposed any child could raise herself without assistance. Even Romulus and Remus had a she-wolf to help them!"

Alexandra laughed. "You are teasing me, my lord! Of course I do not mean I raised myself alone. My aunt and uncle raised me. Actually, they're my great-aunt and -uncle. They took care of my mother when she was a child, and when she died they took care of me."

It occurred to Alexandra as she spoke that the conversation was becoming dangerously personal. At any moment Richard might take it into his head to ask her great-aunt and -uncle's name, and then the fat would be in the fire. Like his sister, he would probably feel a Manning had no business trying to be a governess. He might even feel obliged to send her back to her great-aunt and -uncle. Alexandra decided to change the subject.

"My relatives always took very good care of me, but of course it was lonely growing up without other children around," she told Richard. "That is why I can sympathize with Lady Margaret. I wish she had the opportunity to be with other girls and boys. Are there no other children her age hereabouts?"

Richard frowned. "I don't really know. Presumably some of my neighbors have small children, but I haven't done much socializing in recent years. I've rather lost track of who does and doesn't have children and how old they are." His face suddenly cleared. "But I will be seeing most of them at Christmastime. We are having some entertainments then—a dinner or two, and a ball on Christmas Day. Perhaps I can make some inquiries then."

"That would be wonderful," said Alexandra with enthusiasm. She smiled at Richard. "I have already heard there are to be parties at Brentwood this Christmas, my lord. Rachel, the nurserymaid, has been full of nothing else these two weeks."

Richard laughed. "Yes, we will certainly be having parties at Brentwood this Christmas! Not just for a day or two, but for weeks on end. I have some guests coming next week who will be staying through Twelfth Night, and I know my sister means to keep us in a whirl of gaiety the whole time." He paused a moment, then went on with an air of diffidence. "I had thought, Miss DiMarco, that you might take part in some of the festivities. As a companion to my daughter, you know," he added quickly. "I am much pleased by Margaret's behavior of late, but I would not trust her at a formal party without someone in attendance."

"Of course, my lord. If Lady Margaret is to attend, then of course it is my duty to do so, too, as her governess." Alexandra spoke dutifully, but her heart leaped with joy at the picture Richard's words had drawn for her. Even at Mannington Christmas had been a festive season, a welcome respite from the monotony of the other eleven months, but it had never encompassed anything as exciting as a ball or a large house party. The word "ball" in particular struck enticingly upon Alexandra's ears. She knew nothing of balls apart from what she had read in various novels, but the prospect excited her tremendously. Even to sit on the sidelines with Lady Margaret and watch, which was as far as her imagination allowed her to go, seemed a treat such as she would never have dared hope for.

Richard looked at her anxiously, wondering if she were as reluctant as her voice sounded. For several weeks he had been meditating the invitation he had just made. It was something he had wanted to do ever since the idea of the house party had first been put in motion, but for a long time he had held off, telling himself that he was a fool to think of including Alexandra in the festivities. There was no reason to invite her even if, as he suspected, she was not a governess at all but a young lady of quality. Especially if she was a lady of quality. It had occurred to him once or twice that Alexandra's unheralded appearance at Brentwood might be part of an elaborate plot to entrap him into matrimony.

He had heard of such things being done before. Enterprising young ladies in quest of titled husbands had been known to do even more outrageous things than impersonating a governess for a few weeks. The idea that Alexandra might have come to Brentwood in quest of his title would not have disturbed Richard so much had he not felt himself so susceptible to her charms. But it had occurred to him, the evening he had kissed her hand, that if her intention were really to seduce him into matrimony, then she was finding her task laughably easy.

This idea had inspired him to adopt a more formal and

distant manner during his ensuing interviews with Alexandra. But instead of pursuing her receding prey, she had responded by becoming formal and distant herself.

He was pretty sure now that he had been mistaken in supposing Alexandra an adventuress. But though he had decided she was not an adventuress, he was still no closer to determining exactly what she might be.

Clearly she was of gentle birth, and equally clearly she had had no expense spared on her upbringing, education, and wardrobe. She was incredibly wise and learned in academic matters, yet incredibly naive about such matters as pastrycooks and governesses' salaries. She was in fact an enigma. She was like no other girl Richard had ever met, and various half-formed notions and intentions flitted through his mind as he watched her happily consuming her tea and pastries. At all costs, he was determined to investigate this enigma further.

Alexandra, for her part, was very happy. She was happy at having found the proper materials for Lady Margaret's gift and at the prospect of attending the Christmas festivities Richard had spoken of. And though she did not consider the matter, part of her happiness had to do with Richard himself. He had been so friendly and thoughtful that afternoon, so generous about buying her cakes and such enjoyable company while eating them, that Alexandra felt in quite a glow of spirits.

Her happy mood continued all the way back to Brentwood. Having assisted Richard in choosing a new pair of gloves (his ostensible purpose in driving into the village), she had accepted his invitation to be driven home and had taken up her seat beside him in the curricle once more. They had chatted like old friends during the drive home, discussing Lady Margaret's Christmas gifts and her probable reaction when she saw them. When they reached the house, Alexandra had bade Richard good-bye with profuse thanks and went upstairs to the nursery, humming a little tune under her breath.

In the nursery she had found Lady Margaret drawing pictures by the fire, while Rachel sat sewing in a chair beside her.

"Here I am, Rachel," said Alexandra, greeting the nurserymaid pleasantly. "You see I got back from the village a little early. Lord Brentwood was good enough to take me up in his curricle."

"I like Papa's curricle," said Lady Margaret, looking up from her drawing. "I like it when he makes the horses go very fast. Did he make the horses go fast when you were with him, Miss DiMarco?"

"Mercifully not," said Alexandra, laughing. "He must have taken pity on me, seeing that I was not used to open carriages."

"Or it may be that he just wasn't in any hurry to have the journey over," observed Rachel. Her voice was innocent, but the look she cast Alexandra was replete with significance. With a curtsy, she folded up her sewing and passed out of the room.

Alexandra stood looking after her with surprise, until roused by Lady Margaret. "Can we play a game?" asked Lady Margaret, tugging at her sleeve. "Can we play Hide the Thimble, like we did last Saturday?"

"We can, once I have taken off my outdoor things," said Alexandra, rousing herself from her abstraction. She removed her bonnet, gloves, and spencer, then settled down to play Hide the Thimble with Lady Margaret.

Inwardly, however, she was full of perturbation. It was clear from Rachel's remarks that the nurserymaid suspected her and her employer of carrying on some kind of romantic intrigue. Nothing could be further from the truth, as Alexandra assured herself indignantly. And yet, when she examined her behavior that afternoon, she found several points which gave her pause.

Perhaps it had been indiscreet of her to let Lord Brentwood drive her to and from the village. Even if he had business of his own in the village, his being seen with her in his curricle was the kind of incident that could easily give rise to gossip. And surely it had been indiscreet of her to let him buy her tea and cakes at the village pastrycook's!

But it was not so much what she had done as how she felt that disturbed Alexandra. For when she went to examine her feelings for Richard, she found that she did in truth cherish a warm regard for him—a warmer regard than was perhaps proper under the circumstances. Because, like it or not, she was at Brentwood in the capacity of a governess. Alexandra thought with distaste of *Pamela* and of various other works of fiction in which scheming serving-girls sought to marry their masters. That was the kind of behavior she was suspected of in the servants' hall! Alexandra rued the inexperience that had led her into such indiscretion.

"I do like him," she owned to herself. "He is a handsome, intelligent, personable man, and he has been very kind to me. It would be strange if I did *not* like him—but at the same time, I must not allow myself to like him too much.

"It's quite lowering to think how I used to sneer at those foolish girls in novels, who fall in love with the first good-looking man they see! I never supposed I would be so susceptible. But then, it's not just Lord Brentwood's looks that appeal to me. He is such a kind, considerate man, and so entertaining, too—oh, dear, I mustn't be thinking of that. He is my employer, and I had better start thinking of him as such if I don't want to get myself into difficulties."

It was some comfort to Alexandra to reflect that Richard could hardly be aware of her feelings. Since she had only

just become aware of them herself, it stood to reason that
he could have no suspicion that she cared for him more
than a well-conducted governess ought to care for her employer. But it would behoove her to keep a tight rein on
her behavior if she wanted him to remain in ignorance.
She had preached discipline and self-control to Lady Margaret; now it would be for her to practice the same useful
qualities if she were not to disgrace herself and perhaps
bring embarrassment upon her employer.

"Goodness knows, he has suffered enough from unbalanced women," she told herself. She recalled all Lady
Eleanor had told her about the late Countess of
Brentwood. Truly Lord Brentwood had been unfortunate
in his choice of wives. Or rather, Alexandra corrected herself, he had been unfortunate in his choice of *first* wives.
He was a widower now, and Lady Eleanor had hinted that
he was on the road to recovery. Did that mean he was
contemplating a second marriage?

Alexandra saw at once that nothing could be more likely.
Lord Brentwood was a nobleman with a title and ancestral
estates. It was natural that he should want a son to succeed
him in these dignities. It was also natural that he should
want a stepmother for Lady Margaret. Alexandra had to
fight back an incipient pang of jealousy when she envi-
sioned another lady supplanting her in Lady Margaret's
affections. More painful still was the idea of that same lady
enjoying the affections of Lord Brentwood.

I am a fool, Alexandra told herself, but still she continued
to be plagued by jealousy when she imagined the happiness that would be enjoyed by Lord Brentwood's second
wife. She wondered if he had fixed on any particular lady
for that role, and if so, who the fortunate lady might be.
Was it not possible that she might be one of the guests at
the upcoming house party?

Alexandra thought it extremely probable that this was
the case. She recalled Richard's diffidence in speaking of

his party, and his wish that she and his daughter should be present at the festivities. No doubt this was so that his daughter might meet and become acquainted with her future stepmother.

And it would be very good for Lady Margaret to have a stepmother, Alexandra told herself stoutly. *I'm just being selfish in wishing to keep her for myself. After all, I don't intend to stay here at Brentwood for more than a few more weeks. Poor thing, she deserves something better on which to fix her affections than a temporary governess!* Lord Brentwood, too, deserved to be happy after his first disastrous experiment in matrimony. Alexandra could only hope, with disinterested fervor, that he would be more fortunate in his choice of second wives than in his first.

TEN

The house party arrived on the fifteenth of December. It was the beginning of a most hectic and exciting period at Brentwood.

Things had been hectic enough in the weeks preceding the party's arrival. The household staff had early begun their preparations for the guests who were to pass the Christmas holidays at Brentwood. The maids beat rugs and turned mattresses in bedchambers long disused, while the reception rooms downstairs were brought into a state of shining perfection. Cook in the kitchen baked cakes and stirred up puddings with the assistance of her satellite kitchen maids, while in the stableyard the grooms and stable boys prepared for an influx of visiting carriages. And almost every day a footman was dispatched to the village to buy commodities ranging from soap to sherry.

Even up in the nursery, Alexandra and Lady Margaret were affected by the excitement. Lady Margaret found it hard to concentrate on her lessons when there were so many intriguing things going on belowstairs. Alexandra thoroughly sympathized with her difficulties, for she, too, found it hard to keep from rushing to the window every time a wagon loaded with supplies went rattling by. She tried to help by giving the lessons a holiday theme wherever possible. Lady Margaret practiced Christmas songs on the pianoforte and studied Christmas customs of other

lands for geography. She learned how to say "Merry Christmas" and "King's cake" in French, and when she did
sums, she added quantities of sugarplums and subtracted
chestnuts, raisins, and oranges.

Alexandra also taught her a few simple stitches so she
might make gifts for the different members of the household. At Mannington, present-giving had been an important part of the holiday, and Alexandra assumed it must
be the same at Brentwood. She herself had been diligently
working on the new wardrobe for Méchante in her spare
hours, and it was nearing completion on the afternoon
the guests arrived. She hastily put aside her work on a
fancy petticoat as Lady Margaret came whooping into the
nursery.

"There's a carriage coming down the drive, Miss Di-
Marco! Not a gig or a tradesman's wagon, but a grand
carriage with a coachman and footmen. Can I get ready
for the party now?"

"Quite soon now, anyway," said Alexandra with a smile.
Lady Margaret had been agitating to put on her party raiment ever since she got up that morning. She had been
tremendously excited by the news that she was to dine
downstairs with the grown-ups that evening, and she had
given much anxious thought to her dress and behavior for
the occasion, as if she were a debutante making her bows
at St. James's.

The new dresses which her father and Alexandra had
chosen were of course a secret to her, being destined for
Christmas presents. But Alexandra had let down and fur-
bished up one of her older dresses for this occasion, a
white muslin figured in red with a red satin sash. Lady
Margaret was highly pleased with it. She rushed over to
the wardrobe and brought forth the dress now, waving it
back and forth and squinting anxiously at the nursery
clock in an effort to divine its mysteries.

"It's half past six now, Miss DiMarco. Don't you think I ought to put on my dress?"

"It's half past three," corrected Alexandra, with a glance at the clock. "And if you put on your dress now, it will become rumpled long before dinnertime."

"No, it won't. Once I'm dressed I'll sit very quietly here by the window, and my dress won't get rumpled a bit. Can I please, Miss DiMarco? I promise I'll be very careful."

Alexandra, after much coaxing and teasing, finally gave way and allowed her happy pupil to change her dress. She decided she might as well go ahead and change into her own dinner dress, too. Like Lady Margaret's, her dress for the occasion was of white muslin—a sheer white muslin, worn over a sarcenet slip with a narrow lace edging. It seemed to her an appropriately self-effacing dress for a governess to wear. Once she was dressed, she brushed out, rebraided, and neatly repinned her hair, with an inward sigh for the absent Marie.

Lady Margaret was good as her word and sat quietly by the window, trying to attend to her lessons but a good deal distracted by the carriages which arrived at intervals throughout the afternoon. Equally distracting was the sound of laughter and voices that now and then came drifting up from downstairs. Once or twice Alexandra could distinguish Richard's voice above the others. She found herself quite curious to know what he was saying, and to whom he was saying it. Not a few of the arriving carriages had contained lady guests, and—as nearly as she could ascertain from her window vantage point—several of these were both young and pretty. To judge from the amount of laughter coming from the drawing room, they were certainly a lively party, whatever their constituency might be.

"Ooh, miss, it's so exciting," said Rachel, who had been in and out of the nursery all afternoon with periodic bulletins. "Ever such a good-looking young gentleman has

just arrived," she reported on one of these occasions.
"Looks just like one of the illustrations in my Lady
Eleanor's fashion papers." On another occasion she reported the arrival of a Scottish lady who, she said, had put
the whole party in stitches with her funny remarks. "You
ought to go on down to the drawing room, miss," she told
Alexandra, running an admiring eye over Alexandra's costume. "His lordship said as how you and Lady Margaret
was to join the party, didn't he?"

"Yes, but I do not know that he wants us down so early
as this," said Alexandra, eyeing the clock a little wistfully.
"I had thought when the first bell rang for dinner it would
be soon enough. I am afraid we should only be in the way
if we went downstairs now, when people are still arriving."
Much as she longed to join the party, she was determined
not to obtrude herself where she was not wanted. But as
the afternoon wore on, punctuated by intriguing bursts of
laughter and merriment from below, Alexandra felt inclined to complain, like Lady Margaret, that dinnertime
would never come.

Come it did at last, however. As Alexandra prepared to
go downstairs with her pupil, she was conscious of a nervous flutter in the pit of her stomach. It might be only a
dinner party, but it was the first dinner party she had ever
attended where the guests were not all old enough to be
her grandparents. She was quite thankful for Lady Margaret's presence beside her as she went down the stairs
and into the drawing room.

She had been briefly once or twice in the drawing room
since her arrival at Brentwood, but it looked very different
this evening. For one thing, it was literally ablaze with light.
Dozens of candles burned in branches along the walls, and
hanging lamps cast an additional glow over the gathering
below. More light came from the roaring fires in the twin
fireplaces that faced each other across the room. But it
was chiefly the people that distinguished the room on this

occasion. To Alexandra's dazzled eyes the drawing room appeared to contain hundreds of people, all dressed in the most lavish of finery. And they all seemed to be looking at her.

"Ah, here is Margaret—and here is Miss DiMarco." These words, spoken in Richard's familiar voice, sounded most gratefully in Alexandra's ears. She turned and saw him advancing toward her, a smile on his face.

He was wearing formal evening clothes, such as she had not seen him wear since coming to Brentwood. His black coat fitted without a wrinkle across his broad shoulders; his neckcloth was ornately knotted at his throat; his linen was immaculate. Alexandra was struck by what a handsome appearance he made in this costume. So struck was she indeed, that she could hardly murmur out a response to his greeting.

If she had been paying attention, she might have noticed that Richard was looking struck, too. He had never seen Alexandra in anything resembling formal dress before. Robed in misty white, her head crowned with a braid of honey-colored hair and her eyes brilliant as sapphires, she was a vision to take his breath away. He might have gone on looking at her longer than was prudent if it had not been for Lady Margaret. Impervious to any tension between her father and her governess, she tugged at Richard's sleeve.

"Papa, I'm hungry," she announced in her clear voice. "Is it time to eat yet?"

Most of the guests laughed, and one or two ladies murmured fondly that Lady Margaret was "a perfect doll" or "a little love." About Alexandra they said little, merely regarding her with raised eyebrows. Richard, recovering his composure, began to move about the room, introducing Alexandra and his daughter to his guests.

Alexandra, too, was recovering from her initial shyness. She looked with interest upon the members of the house party. There proved not so many as she had first supposed: some two dozen in all, and most of them seemed quite pleasant, ordinary people. One or two stood out by virtue of some distinguishing characteristic. There was one gentleman, for instance, whom she had no difficulty as recognizing as the object of Rachel's earlier eulogies. Introduced to her as Sir Maximilian Savage, he was a handsome, indolent-looking creature with sleek fair hair and a style of dress even more foppish than the notable Mr. Taft's.

"My dear Brentwood, never say this is a governess," he drawled, scanning Alexandra through his quizzing glass with lazy appreciation. "If so, the breed has improved since I was a boy. You must sit by me at dinner, Miss DiMarco, and tell me all the latest tricks to the governess trade."

Alexandra, misliking this style of speech, gave Sir Maximilian a brief smile by way of response and moved on quickly. The next guest she was introduced to was a Lady Rosalie Banks, a handsome auburn-haired lady some years older than herself.

Like Sir Maximilian, Lady Rosalie seemed to possess an indolent temperament. On hearing Alexandra's name and title, she merely opened her half-closed green eyes a little wider and said, "Oh!" Her demeanor was not unfriendly, however, and it seemed positively effusive compared to the behavior of Miss Spence, the next lady Alexandra was introduced to. Miss Spence was a dark-haired young lady of autocratic bearing and supercilious manner. She lifted her brows in a contemptuous way when she and Alexandra were introduced and made no response to the latter's polite "How do you do?" Over Lady Margaret she fussed for a considerable time, however, telling Richard over and over that she was a little beauty and the most adorable child imaginable.

Alexandra was rather nettled by this behavior. The rudeness to herself she could have overlooked, for she supposed a governess was entitled to no particular notice in such a gathering. But Miss Spence's behavior toward Lady Margaret seemed to her both ill-judged and highly transparent. It was obvious that her remarks were aimed not at Lady Margaret, but at Lady Margaret's father, and that by doting on his child, she hoped to convince Richard that she would make a fitting stepmother for his motherless daughter.

Alexandra hoped earnestly that Richard would not be taken in by such a ploy. If ever the signs of ill-temper were stamped upon a countenance, that countenance was Miss Spence's. Alexandra had disliked her on sight and had no doubt that she would prove as intractable as Lord Brentwood's first wife if he were mad enough to marry her. If he must marry one of the ladies of the house party, then she hoped it would be Lady Rosalie, who seemed at least to possess the merit of good humor.

No other lady among the guests seemed to embody the qualities an earl would necessarily demand in his wife. So Alexandra supposed on first looking around the room, at least, but she was forced to revise this estimation upon being introduced to Miss Henrietta McBride. Miss McBride was certainly not a conventional beauty, being stout, red-faced, and in her middle thirties. But she possessed a charm of manner sufficient to outweigh disadvantages far more material than these.

"I'm verra pleased to meet you, Miss DiMarco," she said, smiling and putting out her hand to Alexandra. "You may as well call me Hattie like everyone else. So you're Lady Margaret's governess, are you? A bonny bairn she is, and you're a bonny lass yourself. Are you from hereabouts, or a foreigner like me? You know these English consider everybody a foreigner that doesn't hail from their particular bit of country."

"I suppose I would be considered a foreigner, then," said Alexandra, smiling. Under the warmth of the Scottish

woman's interest she found herself expanding on this
statement, describing Mannington-on-the-Marsh and her
great-aunt and -uncle's home. She remained talking to
Miss McBride for some minutes, until the bell rang for the
party to go in to dinner. It occurred to her that the charm
of the Scottish woman's manner might have led her to
reveal more about herself and her background than was
really prudent. But as there seemed to be nothing more
than friendly interest behind Miss McBride's questions, Alexandra brushed the matter aside.

Others besides Miss McBride were interested in
Brentwood's new governess, however. As she went in to
dinner, Alexandra saw several ladies scrutinizing her toilette very closely. She also overheard one elderly dowager
whisper to Lady Eleanor, "My dear, never say that girl is
really a governess! This is one of your jokes, is it not?"

Alexandra was glad to hear Lady Eleanor protest this
statement most earnestly. She had thus far had no reason
to believe that Lady Eleanor had betrayed the secret of
her parentage. Having collected her pupil, Alexandra took
Lady Margaret into the dining room, found her her seat,
and settled back in her own seat to enjoy the dinner.

It was a formal dinner, encompassing three full courses
as well as diverse removes. There was turtle and mulliga-
tawny soup to begin with, followed by salmon with shrimp
sauce and collops of oysters. A saddle of mutton and a
mighty roast of beef came next, accompanied by potato
croquettes, carrots in cream, and an assortment of other
entrées. Roast chicken, tongue, and ham followed with
their own proper accompaniments—cauliflower and pars-
nips, pancakes and giblet pie, jellies and fritters. Lastly
came dessert, a delicious medley of cakes, sweet pastries,
preserved fruits, and ices.

Alexandra thoroughly enjoyed the dinner. She was
proud to see that her pupil's manners throughout the
meal did her the greatest credit. Lady Margaret sat very

straight in her chair, conscious of her unaccustomed finery and of her own dignity in being elevated to the hon-
ors of the dining room. She spoke only when spoken to,
and accepted and refused the dishes that were offered
her with such a perfect imitation of a grown-up manner
that more than once Alexandra had to turn away to hide
a smile.

On one of these occasions she happened to catch Richard's eye. He returned her smile with a warmth that
brought a glow to her heart. *I mustn't give way to this,* she
reminded herself, and determinedly averted her gaze from
his. In doing so, she encountered Miss McBride's keen
gray eye, a circumstance that would have been rather disconcerting had not the woman immediately given her a
reassuring smile.

After dinner, the ladies adjourned to the drawing room.
Alexandra thought it best that she and Lady Margaret
should not obtrude on the conversation of the others and
so she led her pupil to the adjoining music room where
Lady Margaret might relieve her pent-up animal spirits by
romping about among the furnishings, playing over some
of her favorite songs on the pianoforte, and volunteering
countless ingenuous comments about the meal she had
just enjoyed.

Half a dozen other ladies soon came over to join them,
among them Lady Eleanor and the genial Miss McBride.
Alexandra was surprised to find herself the center of a
little group. She was also surprised by the amount of attention which that group showered upon her. Not only
Miss McBride but several other ladies seemed very interested to hear about her background and antecedents.
Their interest would have made her quite shy, but fortunately Lady Eleanor shielded her from their questions with
various laughing remarks and humorous diversions. Miss
McBride, who had apparently already satisfied her own curiosity concerning Alexandra, joined with Lady Eleanor in

this endeavor and was quite successful in distracting the group's attention. They were all laughing over one of the Scottish woman's quaint observations when Miss Spence came over to join them.

Miss Spence was wearing a dinner dress of primrose crepe with silver trimmings. Her dark hair was dressed in antique Roman fashion with a silver bandeau tied around her forehead. Alexandra had to admit that she looked extremely handsome thus attired, but the disagreeable expression on her face was very pronounced as she glanced from Alexandra to the rest of the group.

"I wondered where you had gone, Lady Eleanor. And you here, too, Hattie! Ah, I see you are entertaining my friend Lady Margaret." She stooped to address Lady Margaret in a saccharine voice. "You behaved very well tonight at dinner, my dear. I was very proud of you, and I am sure your papa must have been very proud of you, too."

Lady Margaret gave Miss Spence a surprised look, but responded politely, "Thank you, ma'am."

Miss Spence smiled fondly upon her. "What pretty manners you have! I must confess, however, I am surprised to see your governess lets you sit up so late." She threw Alexandra a meaning look. "But perhaps she has been so busy talking that she has failed to observe it is past nine o'clock."

Alexandra was amazed by this attack and rather incensed by it, too. But she sought to respond to Miss Spence's words with quiet composure. "On the contrary, I checked my watch only a moment ago," she said, displaying the timepiece at her waist to Miss Spence. "I saw it was after nine, but since Lord Brentwood said Lady Margaret might sit up late tonight, I saw no reason why we should not remain at least till the tea tray came in."

The sight of Alexandra's watch seemed to divert Miss Spence. She came over and took it into her hand, quite

We'd Like to Invite You to Subscribe to Zebra's Regency Romance Book Club and Give You a Gift of 4 Free Books as Your Introduction! *(Worth $19.96!)*

If you're a Regency lover, imagine the joy of getting 4 FREE Zebra Regency Romances and then the chance to have these lovely stories delivered to your home each month at the lowest prices available! Well, that's our offer to you and here's how you benefit by becoming a Zebra Home Subscription Service subscriber:

- **4 FREE Introductory Regency Romances** are delivered to your doorstep

- **4 BRAND NEW Regencies** are then delivered each month (usually before they're available in bookstores)

- **Subscribers save almost $4.00 every month**

- **Home delivery is always FREE**

- **You also receive a FREE monthly newsletter,** *Zebra/Pinnacle Romance News* which features author profiles, contests, subscriber benefits, book previews and more

- **No risks or obligations...in other words you can cancel whenever you wish with no questions asked**

Join the thousands of readers who enjoy the savings and convenience offered to Regency Romance subscribers. After your initial introductory shipment, you receive 4 brand-new Zebra Regency Romances each month to examine for 10 days. Then, if you decide to keep the books, you'll pay the preferred subscriber's price of just $4.00 per title. That's only $16.00 for all 4 books and there's never an extra charge for shipping and handling.

It's a no-lose proposition, so return the FREE BOOK CERTIFICATE today!

ZEBRA HOME SUBSCRIPTION SERVICE, INC.

120 BRIGHTON ROAD

P.O. BOX 5214

CLIFTON, NEW JERSEY 07015-5214

as if it were her property rather than Alexandra's. "Is this yours?" she demanded sharply.

Alexandra nodded, wondering at her tone. "Where did you get it?" was Miss Spence's next question, spoken in an even sharper tone. "You cannot possibly have purchased it yourself."

"As a matter of fact, I did not purchase it myself," said Alexandra, gently but firmly removing the watch from Miss Spence's grasp. "It was a gift."

Miss Spence's eyebrows rose. She glanced around at the others with a significance Alexandra did not understand. "A gift," she repeated. "And who was generous enough to give a governess a Breguet, may I ask?"

Although Alexandra did not understand the direction of Miss Spence's speech, she could not fail to understand that some disrespect to herself was intended. Drawing herself up, unsmilingly she looked Miss Spence in the eye. "My great-aunt and -uncle gave me the watch," she said. "It was indeed very generous of them, and I treasure it accordingly. Is there any reason I should not?"

Miss Spence seemed a little taken aback by this forceful counterattack, but she managed a dry laugh. "No reason at all," she said. "But such a watch is hardly a suitable ornament for a governess, you must admit."

"Ah, but Miss DiMarco is a very superior governess," put in Lady Eleanor, shooting Alexandra a conspiratorial smile. "When you know her better, Miss Spence, as I daresay you will, you will see that there is nothing out of place about her possessing and wearing such a fine watch."

Alexandra was surprised and gratified by Lady Eleanor's defense, though she thought the latter part of it a trifle fanciful. She was even more surprised when Miss McBride took up the cudgels in her defense. "Dinna be disagreeable, Eva," the Scottish woman told Miss Spence in her downright way. "I dinna ken why Miss DiMarco mayna wear her watch if she's a mind to. You've enough fine feathers of your own not to grudge her a wee baubee like that."

Miss Spence, discomposed by this unexpected partisanship among the ladies, muttered something inaudible and moved off. Lady Eleanor watched her go with a faintly regretful eye. "And to think I once thought she and Richard might suit," she remarked conversationally. "It just goes to show what a fool one can be, doesn't it?"

"Ah, well, Eva isna showing to advantage right now," said Miss McBride tolerantly. "People seldom do when they've a touch of the green-eyed monster, I trow." She smiled directly at Alexandra.

Alexandra hardly knew where to look, but happily her embarrassment was not destined to be of long duration. The gentlemen had begun to drift in from the dining room, and their entrance provided a welcome diversion. Richard was among the earliest arrivals. He did not linger in the drawing room, but came directly into the music room where Alexandra and the others were sitting.

"What's this?" he asked, smiling around the group. "I have not interrupted the sitting of some purely feminine conclave, have I?"

"Papa!" shrieked Lady Margaret, dashing toward him.

"As you can see, one member of our group doesna mind your interrupting us," said Miss McBride, smiling at him. "As for the rest of us, we'll pardon you, seeing it's your house we're sitting in!"

"I am glad to hear it," said Richard, smiling round the group once again. He tried hard not to let his gaze linger longest on Alexandra, but it was a struggle. She looked so lovely, sitting there on the pianoforte bench with her white draperies flowing around her.

Lady Margaret, meanwhile, was dancing about him in a distracting way, begging to be picked up. Alexandra called to her and seated the child on the bench beside her. Richard found himself envying his daughter's position. Averting his eyes, he spoke to the group.

"I hope, at least, none of you are complaining about the dearth of entertainment. We have several formal parties planned for later on, but for tonight I thought tea and conversation would suffice."

Miss McBride shook her head. "Ah, 'tis a sad thing to see the cheese-paring ways of the English aristocracy," she observed with mock gravity. " 'Tis usually the Scots who are given a reputation for parsimony."

Richard laughed. "Yes, it's a sad thing, Hattie. But you know I am depending on you to help me conceal the inadequacies of the entertainment."

"Aye, to be sure," replied Miss McBride with composure. "I didna suppose you invited me for any other reason."

The conversation went on in this way until the tea tray was brought in, with Richard and Miss McBride trading jibes and the others laughing and egging them on. Alexandra did not contribute to the conversation, but she listened with enjoyment and a certain amount of envy.

Richard and Miss McBride were obviously very old friends. It was clear from their conversation that they regarded each other with affection. Perhaps their affection was more than that of mere friendship. It seemed a not-inconceivable idea to Alexandra. Miss McBride might be Richard's senior by a few years, but she was by no means elderly, and her lack of conventional beauty could not diminish her very real charm. Alexandra chided herself for the pang that arose in her heart when she thought of Richard and Miss McBride together. Painful as the thought of such an alliance might be, it would be better than seeing him marry someone like Miss Spence.

As long as he's happy, she told herself firmly that night, as she made herself and her weary pupil ready for bed.

All I want is to see him and Lady Margaret happy. If they're happy, then I am happy, too. And if Miss McBride is as nice as she seems, then probably she would do very well for them both.

ELEVEN

The ball Lady Eleanor had planned was to be held on Christmas Day. This made Christmas Eve the focus of much preparation at Brentwood, even apart from the normal preparations due the day.

The members of the house party joined with the household staff in decking the house with Christmas greenery. Early in the afternoon they went out to the woods surrounding Brentwood and returned laden with boughs of holly, ivy, laurel, and mistletoe. Much merriment ensued as these were distributed throughout the house, especially when it came to the hanging of the mistletoe. Miss McBride dryly observed that if the old adage held true that every girl kissed beneath the mistletoe had a chance of marrying in the New Year, then their party had already ensured that the churches and clergymen would not lack for business in the coming year.

Alexandra and Lady Margaret took part in these festivities, though their role was necessarily a minor one. Lady Margaret trotted about the woods, diligently gathering a fine assortment of evergreen branches—twigs, really, since anything larger was beyond the strength of her small hands to cut. These Alexandra tactfully eked out with an armful of larger boughs.

"I wonder," she said, when these had been deposited

in the basket she had brought for that purpose. "I wonder if there's a small evergreen tree we might take."

"A tree?" said Lady Margaret, looking about the wood with puzzlement. "There are lots of trees here. What do you want a tree for, Miss DiMarco?"

"To decorate for Christmas," explained Alexandra. "At my great-aunt and -uncle's house we always cut a tree at Christmastime and brought it indoors to decorate with nuts and paper chains and candles. It's a German custom, I believe. My great-uncle's mother was a German lady."

"Oh, yes, I remember we talked about it during my geography lesson. Christmas trees, Knocking Nights, and Frau Frick," said Lady Margaret, glibly rattling off this list. Once more she looked around the grove. "That's a nice tree over there," she said, pointing to a handsome Scotch pine some sixty feet in height. "Is that the kind you want?"

Alexandra laughed. "No, although it would certainly make a magnificent Christmas tree! But I was wanting a little tree, something we could use to decorate the nursery. Something about this size." She indicated a small fir standing nearby.

"Oh, yes, that would be very pretty in the nursery," said Lady Margaret with enthusiasm. "Let's take it, shall we?"

"I'd like to, but I can't cut it without an ax," said Alexandra, looking around the grove. "And I think we ought to ask your father first, before cutting down a tree."

"Papa won't mind," said Lady Margaret confidently. "Not just one little tree like this."

"Nevertheless, I should prefer to ask him," said Alexandra. Once more she looked about the grove, hoping to catch a glimpse of Richard's tall figure. What she saw instead, however, was the elegant figure of Sir Maximilian Savage, leaning against a tree trunk not far away. There was a look of ineffable boredom on Sir Maximilian's face. On seeing Alexandra, however, his expression became marginally less bored. He straightened himself, brushed an imaginary speck of dust from his coat sleeve, and came over to join her and Lady Margaret.

"Good afternoon, Miss DiMarco," he said, removing his hat from his head and sweeping her a graceful bow. "A pleasure to see you again." He surveyed Alexandra's blue-velvet-and-chinchilla-trimmed costume with admiration. "You cut an elegant figure amid these bucolic pleasantries."

Alexandra thanked him, albeit with no very marked enthusiasm. "What's 'bucolic?'" Lady Margaret wanted to know. "What are 'bucolic'—whatever he said?"

"Bucolic means having to do with the country," explained Alexandra. "So 'bucolic pleasantries' would be country diversions, such as we are enjoying today as we gather our Christmas greenery."

"Such as some of us are enjoying," corrected Sir Maximilian. "I, for one, have no taste for the bucolic." He rolled a contemptuous eye toward a young gentleman who was terrorizing several of the lady guests with a large bunch of mistletoe.

"Have you seen Lord Brentwood about?" asked Alexandra. "I saw him a few minutes ago, but he seems to have disappeared."

"We want to ask him if we can cut this little tree," explained Lady Margaret. "Miss DiMarco wants it to decorate the nursery."

This speech brought Sir Maximilian's eyes back to Alexandra. "So Miss DiMarco wants a tree, does she?" he drawled. "Well, and why not? Among so many trees, Brentwood can certainly spare one to the nursery."

"Yes, that's what I thought," said Lady Margaret with a satisfied nod. "But we cannot cut it ourselves, you see. And so we need Papa to cut it for us."

Sir Maximilian glanced at the tree, debated a moment, then began to remove his greatcoat and topcoat with deliberate care. "Although it is an exercise I do not normally practice, I am quite capable of cutting down a tree," he told Lady Margaret with a whimsical smile. "And I should regard it as a privilege to cut this one for you and Miss DiMarco."

"Please don't bother, Sir Maximilian," said Alexandra hurriedly. "I would not want you to injure yourself or your clothes. Besides, I should not feel right about cutting a tree without getting Lord Brentwood's permission first."

Sir Maximilian waved this objection aside and went off to find an ax. Obtaining one from Richard's serving men, he returned and began to hack away at the trunk of the small fir. "Please don't," begged Alexandra again, looking about the grove nervously. "I am sure—quite, quite sure— we ought not to be doing this without Lord Brentwood's permission."

"What ought not you to be doing without my permission?" demanded a voice behind them.

Both Sir Maximilian and Alexandra turned around and saw Richard, booted and greatcoated, standing at the entrance to the grove where they were working. There was an expression of mild incredulity on his face as he regarded Sir Maximilian and the ax. "What the deuce are you doing to my tree there, Max?" he asked. "Do you know what the penalty is for poaching timber nowadays?"

Sir Maximilian, breathing rather hard from his exercise, gave Richard a tight-lipped smile. "Don't be an ass, Brentwood," he said. "Miss DiMarco wanted a tree for the nursery, so I am merely undertaking to gratify her wish. Surely you don't begrudge her a single tree?"

"This was your wish, Miss DiMarco?" said Richard, looking at Alexandra in surprise.

Alexandra felt as though she could have wept with vexation. "My lord, I am so sorry," she said unhappily. "I did tell him we ought to get your permission first. Upon my word, I did. If the tree is a valuable one, then I will pay for it. You may deduct its cost from my wages."

"The devil he will!" exclaimed Sir Maximilian, looking indignantly at Richard. "If Lord Brentwood insists on being paid for his scrubby little tree, then I shall pay for it. I'm the one who's cutting it down, after all."

"Trying to cut it down, you mean," corrected Richard, who had been inspecting Sir Maximilian's work with raised eyebrows. "You're not going the right way about it, Max. Give me the ax, and I'll take care of it."

"I'm damned if I will," said Sir Maximilian, gripping the ax possessively. "I started this job, and I intend to finish it."

"Not at the rate you're going," returned Richard, and advanced on Sir Maximilian. A brief physical struggle ensued, which Lady Margaret and Alexandra watched wide-eyed. Richard was the victor and emerged bearing the ax triumphantly aloft, while Sir Maximilian took himself off, brushing the pine needles from his raiment with a sulky air.

"Papa won! Papa won!" cried Lady Margaret, dancing about exultantly.

"Hush," said Alexandra, looking rather anxiously after Sir Maximilian. He had heard, however, and turned to regard Lady Margaret with a grim smile.

"Yes, Papa won, but he may be grateful to you that the matter rests there," he told her. "By rights I ought to call him out over this piece of injustice. But because I have a decent respect for the claims of women and dependent children, I will refrain from making you an orphan."

"I'm sure we're all much obliged to you, Max," said Richard, shouldering the ax with a cheerful smile. In a few strong blows, he finished chopping down the tree. "Now what, Miss DiMarco?" he asked. "Do you want me to cut the branches off?"

"No, I need it left whole," said Alexandra. She picked up the tree rather gingerly, trying to avoid contact with the sap that was oozing from its trunk. Richard promptly took it from her.

"Let me carry that, Miss DiMarco. You want it taken to the nursery?"

"Yes, but I can carry it, my lord. It is no great weight, after all."

"No, but it's rather messy. You'd better let me do it." So saying, Richard began to carry the tree back toward the house.

Alexandra and Lady Margaret trailed after him, the latter busily picking up pine cones and sprigs of greenery as she went. When they reached the nursery, Richard laid down the tree and looked at Alexandra. "What do we do with it now?"

"We ought to have a pail of wet sand to stand it up in," said Alexandra, looking about the nursery rather helplessly. "That is how we did it in my great-uncle's house. But I'm not sure there's anything suitable here. We shall have to improvise, I suppose."

Before she had finished speaking, Richard reached for the bell rope and gave it a couple of swift jerks. When Rachel appeared in answer to its summons, he said concisely, "We need a bucket of wet sand, Rachel. As soon as possible, if you please."

"Yes, my lord," said Rachel, looking wonderingly at him and dubiously at the tree lying on the nursery rug. She returned a few minutes later bearing a pail half full of sand.

"Is this enough?" asked Richard, showing the pail to Alexandra.

"I think it will do," she responded. "It's not a very large tree after all. We just stand the tree up in the sand, so—and that is our Christmas tree."

"It looks very nice," said Richard, regarding the tree with approval. "A pleasant variation from our usual wreaths and garlands."

"Beautiful," agreed Lady Margaret rapturously.

Alexandra laughed. "Ah, but it's not done yet," she said. "Just you go back to your party, my lord, and let Lady Margaret and me tend to things here for a few hours. And then you will see what a Christmas tree really looks like."

Richard hesitated. "You don't think I could help?" he said. "What I mean is, I would be happy to assist you in any additional work that needed doing. If you wanted anything else chopped or fetched or carried, for instance—"

"No, I am sure Lady Margaret and I between us can do all that is necessary," said Alexandra, flashing him a grateful smile. "And then, of course, you must get back to your guests, my lord. We cannot keep you up here simply to help decorate our tree."

"No, I suppose not," said Richard. He said it rather wistfully, however, and there was regret in the look he cast over his shoulder as he left the nursery.

"I don't think Papa *wanted* to go back to his guests," said Lady Margaret shrewdly. "I think he wanted to stay here and help us."

"Do you think so?" said Alexandra, busily getting out gold and silver paper and paste. In her heart she regretted the necessity of sending Richard away, but she told herself firmly that she had done the right thing. She had already shown herself so susceptible to her employer's charm that it was better not to spend any more time in his company than was absolutely necessary. And of course it was quite true that he ought to stay with his guests instead of isolating himself in the nursery with her and Lady Margaret. It would have been mere selfishness to have kept him there— selfishness and a kind of self-indulgent weakness which Alexandra was determined not to give way to.

"Of course it would have been nice if your father could have stayed, but we will do very well by ourselves," she told Lady Margaret cheerfully. "We will make lots of gold and silver paper flowers to decorate the tree, and perhaps Cook

will let us have some nuts and apples to hang on it, too
And we will have candles also, if I can find some way to
fasten them to the branches. At home we have special little
holders which my uncle had sent over from Germany."

The next few hours were very happily employed in deco
rating the nursery Christmas tree. Cook obliged not only
with nuts and lady-apples, but with some little wafer-cake
much like the ones that habitually figured on the Man
nington Christmas tree. Alexandra carefully made hole
in these with a hat pin and tied them with ribbons to the
tree branches. Candles proved more difficult to manage
but by dint of using slender tapers, more ribbon, and a
good deal of melted wax, she was able to secure some
dozen or so to the stronger branches. "We wouldn't dar
burn them for long like this, but we can at least light them
and see how they look," she told Lady Margaret. "Now
let's put some greenery on the mantel and around the
doorways, and then things will be all ready for Christmas."

Richard returned to the nursery early that evening, jus
as dusk was beginning to fall. It had been a struggle to
stay away so long, but he had not dared disobey the in
structions Alexandra had given him. Indeed, his con
science assured him that she was quite correct in saying
he owed a duty to his guests. Yet all that afternoon as he
had laughed and joked, hung greenery and helped hau
in the Yule log, he had been mentally counting off the
hours until he might reasonably present himself in the
nursery. He quietly opened the door, then stopped on the
threshold, looking with amazement at the transfigured
tree.

"What a gorgeous thing," he exclaimed.

Alexandra had just finished lighting the candles for the
very first time. It had been a tenuous business, and she
still held a taper in her hand lest her makeshift holder

require bolstering with extra wax. She turned around to smile at Richard. "It looks very different now, does it not, my lord?"

"I should say so," said Richard, coming over to inspect the candle-lit tree more closely. Lady Margaret accompanied him, swinging Méchante in her arms and gazing rapturously at the tree.

"Isn't it beautiful, Papa? Miss DiMarco and I made it all ourselves, except that Cook gave us the cakes and apples and things. I made that rose there." She pointed to a misshapen silver flower decorating one of the branches. "And I also made that one, and that one. Miss DiMarco made the others. It's very nice, isn't it, Papa?"

"Very nice indeed," said Richard. He turned to look at Alexandra. "This is a lovely idea, Miss DiMarco," he told her. "So lovely that it seems a shame to keep it shut away up here in the nursery. Do you think we might take it downstairs so everyone might enjoy it?"

"To be sure, but I don't know how movable it is," said Alexandra, regarding the tree with a dubious eye. "I barely got those candles to stay on in the first place."

"I'll be very careful," Richard promised. "I'll take it down personally, and if any candles come off, I will help you put them back on again."

"But it's ours," protested Lady Margaret. Her lower lip quivered as she added, "Miss DiMarco and I made it, and it isn't fair that anyone else should have it."

Alexandra opened her mouth, but Richard forestalled her. He squatted down to address his daughter eye to eye. "It wouldn't be a case of anyone else having it," he said gently. "The tree would still be yours and Miss DiMarco's, only it would be downstairs where everyone else could admire it. Just for this evening, Margaret. We could take it down now, and bring it up again when it is time for you to go to bed. Wouldn't you like to have the tree downstairs, where everyone could admire your handiwork?"

Lady Margaret considered. "Could it go on the big table?" she asked. "The big table in the dining room?"

"What, the dinner table?" said Richard, startled.

Lady Margaret nodded firmly. "Yes, the dinner table. It could go right in the middle of the table, just like that big silver thing we had there last night with the flowers and fruit."

"The epergne," said Alexandra with unsteady lips.

"I don't think it should go *on* the dinner table," said Richard, also repressing a smile. "But it could go *beside* it—over in the corner of the room, perhaps. We could bring in a small table to put it on, so it would be properly displayed."

Lady Margaret, after due consideration, decided this was an acceptable compromise. Alexandra, too, consented to have Richard carry the tree down. "But if I had known everyone would see it, I would have taken more pains with it," she told him. "And I definitely would have thought of a better way to fix on those candles. If you intend to burn them as they are, my lord, I would suggest you appoint one of the servants to stand by with a pail of water. My great-uncle always does that at home anyway when our Christmas tree is lit," she added irrelevantly. "He believes trees and candles together pose a great risk of fire."

Richard looked at her, but she seemed unaware that her remark betrayed a background of considerable affluence. He therefore held his tongue and devoted himself to carrying the tree down to the dining room. When it had been successfully installed on a small table in the corner and the servants had been instructed about lighting the candles and standing by in case of fire, Richard took his leave of Lady Margaret and Alexandra. "I must go and change for dinner," he told them with a smile. "And I suggest you do the same. But I'll see you downstairs in a half hour or so."

* * *

It proved to be an altogether magical Christmas Eve. The dinner was both lavish and delicious, and the Christmas tree was praised enough to reconcile Lady Margaret to its relocation. Richard was rather annoyed because Sir Maximilian insisted on taking partial credit for it, but charitably he put aside his annoyance, reflecting that he himself had had the superior pleasure of assisting Alexandra in its installation.

After dinner the Yule log was ceremoniously lit, and the party settled down to the traditional Christmas Eve pastime of playing cards.

Alexandra, judging whist to be beyond her pupil's capabilities or interest, set up a private game of lottery tickets in one corner of the drawing room. But an amazing number of other guests drifted over to join them, including Miss McBride and Lady Eleanor. To Alexandra's surprise, even the indolent Sir Maximilian Savage opted to join the lottery-ticket table. Sir Maximilian seemed to have shed his habitual indolence for the evening. He became quite the life of the party, bargaining, bluffing, and scheming for his cards with the skill of a wily politician. Alexandra, having watched him cheat himself so that Lady Margaret might win, decided he was much nicer than she had first supposed, but she still could not like him so well as Richard.

This would have been a comfort to Richard had he known it. As it was, he could only regret that his role as host kept him from entering into the fun at the lottery-ticket table. He went to bed that night disconsolate and determined that another day would not go by without his making some declaration to Alexandra.

TWELVE

Alexandra was wakened early Christmas morning by a joyful cry in her ear. "Miss DiMarco, it snowed last night! It snowed! Just in time for Christmas. Do come and see, Miss DiMarco. Everything's white all over!"

Alexandra opened bleary eyes to see Lady Margaret's small face suspended over hers. The face wore a beatific smile. It was a smile such as warms the heart of even a sleepy governess. Alexandra sighed, rubbed her eyes, and smiled back at her pupil. Lady Margaret tugged urgently at the sleeve of her nightdress. "Come look out the window, Miss DiMarco! It's so pretty outside. You never saw such a pretty sight."

Alexandra, standing side by side with her pupil at the window a moment later, was inclined to agree with this statement. The now familiar grounds of Brentwood were transfigured by snow into a landscape of glittering white. A few flakes still swirled in the air, but the sun was peeping over the horizon, and the day promised to be an uncommonly beautiful one. "We must get you dressed," Alexandra told Lady Margaret. "We are to eat breakfast downstairs today, and then go to church afterward. Since you're up so early, you might as well have a bath while we're at it."

The tub and bathwater were sent for, and when eventually Lady Margaret went downstairs for breakfast, she was well scrubbed and neatly attired in a red merino dress a little too short for her. Alexandra smiled, thinking of the new dresses that were awaiting her upon her return from church. It was obvious Lady Margaret was looking forward to the gift-giving time, too. "I wish I could give Papa his present now," she whispered to Alexandra as they took their places at the breakfast table. "Do you think he will like it, Miss DiMarco? I didn't get the stitches quite straight, you know."

"No, but your father would rather have a handkerchief you have made yourself than one with the straightest stitches imaginable," said Alexandra with conviction. "Just you wait and see what he says." She had no doubt Richard would accept his daughter's gift in the proper spirit and overlook any little deficiencies in its manufacture. He was a wonderful father—a wonderful man altogether, in fact. Looking to where he sat at the head of the table, she felt a wave of love and longing wash over her.

At that same moment, Richard looked up and caught her eye. Alexandra was filled with confusion. She looked hastily away, but she felt quite sure that she had betrayed herself in that glance and that her heart had been in her eyes, plain for anybody to see. She could only hope Richard had not seen it, or that if he had, he would attribute it to the holiday excitement in the atmosphere. It was a fortunate thing it was Christmas, Alexandra told herself, as she bent over her plate of ham and hot rolls. Holiday high spirits could excuse any number of behavioral lapses. And with any luck at all, Miss Harcourt would soon be able to leave her mother, and she would be able to resign the position that had become at once such a delight and such a burden to her.

Alexandra was right in supposing Richard had noticed her looking at him. He was far from giving her lovestruck gaze its proper interpretation, however. Looking into her eyes, all he could think was how beautiful she was and how much he desired her. Not only in the physical sense, as he assured himself. The happiness he got from merely being in her company was proof that it was more than her lovely face and form that attracted him.

He stole frequent, wistful looks at her as the morning wore on. When breakfast was over and the party were preparing to go to church, he contrived to be in the same carriage with her and Lady Margaret, and when they reached the church, he made sure they were seated where he could keep an eye on them both. He stole frequent looks at them throughout the service. It gave him pleasure to see his daughter's evident attachment to Alexandra, and even more pleasure to see that the attachment appeared to be reciprocated He reckoned that this would make it easier to induce Alexandra to assume Lady Margaret's care on a permanent basis. Indeed, he was not sure this was not the proper way to approach her on the matter. Of her feelings for him he was uncertain, but he had no doubt she cared for his daughter. Perhaps an appeal to her maternal instincts would be more successful than a profession of his own love and esteem for her.

Richard pondered this matter all that morning, observing and enjoying the merriment going on around him in an abstracted way but meditating all the while on how best to plead his cause to Alexandra. He was no nearer a decision when the moment arrived which Lady Margaret had been anticipating all morning: the moment when the Christmas presents were to be distributed.

Lady Margaret took precedence in this matter, insisting on distributing her own crudely wrapped presents even before everyone was seated in the drawing room. Her gifts were all things she had made herself—handkerchiefs, mostly, rather unevenly hemmed and marked with a crooked letter or two. But the recipients of these tokens all professed themselves delighted with them. Alexandra, smoothing her own gift handkerchief (which had come as little surprise to her, seeing that she had supervised its construction) smiled at her pupil. "I shall treasure it always, Lady Margaret," she said. "Now let me give you *my* gift."

Lady Margaret excitedly tore open the bundle which Alexandra placed in her lap. "It's clothes for Méchante!" she cried. "Lots and lots of dresses—and a lovely cloak— and underclothes, too. Oh, Miss DiMarco, how beautiful! Méchante will look fine as a star." She held aloft a handful of doll clothes.

The other lady guests crowded around curiously to see. "How lovely," drawled Lady Rosalie, looking with interest at the doll wardrobe. "You are an accomplished seamstress, Miss DiMarco."

"Indeed she is," said Miss McBride heartily. "I never saw such a canty doll's kit."

"Nor I," agreed Lady Rosalie. Touching a diminutive morning dress, she added with perfect seriousness, "I wouldn't mind something like this myself. Would you be willing to make me one if I bought the material for it, Miss DiMarco?"

Miss Spence, who had been regarding the doll clothes with a jealous eye, gave a short laugh. "Don't be a goose, Rosalie," she said. "Miss DiMarco is a governess, not a dressmaker."

Alexandra laughed. "Yes, and I'm afraid I haven't time for any full-scale dressmaking, Lady Rosalie. But I thank you very much for the compliment." In a thoughtful voice, she added, "Perhaps I could make a sketch of the dress for you, so you could take it to your regular dressmaker and have her make one up for you after the same pattern."

"That would be lovely," said Lady Rosalie with obvious sincerity. Seating herself beside Lady Margaret, she began to inspect the rest of the doll clothes with a connoisseur's eye.

Lady Eleanor, who was among the ladies crowded round the doll clothes, gave Alexandra a conspiratorial smile. "You know not how highly you are complimented, Miss DiMarco," she said in a low voice. "Lady Rosalie prides herself on being the best-dressed woman in London."

"Well, *I* am not likely to criticize her taste," said Alexandra with a smile. Lady Eleanor patted her shoulder and then, to Alexandra's surprise, deposited a slim box in her lap.

"Merry Christmas, Miss DiMarco," she said. "I hope you will do me the honor of wearing these at the ball tonight."

The package proved to contain a pair of long white kid gloves. "Thank you very much, ma'am," said Alexandra, regarding them with mingled pleasure and surprise. "Of course I shall wear them tonight, and wear them with pleasure." In a dubious voice she added, "But are you sure I ought to wear anything so formal? I had thought that since I am attending as Lady Margaret's governess, it would be out of place for me to wear full evening dress."

"Oh no," said Lady Eleanor with a vigorous shake of her head. "You are a guest like all the others, and it is only right that you should be properly dressed. You know that everyone wears their finest clothes and jewels to a ball." With an anxiety Alexandra found surprising, she added, "Have you an appropriate dress with you, Miss DiMarco? If you have not, I would be happy to loan you one. I know we are rather different sizes, but my maid is very clever, and I am sure she can contrive to make one of my dresses fit you between now and tonight."

Alexandra's mind flew to the blue taffeta, still packed in tissue paper in her bottommost trunk. "No, I have an appropriate dress," she said slowly. "At least I think it is appropriate. But I would appreciate your giving me an opinion on the matter, ma'am. If you would drop by my room sometime before dinner this afternoon—"

"I would be happy to," said Lady Eleanor, and gave her arm a squeeze.

The guests, meanwhile, were busy exchanging gifts among themselves. The drawing room was soon littered with shreds of gold and silver paper, as handkerchiefs, purses, books, boxes of bonbons, fans, and similar trifles were discovered amid the holiday wrappings. Richard, as host, received more than his fair share of these tokens. He in return gave out small silver trinket-boxes with his coat-of-arms engraved upon them. He found it deeply annoying that some of the lady guests insisted on taking these gifts as a direct and personal tribute to their own charms. Miss Spence, in particular, made a great fuss over her silver box.

"Oh, Lord Brentwood, you should not have, upon my word," she gushed. "And only look! I do believe—yes, I am quite sure—that mine is just a little handsomer than the other ladies'! They will be quite jealous, I vow and declare," she added, with a sly look around the room.

The other ladies declined to respond to this sally, although several were seen to compare their own boxes and Miss Spence's with a jealous eye. Miss Spence continued with her soliloquy. "Whatever shall I keep in such a charming box?" she inquired, opening and shutting the lid. "I declare I have not anything half fine enough."

"You might keep your false hair in it," suggested Miss McBride with a straight face. One or two of the other ladies snickered. Miss Spence reddened and put a hand self-consciously to the handsome chignon at the back of her head.

"Hattie, how can you be so absurd?" she said with a forced laugh. "You must know my hair is all my own." Lest anyone be tempted to challenge this statement, she hurried on, not giving the others a chance to speak. "I must thank you, my lord, for your munificent gift," she told Richard. "Be sure I shall treasure it as it deserves."

Richard murmured that he was much obliged, but was
relieved to turn from Miss Spence to his daughter, who
came rushing up just then to show him Méchante in one
of her new dresses. "Perhaps someone else could use some
new dresses, too," he said, presenting her with the box
containing her new clothing.

Lady Margaret's eyes were round as saucers as she
opened the box. On top was the pink satin dress. She regarded it speechlessly for a moment, then let out a cry
that made everyone in the room look around. "Oh! Oh,
it's a dress like Méchante's! Look, Miss DiMarco, only look
at what Papa has given me! It's a dress exactly like
Méchante's."

Alexandra came over to see and admire the pink dress.
Of course its similarity to Méchante's came as no surprise
to her; likewise, she was unsurprised to find that a great
many of Méchante's new dresses bore a striking resemblance to her mistress's. She had fashioned much of the
doll wardrobe from scraps left over from making Lady Margaret's new dresses, and she felt fully repaid now for her
labors with the needle as she observed her pupil's evident
delight.

It was, beyond doubt, the pink satin dress that delighted
Lady Margaret most. "Can I put it on now?" she begged.
"Please, oh please, Papa, may I put it on now? Please, Miss
DiMarco?"

Richard looked at Alexandra. Alexandra put her arms
around Lady Margaret and hugged her. "No, not now,
dearest, but you may wear it tonight for the party," she
told the little girl. "It would be better if you put on one
of your other new dresses now—the green merino, perhaps. And Méchante may change into her green merino,
too, and save the pink satin for tonight."

"Before you do that, though, there are one or two other
packages you might open," suggested Richard. Lady Margaret pricked up her ears at these words and immediately

signified her willingness to open more packages. The wooden animals delighted her, as did the books, and when she went upstairs a little later, she was clutching to her chest the animals, the books, and her own and Méchante's pink satin dresses.

"Well, that was a notable success," Richard told Alexandra as they followed behind, carrying the rest of Lady Margaret's bounty. "I must thank you, Miss DiMarco, for assisting me in choosing my daughter's gifts."

"It was a pleasure," said Alexandra. She smiled at Richard as she spoke, but her smile was a trifle forced. Happy as she was at the success of her gifts, happy as it made her to see Lady Margaret's childish glee, she was still prey to a faint feeling of discontent.

In her room was another gift, a beautifully framed crayon portrait of Lady Margaret which she had made for Richard. She had embarked on the project a bit hesitantly, feeling she ought not to indulge herself in what was admittedly a labor of love. Still, she could not resist making her employer a gift, especially since she reasoned he would probably make her one, too, and it would be only polite to reciprocate. But he had not given her a gift. He had not even given her the purse and money he had given the other servants. He had given everyone in the house something except her.

Alexandra had done her best to rationalize this behavior. She was a governess, she reminded herself, and as such she occupied a unique position at Brentwood: neither servant nor guest, but something in between. And it was not as though she were not being compensated for her work. Conversation with Rachel and the other servants had revealed to her that she was being paid more than any servant in the house—more even than the culinary artist who presided over the kitchens, or the hard-working bailiff who oversaw Richard's tenants and home farm.

Alexandra told herself she was lucky to have received as

much as she had from Richard. She could not reasonably expect more than the munificent salary and unstinting praise he had bestowed upon her ever since she had arrived at Brentwood. Besides, his family had given her such generous Christmas gifts that it would have been redundant for him to do the same. Lady Margaret's handkerchief might have little intrinsic value, but the gloves from Lady Eleanor undoubtedly had been costly, and even Mr. Taft had given her a gift—a ponderous tome in Latin, which he had proudly announced was a tribute to her skill with languages.

Alexandra had not any reason to feel neglected, therefore. And yet she did feel neglected. She tried to smile as Richard, having deposited his own burden of toys and clothes within the nursery, returned to take the things she was carrying. "Thank you, my lord. If you will just leave those things in a pile, Lady Margaret and I will see about putting them away properly," she told him.

He nodded, but instead of returning downstairs, as she expected, he lingered in the nursery. If Alexandra had glanced in his direction, she would have seen he was regarding her with an indecisive expression. She kept her eyes firmly averted, however, as she began to place Lady Margaret's new books upon the nursery shelves. The thought of that picture in her room was painful to her.

She chided herself for having cherished so many foolish, romantic fantasies in connection with her employer. Clearly he regarded himself as nothing more than that, and the sooner he left, the sooner she might dispose of her lovingly made but ill-judged gift. She would then devote her remaining time at Brentwood to seeing that she never again indulged in such folly.

Lady Margaret was frolicking about the nursery, embarked on an elaborate play wherein Méchante attended a ball given by a family of bears. Alexandra watched her absently. Gradually it dawned on her that she herself was being watched. She looked up to encounter Richard's gaze.

"Miss DiMarco, I hope—" he began, then stopped.

Alexandra waited, her dejected mood giving way to one of curiosity. He looked so solemn, and at the same time so embarrassed, that she could not imagine what he was about to say.

After a minute Richard went on. "Miss DiMarco, I hope you won't think it presumptuous, but it happens I have a present for you," he said. "A Christmas present, I suppose you might call it. I didn't want to give it to you downstairs . . ." Again he stopped.

Alexandra's dejected mood evaporated completely at these words. "You have a present for me?" she said, trying to conceal her joy. "Oh, but it happens that I have one for you, too, my lord. Wait just one moment, and I'll get it."

Not giving Richard time to reply, Alexandra hurried into her bedchamber. She returned a moment later carrying the picture. "Here you are, my lord," she said, presenting it to him with a curtsy. "It's nothing very much—only a drawing of Lady Margaret which I made a few weeks ago when I was trying to amuse her on a wet day. But it came out rather nicely, I thought—and so I thought you might like to have it."

A moment of silence followed, as Richard looked down at the picture. Alexandra felt all at once that she had done something presumptuous. She stood looking at her feet, not daring to speak, until at last Richard's voice broke the silence.

"This is beautiful," he said. "Did you truly make it yourself, Miss DiMarco? I am honored that you should have spent so much time and labor on my behalf." He hesitated again, then went on in a rush. "I hope you won't mind very much, but I think—I rather believe—that I would prefer to give the present I have for you at the ball tonight.

Would you mind waiting very much?" He looked at Alexandra earnestly.

Alexandra was disappointed, but also greatly intrigued. What could his gift possibly be? And why would he prefer to give it to her at the ball? "Of course I do not mind, my lord," she said firmly. "Indeed, you must not feel you must give me a present at all. After all you have done for me—"

He stopped her with a smile. "No, the obligation is all on my side, I assure you. But never mind that now. I can better make that clear to you tonight." In a diffident voice, he added, "Would it be too much to hope you might save me a dance or two tonight, Miss DiMarco? I would like very much to dance with you."

Alexandra blinked. "Yes, of course. Although that is not really necessary, my lord. I do not expect to dance many dances since I am attending the ball as Lady Margaret's governess. Indeed, perhaps it would be better if I did not dance at all. I doubt whether it would be fitting—"

"It would be perfectly fitting," said Richard firmly. "And I insist on your dancing, Miss DiMarco. Which two dances will you give me?"

Alexandra laughed. "As to that, I doubt not you may have your pick, my lord. As I said before, I shall be attending as Lady Margaret's governess, and I don't expect there will be much demand for me on the dance floor." Smiling, she gave her hand to Richard. "But I shall be looking forward to dancing with you, my lord. And I am burning with curiosity to see your gift! Until tonight?"

"Until tonight," agreed Richard. Taking her hand in his, he raised it to his lips.

THIRTEEN

Alexandra was both excited and nervous as she made herself ready for the ball that evening.

She told herself it was no wonder she was a trifle excited. The day had been an eventful one—the most eventful day of her life, without doubt. The morning service at church; the holiday gift-giving and jollity in the afternoon; Lady Margaret's childish delight in her new gifts—all had left a vivid and indelible impression on Alexandra's memory. And now there was the ball to look forward to. Alexandra had been eagerly looking forward to it ever since she had learned there was to be a ball, but her eagerness had been intensified a hundredfold by Richard's announcement that he meant to give her a Christmas gift sometime during the evening's festivities.

This announcement had greatly elated Alexandra. It had also given her a good deal of food for conjecture. What kind of gift did Richard mean to give her? And why did he prefer to wait and give it to her tonight at the ball rather than giving it to her that afternoon with the other guests' presents? Alexandra could think of several reasons for such behavior, but her common sense rejected them all as romantic folly. Yet so strong an impression had Richard's manner made on her that the sensible, commonplace explanations which her intellect offered as substitutes did not satisfy her, either.

Consequently she was in a flutter of nerves as she go
herself and her pupil dressed and ready. Lady Margare
also seemed to have partaken of this mood, for she said
not a single word as Alexandra brushed out her hair and
buttoned her into the pink satin dress. She then sat quietly
looking through one of her new books while Alexandra
took a bath and washed her hair. It took some considerable
time to brush her hair dry before the fire, but the job wa:
finished at last, some thirty minutes before the party wa:
due to go down to dinner. Alexandra was standing in her
chemise, looking dubiously at her blue taffeta gown, wher
Lady Eleanor came into the nursery.

"Oh, Aunt Eleanor, what a lovely dress! You look like a
queen," cried Lady Margaret, dropping her book and running to greet her. Lady Eleanor was gorgeously appareled
in a red brocade gown embroidered in gold. A handsome
set of rubies hung about her neck and glowed in a tiara
atop her dark head. She laughed at her niece's exuberan
greeting and bent down to embrace her.

"Thank you, my sweet. You look very lovely, too. And
look at Méchante! What an elegant pair you make, to be
sure." She curtsied gravely to Lady Margaret and her doll
then turned to look about the nursery. "Where is your
governess, my child?"

"In here," called Alexandra. Lady Margaret crossed the
nursery and schoolroom and came to stand in the doorway
of Alexandra's room.

"I have come to offer you advice about your toilette, a:
you requested," she said gaily. Half curiously, half critically
she surveyed Alexandra's chemise-clad figure. "It must be
nice to have a natural figure," she remarked. "Without
my corsets, I would look as shapeless as a bolster. But i
could be worse. I could have to wear a wax bosom like
Miss Spence!"

"A wax bosom?" said Alexandra, looking at her disbe
lievingly. "Does Miss Spence wear a wax bosom?"

Lady Eleanor laughed. "Yes, to be sure. Don't say you have never heard of such things? What a delightful innocent you are, Miss DiMarco. And yet there's a touch of the serpent about you, too. No wonder Richard——" She broke off abruptly, with a conscious smile. "But there, I do not mean to talk out of turn. My purpose in being here is to help you dress for the ball." Briskly walking over to where Alexandra was standing, she took the blue taffeta dress out of her hands. "Is this what you were planning to wear? It looks as though it would do very nicely."

"Do you think so?" said Alexandra, pleased but a little doubtful. "I had feared it might be a trifle elaborate."

"No indeed," said Lady Eleanor with decision. "You must know nothing can be too elaborate for a ball, my dear."

"I am sure that is true for an ordinary guest," said Alexandra, as tactfully as she could. "But you know I am not an ordinary guest, Lady Eleanor. I am your niece's governess—yes, indeed I am, no matter who I am, or what my parents may have been. And I am afraid wearing such a dress as this would look out of place."

"Nonsense," said Lady Eleanor robustly. "You make too much of it, my dear. The dress is perfectly correct, and if anyone criticizes it—why, you may be sure it will merely be some lady who is jealous because you look more elegant than she does."

Alexandra looked again at the blue taffeta dress. It was a beautiful dress, and she wanted in the worst way to wear it—not so as to flaunt herself before Richard, as she assured herself hastily, but merely because she wished her appearance to do him and his household credit. And if she believed Lady Eleanor, there was nothing wrong about her doing so. She could not help being a little surprised that Lady Eleanor should urge her so strongly to make herself fine, but the fact remained that she had no experience in such matters while Lady Eleanor had a great deal.

Why should Lady Eleanor deceive her, after all? There could be no possible reason.

So Alexandra stood still meekly and let Lady Eleanor button her into the blue taffeta dress. When it was on, Lady Eleanor scrutinized her with a furrowed brow. "It fits you to a nicety, my dear. You look very lovely indeed. But I think you would look even better with some kind of ornament. A string of pearls, perhaps. . . ."

Alexandra, remembering how spiteful Miss Spence had been over the matter of the watch, was surprised by this advice, but once again she assumed Lady Eleanor must know best. "I have some sapphires that my uncle bought me a few months ago," she offered diffidently. "They go very nicely with this dress, I think. But if you advise it, I will wear my pearls instead."

For some reason, this speech made Lady Eleanor go into paroxysms of hysterical laughter. "No, indeed, my love," she said, in a voice that shook with mirth. "Now that you mention it, I am sure sapphires would be more becoming. Get them out, if you please, and I will help you put them on."

Alexandra obediently complied with these instructions. She was likewise compliant when Lady Eleanor suggested calling in her maid to assist with the dressing of her hair. "Braids do very well for every day, but for a ball you need something more elaborate," decreed Lady Eleanor. "Ringlets, I think, Hawkins, with the back hair done up behind, perhaps."

Lady Margaret was in raptures while this process was going on. She sat on Alexandra's bed, watching with round eyes as Hawkins deftly set the finishing touches on Alexandra's coiffure. "You look so beautiful, Miss DiMarco," she kept saying. "You will be the beautifullest lady at the ball."

"Most beautiful," Alexandra corrected absently. She surveyed herself in the glass. The sight of her reflection came as a shock to her, for she had grown used to seeing herself with plain braided hair, little or no jewelry, and dark gowns that covered her arms and shoulders. Now both arms and shoulders were bared by the low-cut corsage of her ball dress, and her hair hung in clusters of ringlets around her ears. The sapphires glittering on her breast and in her ears added the final finishing touch.

Alexandra was pleased with her appearance, although she could not quite concur with Lady Margaret's extravagant praise. In her own mind, her looks were definitely inferior to Miss Spence's and Lady Rosalie's. The contrast would probably be all the greater tonight, for on such a gala occasion the ladies of the party would have spared no labor or expense to set off their beauty. But when she recalled Lady Eleanor's remarks about wax bosoms—and Miss McBride's thrust about false hair—she felt no reason to be jealous of Miss Spence at least. Nor did she really envy Lady Rosalie her opulent beauty, much as she might admire it. She was content to be herself tonight—Alexandra Elizabeth Manning DiMarco, on the eve of her first ball. And not just any ball, she reminded herself, but the ball whereat she was to receive a Christmas gift from the man whom she loved above all others.

The thought made Alexandra blush and look guiltily at Lady Eleanor and Lady Margaret. Fortunately, neither of them was looking at her. Lady Margaret was attempting to arrange Méchante's hair in ringlets, and Lady Eleanor was dismissing her maid with instructions not to sit up for her. "We will undoubtedly be up very late," she said in a voice of satisfaction. "I never consider a ball really successful unless everyone is up to see the sun rise the next morning."

"Will I be up to see the sun rise tomorrow morning, too?" asked Lady Margaret in a voice of awe.

"Oh, my dear! I am sure you will be asleep long before midnight," said Lady Eleanor, laughing. Alexandra shook her head at her violently, but it was too late. Lady Margaret's face took on the familiar look of stubborn determination.

"I can too stay up past midnight. I stayed up past midnight all the time when I lived with Mama. And I'm sure I could stay awake all night if I wanted to. You just wait and see, Aunt Eleanor. Papa said I might sit up late tonight, you know."

Lady Eleanor threw Alexandra a look of laughing dismay.

Alexandra responded instantly. "Yes, and I am sure you could stay awake all night if you wanted to," she told Lady Margaret. "None of us doubts that you *could*. But you must consider whether you really want to, Lady Margaret. You remember we have talked before about how important it is to decide things for yourself rather than letting other people's words and actions influence you. It would be silly to stay up all night just to show us you could, when it means you would feel tired and cross all the next day. Why don't you wait and see how you feel tonight before deciding when you will go to bed?"

"How clever you are," murmured Lady Eleanor admiringly. Alexandra merely shook her head. Her eyes were on Lady Margaret, who was considering her words with an earnest frown.

"All right," she said at last. "I'll wait and see. But I know I won't want to go to bed until midnight at the least."

"I don't think it would be unreasonable for you to stay up that late," said Alexandra, giving her a hug. "I doubt I shall stay up any later than midnight myself."

Her words elicited a startled glance from Lady Eleanor. At the first opportunity, Lady Eleanor bent to whisper in her ear. "My dear, you do not really mean to retire at midnight? Why, the party will be just beginning!"

"Will it?" said Alexandra naively. "I should hate to miss any of the festivities, but you know Lady Margaret must be my first care. And I don't think it healthy for her to sit up too late."

"Yes, but—" Lady Eleanor looked dissatisfied, but said no more as long as Lady Margaret was in earshot.

When they were going down the stairs, however, with Lady Margaret running ahead of them, she spoke again. "I cannot like to see you sacrifice your pleasure for a child, Miss DiMarco. Perhaps Rachel might take charge of Margaret for you this evening, so you can really enjoy yourself."

Alexandra gave her a surprised look. "I do not mind taking care of Lady Margaret, ma'am. Strange as it may sound, I really enjoy her company." With a smile, she added, "Indeed, I should feel very uncomfortable attending the party tonight without her. We can have a nice time, you know, watching and listening in some quiet corner. And when Lady Margaret grows tired, we can slip out without disturbing anyone."

Lady Eleanor gave her a long look, but said nothing more. They reached the drawing room without incident and joined the rest of the party that were gathered there, waiting to go into dinner.

As Alexandra had expected, all the ladies were looking their best in honor of the evening's festivities. Lady Rosalie was a vision of voluptuous splendor in a gown of clinging lilac silk, and Miss Spence was dazzling in diamonds and silver lamé. Even Miss McBride had changed her usual mannish garb for a gown of cream-colored sarcenet enhanced with a sash and scarf of plaid silk which she explained was her family's native tartan.

The gentlemen made a fitting foil for this feminine brilliance. Charles Taft wore a blue topcoat with large buttons, broad lapels, and an intricately knotted neckcloth. Sir Maximilian had gone him one better: his buttons were a shade larger, his lapels a shade wider, and his neckcloth so intricate that its bulk nearly forbade him to turn his head. He managed to look very handsome even in this extreme dress, but to Alexandra's eyes neither he nor Mr. Taft nor any of the other gentlemen present could compare to the appearance Richard made in his simple, severely tailored black evening clothes. She watched him admiringly as he stooped to greet Lady Margaret.

"And where is Miss DiMarco?" he asked, looking around the drawing room. His eyes lit on Alexandra, and he was suddenly still, his eyes fixed on her face. The next moment he was smiling again, but Alexandra had observed the pause and the momentary flicker of expression in Richard's eyes. It seemed to her a portent—of what, she could not have said exactly, but the excitement that had been building within her all day flared a little higher. She gave a small, involuntary shiver.

"Are you cold, Miss DiMarco?" The solicitous voice of Sir Maximilian Savage recalled her to a sense of her surroundings. She turned to find him standing at her elbow.

Alexandra smiled and shook her head. "No, thank you, Sir Maximilian. I merely thought I felt a chill for a moment."

"This whole house of Brentwood's is drafty as a barn," agreed Sir Maximilian. His eyes appraised Alexandra greedily, lingering last on her sapphires with a speculative expression. "Allow me to compliment you on your appearance, Miss DiMarco. You look absolutely ravishing."

"Thank you," said Alexandra. The way he was looking at her (as if in truth he wanted to ravish her) made her extremely uncomfortable. To hide her embarrassment, she pretended to look around the drawing room. "Dinner ought to be announced any minute. I wonder who my partner will be?"

"I have that honor," said Sir Maximilian, executing a graceful bow. In an undertone, he added, "I had to bribe Brentwood's butler to switch the cards, but I consider the reward well worth the cost. If you are ready, Miss Di-Marco?" He offered her his arm.

Alexandra took it rather reluctantly. She had not really believed Sir Maximilian's speech—the part about paying for the privilege of partnering her at dinner sounded like purest hyperbole—but she could not fail to understand his voice and manner, both of which were uncomfortably warm. Fervently she wished she had drawn some other dinner partner. Then she reminded herself that it might have been worse. She might have been seated next to Miss Spence, or a perfect stranger. In addition to the party guests, Lady Eleanor had invited a number of friends, relatives and neighbors to dine at Brentwood before the ball. Alexandra felt that even an amorous Sir Maximilian Savage was better than the prospect of trying to converse with a wholly unfamiliar gentleman. Sir Maximilian could hardly make love to her at the dinner table, after all.

So Alexandra sustained the addresses of her partner throughout the meal with the appearance of complacency. In truth, she found Sir Maximilian a diverting companion apart from his propensity to pay her embarrassing compliments. And even these she was able to endure by treating them as jokes. There were only two really uncomfortable moments during the meal. One was when Miss Spence inquired generally of the party whether menials ought to be allowed to wear the finery of their betters. The other uncomfortable moment came toward the end of the meal, when Alexandra was laughing at one of Sir Maximilian's outrageous sallies. She looked up to find Richard's eyes upon her. There was a look of such mingled surprise and disapproval in his eyes that she dropped her own eyes in confusion.

For the rest of the meal, Sir Maximilian found Alexandra a singularly unresponsive companion. This did not prevent him from continuing his pursuit of her, however. He begged her to be his partner for the first two dances with a persistence as unflagging as it was annoying. Alexandra evaded his importunings as well as she could, but was eventually forced to admit she was not engaged for the first two dances. "But you know I must attend to Lady Margaret, Sir Maximilian," she told him. "I doubt I shall be able to dance much this evening and perhaps not at all."

"We'll see about that," he said with a confident smile. "Only promise me that you will not dance the first two dances with anyone else, Miss DiMarco, and I will be satisfied."

Alexandra promised, with a sensation of inward discontent. She could not have said why she was so unhappy about committing herself in this manner. It was not that she had any hopes of dancing the first two dances with Richard. As host, he would naturally be obliged to dance those dances with his most notable lady guest. If he danced with Alexandra at all, it would have to be later in the evening—probably a good deal later. So Alexandra assured herself as she left the drawing room with the other ladies. But she could not resist looking wistfully back at Richard as she went out of the room. And though she was gratified to receive a slight smile and bow from Richard, she was embarrassed to receive a much warmer smile and bow from Sir Maximilian. Averting her eyes, Alexandra left the room with some haste.

There followed an interval in the drawing room during which the ladies gossiped, drank tea, and waited for the gentlemen to join them. Miss Spence made one or two additional catty remarks about Alexandra's dress and general appearance, but Alexandra was able to ignore these without too much difficulty. She had her hands full with Lady Margaret, who was by now bouncing about the room in a state of nearly unbearable excitement. Presently the interval of waiting was over; the gentlemen began to reappear, and it was time to proceed to the ballroom.

There followed another interval of waiting in the ballroom, during which the guests milled about, conversing in a desultory way and waiting for the dancing to begin. The first dance was to commence at nine o'clock. For some time previous to this hour, carriageloads of guests had been arriving, and when the clock finally struck the magic hour, the ballroom was already very full.

Alexandra, who had taken a bench at the back of the room beside Lady Margaret, saw Richard making his way across the ballroom in her direction. Her heart gave a little involuntary flutter at the sight of him. She was even more flustered when he drew closer and she realized that he meant to speak to her. Then she was distracted by a voice in her ear: the voice of Sir Maximilian Savage, who had come up to her quietly while her attention was engaged in watching Richard.

"It's all arranged, Miss DiMarco," he said jubilantly. "Mrs. Renfrew has agreed to sit with Lady Margaret while you dance with me." He indicated the plump and smiling lady at his elbow, whom Alexandra recognized as one of the house party guests.

Mrs. Renfrew laughed and struck Sir Maximilian's arm lightly with her fan. "Yes, I am getting too heavy to dance, not to mention too old, though Max was not unkind enough to say so. But I don't mind playing chaperone to this little lady while you young folks dance." She smiled at Lady Margaret.

As Alexandra was searching for some way to politely decline Mrs. Renfrew's services, Richard came up to join them. He looked frowningly at Sir Maximilian and rather doubtingly at Mrs. Renfrew. When he spoke, however, his words were addressed to Alexandra.

"Good evening, Miss DiMarco. I wondered if you might—"

He got no further, for Sir Maximilian interrupted him in a reproving voice. "No, no, Brentwood, this is no time

to be giving poor Miss DiMarco any orders. She has agreed
to dance this next dance with me."

"Why, how is this?" said Richard, bending a look of surprise and indignation upon Alexandra. "I had thought—"
Collecting himself, he went on in a more formal voice. "I
am glad to hear you find yourself able to dance, ma'am.
Perhaps as that is the case, you will do me the honor of
dancing the second dance with me?"

"Can't be done, Brentwood," said Sir Maximilian exultantly. "Miss DiMarco is engaged to dance the second
dance with me, too."

"I see," said Richard in a tight voice. "Well, I trust you
will not overexert yourselves. Good evening to you both—
and to you, too, Mrs. Renfrew." Bowing, he took himself
off.

Alexandra, looking after him, felt a strong urge to burst
into tears. She also knew a strong urge to slap Sir Maximilian. It was obvious Richard was angry with her. She
supposed he must be angry because she had abdicated her
duty to Lady Margaret to dance with Sir Maximilian. It
could not be because he had wanted to dance the first two
dances with her himself and was peeved at being cut out
by the other gentleman. No, Alexandra assured herself; it
could not be for any such reason as that. Nevertheless it
had looked very much like it. And if such *had* been his
intention, then all had been ruined by Sir Maximilian's
ill-timed presumption.

This idea made Alexandra want to slap Sir Maximilian
more than ever. Sir Maximilian, unaware of her violent
thoughts toward him, smiled at her cheerfully. "Don't fret,
Miss DiMarco. I'll make it all right with Brentwood, you'll
see. He may be in a bit of a snit now because I'm taking
you away from your duties, but hang it, he can't expect a
girl as young and pretty as you to attend a ball and spend
all night sitting. I'll go and talk to him as soon as our
dances are over."

Alexandra declined this generous offer, however. "I thank you, Sir Maximilian, but that will not be necessary," she told him firmly. "I would prefer to explain the circumstances to Lord Brentwood myself."

It seemed, however, she would be denied the opportunity to do so. Richard made no effort to approach her again as the evening wore on. The fact that she was besieged by other potential partners throughout the evening was no consolation. Miserably, Alexandra reflected that her first ball was turning out to be less enjoyable than she had expected.

FOURTEEN

Alexandra was not wrong in supposing Richard was angry. He was angry through and through, with a fury that threatened at any moment to break into forceful self-expression.

As to the cause of his anger, however, Alexandra missed the mark entirely. It was not a cold emotion like annoyance or disapproval that had him seeing red. It was jealousy—a jealousy so potent that it was all he could do to keep from punching Sir Maximilian in the nose. By exercising the most stringent control on his temper, Richard refrained from this action, but he felt no better for his act of self-denial. Indeed, he felt a good deal worse. Punching Sir Maximilian would at least have allowed him to give vent to his feelings. The more civilized course he had chosen allowed no such relief. As Richard walked away from Alexandra, Sir Maximilian, and Mrs. Renfrew, he knew an urge to abandon both guests and party and seek consolation in copious draughts of strong drink.

If he had been capable of self-analysis at that moment, he would have seen that his anger was not directed at Alexandra herself. She had rejected him, true, and that was painful, but he was so diffident where Alexandra was concerned that this was an outcome he had half expected. It was Sir Maximilian Savage for whom he reserved the bulk of his wrath. What right had Max to go thrusting his handsome face between him, Richard Brentwood, and the woman he loved? And why should it be that ninety-nine women out of a hundred should prefer a popinjay like Sir Maximilian to a man of solid worth and genuine feeling?

The idea that Alexandra was no different from other women made Richard feel low indeed. He stalked up to Lady Rosalie and asked her to dance in a tone that would have offended any lady less secure in her self-consequence than that indolent beauty.

Although Lady Rosalie was not Richard's first choice of partners, she proved ideal as his second. She did not speak herself, nor did she seem to expect Richard to talk as they went through the movements of the dance. He was thus able to spend his entire time on the floor watching Alexandra dance with Sir Maximilian and brooding over her treacherous behavior.

It did seem to him that Alexandra was guilty of the utmost perfidy. She had pretended this afternoon that she wanted to dance with him. She had refused to engage herself ahead of time for any particular dance, saying he might have any he pleased when the time came. And then, when he made bold to ask her for one, she had informed him that she had already engaged herself to another man! Was this not perfidy of the most blatant kind?

Richard thought it was. At any rate, he made up his mind that he should not risk a second rejection by asking her to dance with him again. Having resolved on this course, he turned to Lady Rosalie and asked her brusquely to dance with him a second time. Lady Rosalie placidly assented, and they went out on the floor again.

The sight of Richard dancing with Lady Rosalie came as no surprise to Alexandra. She had made up her mind that, whatever Richard's motive in approaching her earlier, it could not have been to ask her to dance the first dance

with him. The most a humble governess like herself could
hope for was that he would invite her to stand up for one
of the later dances. But though she was resigned to playing
second, third, or even fourth fiddle that evening, she
found it still hurt to see him dancing with somebody else.
Especially when the somebody else was as beautiful and
seductive as Lady Rosalie. Alexandra found herself mentally consigning the handsome redhead to the same warm
place to which she had formerly consigned Sir Maximilian.

Anxiously she waited for Richard to approach her again.
She had not forgotten the matter of the Christmas present.
He might be irritated with her, but surely he did not mean
to deprive her of the gift which he had promised on those
grounds? But dance after dance went by, and still Richard
kept his distance.

It began to seem to Alexandra that he was purposely
avoiding her. Of course this must be fancy. She could
hardly be important enough in Richard's life to merit such
a snub. But it felt like a snub to Alexandra when she saw
him dancing with what seemed like every other lady in the
room and not asking her.

Although she might be neglected by Richard, she was
not similarly neglected by other men. She might have
danced every dance if she had chosen to. But in fact she
had no wish to dance if it could not be with Richard. She
excused herself to most of her would-be partners on the
grounds that she could not desert Lady Margaret. One or
two of the more intrepid of these cavaliers followed Sir
Maximilian's example and found some other obliging lady
to watch Lady Margaret so Alexandra might dance with
them. On those occasions she did take to the floor again,
but any pleasure she might have gotten out of the exercise
was negated by the sight of Richard devoting himself to
some other lady.

Meanwhile the hour was growing late. Lady Margaret
stoutly maintained that she was not tired, but Alexandra

could tell by her frequent yawns and lapses of attention
that sleep was gaining the upper hand. Soon she would
be ready to retire, and Alexandra would be obliged to retire with her. And that would be the end of the evening
for which she had held such high hopes.

As Alexandra was meditating on this depressing theme,
she was approached by a rotund gentleman in a florid
waistcoat, who asked her to dance with the air of one con-
ferring a great favor.

"I thank you, sir, but I am not dancing at present," she
told him. "I am Lady Margaret's governess, you see, and
it is necessary that I stay here and bear her company."

The gentleman made a conventional expression of regret, then stalked away with an offended look on his face.
Lady Margaret looked after him rather wistfully.

"You know you do not have to sit here with me all evening, Miss DiMarco," she told Alexandra. "I would not
mind it if you wanted to dance with that man."

"But I did not want to dance with that man, Lady Margaret," said Alexandra. "I would much rather sit here with
you."

Lady Margaret looked pleased but incredulous. "Would
you? I would think you would rather dance. It looks like
such fun." She drew a deep sigh. "I wish I were old enough
to dance!"

An elderly gentleman in an old-fashioned periwig was
passing close by their bench as Lady Margaret voiced this
wish. He paused, regarding her with a kindly smile.

"Well, and why should you not dance, my dear? I'll wager you could foot it as well as any lady in the room!"

Lady Margaret giggled and ducked her head in response
to this speech. The elderly gentleman gave Alexandra a
conspiratorial wink. "Ah, she's coquetting with me,
ma'am, you see! But 'pon my soul, I'm quite in earnest.
'Twould be an honor to partner such a pretty young lady

in the dance. Don't say you're already booked for the evening?"

Lady Margaret, giggling once more, shook her head. The gentleman extended his hand. "Well, then, come out and step with me!" he said encouragingly. "We'll show the rest of these idlers how to dance a country dance, if you please."

"May I, Miss DiMarco?" said Lady Margaret, looking at Alexandra.

"On my honor, I'll take care of her, ma'am," said the elderly gentleman, also looking at Alexandra earnestly. "You can trust me for that. Ask his lordship if you've any doubt. John Tallistand's the name—John Tallistand of Tallistand Farm. Lord Brentwood'll vouch that my character's perfectly respectable."

Alexandra was in a quandary. Although Richard had said his daughter might attend the ball that evening, he had said nothing about her dancing. She supposed she might ask him about it as Mr. Tallistand had suggested, but after the way he had been avoiding her, she was reluctant to approach him even over so small a matter as this. And indeed it seemed a very small matter. Mr. Tallistand looked a harmless sort, and Alexandra reasoned that no one was likely to object if Lady Margaret stood up with him for a figure or two of a country dance.

So she smiled and nodded at Mr. Tallistand. "Very well, sir," she told him. "Lady Margaret may dance this one dance with you, provided she behaves herself."

"Thank you, Miss DiMarco," exclaimed Lady Margaret, bouncing out of her seat. Mr. Tallistand gravely gave her his arm, and together they took their places on the floor much to the amusement to the other dancers.

Alexandra watched them, smiling a little at the mature way Lady Margaret returned her partner's bow in the opening figure. Then she was distracted by a touch on her arm. "I see your charge is presently disporting herself on the dance floor. You can thus have no excuse not to do the same with me."

Alexandra turned and saw Sir Maximilian regarding her with a confident smile. Her heart sank, but the next instant she recalled she had a made-to-order excuse. "Forgive me, Sir Maximilian, but you know I have already danced two dances with you," she said with feigned regret. "I am afraid it would look rather particular if I danced with you again."

Sir Maximilian protested this statement, but Alexandra protested as firmly that she could not think of dancing with him a third time. Finding her adamant on this point, Sir Maximilian cleverly switched his tack. "If you will not dance, then at least you can drink a glass of champagne with me," he said coaxingly. "Come, you cannot be so cruel as to deny me that, Miss DiMarco? All I ask is a few minutes of your company."

Alexandra was heartsick and weary, and at that moment she wished nothing so much as to put an end to Sir Maximilian's importuning once and for all. To accompany him to the refreshment room and drink a glass of champagne with him seemed the easiest way of getting rid of him. And she had an additional motive for wishing to leave the ballroom. Through a gap in the crowd she had just caught a glimpse of Richard and Miss McBride talking confidentially in a corner. The sight of them sitting with their heads together brought back the old, irrational jealousy that she had been fighting so hard against these last few weeks.

"Very well," she said wearily. "I will drink a glass of champagne with you, Sir Maximilian. But you really must promise to ask nothing more of me this evening. I am Lady Margaret's governess first and foremost, and I must devote most of my time to her."

"A woman of conscience," said Sir Maximilian, regarding her with a half smile. "I have always doubted that such a creature existed, but you prove me wrong, Miss DiMarco: you prove me wrong. Of course I will do as you wish, but

I must say that even if you do not resent your position of dependency, I do. It seems wrong that a woman like you must work for a living at a menial job like governessing."

"But it's not menial," protested Alexandra, as she accompanied Sir Maximilian along the corridor to the refreshment room. "Indeed, I enjoy teaching, Sir Maximilian. And I am genuinely fond of Lady Margaret. I have never been happier in my life than I have been during my time here at Brentwood."

Sir Maximilian halted abruptly, looking down at her. "Is that so?" he said. "But I would like to make you happier still, Miss DiMarco."

Before the startled Alexandra realized what he was about, Sir Maximilian had clasped her to his breast in an ardent embrace. A shower of kisses fell upon her cheek and neck, while a passionate litany was murmured in her ear. "I would like to take you away from your servitude and put you where you belong, Miss DiMarco—in a place where your beauty and talents are appreciated as they deserve. I would like to shower you with pretty things and indulge your every whim."

"Oh!" Alexandra cried, too taken aback by this treatment to make any concerted resistance. Sir Maximilian, supposing his advances were meeting with a favorable response, continued his impassioned litany.

"Miss DiMarco, you cannot know how I have longed to do this," he murmured in her ear. "From the moment I first saw you, I have been mad to possess you. Say you will come away with me—now, tonight, this very instant."

"Indeed I will not," said Alexandra indignantly, trying to free herself from Sir Maximilian's embrace. "Sir, you forget yourself!"

Sir Maximilian regarded her with a fondly indulgent smile. "Indeed, I did forget," he said. "You are a woman of conscience, aren't you? Of course you would insist on a marriage license first." He debated a moment, then nodded with sudden decision. "Well, and why not? Even though I have often sworn never to sacrifice myself on Hymen's altar, I am willing for your sake to recant my former creed. Everything shall be just as you wish, Miss Di-Marco. Gretna, or a special license, or even banns if you insist—it matters not to me, so long as you agree to be mine."

As he spoke, he bent to kiss Alexandra again. "No, no," she protested, trying once more to break free. Sir Maximilian was surprisingly strong for his size, however, as well as being very determined. It was not until an ironic voice spoke behind them that he released Alexandra.

"I hate to spoil sport, but I really must ask that you conduct your dalliances in some less public place, Max. At the moment you are obstructing my guests' way to the refreshment room."

Sir Maximilian, startled, released his hold on Alexandra and spun around. Alexandra also turned to look, and what she saw made her heart sink with dismay. Richard stood there in the corridor, regarding her and Sir Maximilian with a contemptuous smile. Beside him stood Miss McBride, a look of concern on her kindly face. Alexandra hardly noticed the Scottish woman's expression, however. It was the look on Richard's face that made her catch her breath. Although his lips were smiling, his eyes were ablaze with a fire that she had never seen there before.

It seemed an eon to Alexandra that she was transfixed by that burning gaze. But when Richard spoke again, his voice was as cool and ironic as before.

"You here, too, Miss DiMarco? I would not have supposed it. I hope Max has not been deceiving you with false promises. My sister tells me it was only a few weeks ago that he was paying tribute to Virginie at the opera."

"That's all over now," said Sir Maximilian. A faint flush stained his cheeks, but he spoke with simple dignity. "I don't deny I was once one of Virginie's admirers, but that all ended as soon as I met Miss DiMarco." He cast a look of admiration at Alexandra. "After knowing an angel like her, I could never look at a girl like Virginie—or at any other girl, for that matter. And all the use you have for her is as governess for your daughter!"

Richard started to speak, then stopped. He regarded Sir Maximilian a moment with an inscrutable expression. "We talk at cross-purposes, Max," he said. "Am I to understand your intentions toward Miss DiMarco are honorable?"

"Dash it, yes! As honorable as you please," said Sir Maximilian warmly. "I'll marry her this minute if you like."

At these words, Alexandra finally found her tongue. "Indeed, you will not!" she said with asperity. "You take a deal too much for granted, Sir Maximilian. I have no wish to marry you. And I would appreciate it if, in the future, you would refrain from—from mauling me about, as you have done this evening."

She looked angrily at Sir Maximilian. Richard and Miss McBride looked at him, too. "This is an unco' awkward situation, Max," said Miss McBride bluntly. "It appears to me that Miss DiMarco doesna welcome your advances. You'd better come away with me now, and let her bide a wee." She extended her arm to Sir Maximilian.

Sir Maximilian hesitated, looking at Alexandra. At last he took Miss McBride's arm. "I beg your pardon if I have discommoded you, Miss DiMarco," he said in a constrained voice. "Please believe I meant no insult. I have only the highest respect and admiration for your character, and it would make me the happiest man alive if I thought you might change your mind and—"

"I am sure Miss DiMarco will let you know if she changes her mind, Max," cut in Richard. His voice still held the note of scorn it held earlier. He gave Sir Maximilian a none-too-gentle push toward the door of the ballroom as he added, "Now, you go on back to the party with Hattie, and don't let me hear of your disturbing any of my staff again."

After Sir Maximilian and Miss McBride had gone off, Richard turned to Alexandra. He was trying to smile, but Alexandra thought his eyes were still angry. "This is quite a coup for you, Miss DiMarco," he said. "I know of no other lady who has managed to extract a marriage proposal from Max. You are to be congratulated."

Alexandra had suffered a great deal already that evening. This biting speech, coming from the man who had indirectly caused most of her suffering, was too much to be borne. She turned on Richard with flashing eyes.

"No, I am not to be congratulated!" she said hotly. "I didn't 'extract' a marriage proposal from Sir Maximilian, as you put it! I had no idea he intended to propose to me this evening. If I had, I would have done my best to discourage him. Indeed, my lord, I can do without your congratulations. Mine has been the victim's role this evening."

Her voice shook as she spoke, and she felt herself perilously close to tears.

Richard came closer, looking searchingly into her face. "Indeed," he said, "if that be so, then I apologize, Miss DiMarco. But when I saw Max kissing you, I thought—" He stopped abruptly.

"You thought what?" demanded Alexandra. "That I had been encouraging him? Oh, but that is unjust, my lord! Unjust, and infamous, and vile."

Richard shook his head. "Now *you* are being unjust, Miss DiMarco," he said. "My thought was of something quite different, I assure you."

"Then what was it?" said Alexandra, looking up at him. He returned her gaze steadily, with an expression which she could not understand.

"You truly want to know?" he said at last. "Well, why not? I thought— I thought that I would like to kiss you myself, Miss DiMarco."

"Oh," said Alexandra. She gazed at him blankly. Richard took a deliberate step toward her, laying his hands on her shoulders. A tremor went through her body, but she did not make any protest. She only went on gazing up at him with wide, dark-fringed eyes. Their beauty acted on Richard like a powerful intoxicant. Gathering her in his arms, he lowered his lips to hers.

A thousand thoughts went through Alexandra's head in that instant. She reflected that the whole situation, which had been like a nightmare a short while ago, now seemed like a dream—an impossibly lovely dream from which she feared she might awake at any moment. She was keenly aware of Richard's nearness to her: the strength of his arms, the pressure of his lips, the warmth of his body against hers. She reflected how heavenly it was to be kissed by Richard—and how completely different it was from being mauled by Sir Maximilian. And it was here that Alexandra's thoughts came back to earth with a jerk.

Sir Maximilian had been both rude and overbearing in his actions, but it had been obvious that his actions were prompted by a genuine passion. This was demonstrated both by his private avowal of devotion and by his public offer of marriage.

But Richard had claimed no such passion. He had said merely that he wanted to kiss her—and he had kissed her. And what did that signify? Nothing, except that he thought her depraved enough to welcome the embraces of two men in one evening.

The thought made Alexandra go suddenly rigid in Richard's arms. "No!" she cried, taking a step backward. "You must not, my lord. Indeed, you must not."

Richard felt as though his fondest hopes had been dashed to pieces. His decision to kiss Alexandra had been prompted partly by impulse, partly by frustrated passion, and partly by an obscure but overpowering conviction that the time had come for him to reveal his feelings for her.

Now it was all too evident that he had made a miscalculation.

"I'm sorry," he said uncertainly. Alexandra merely shook her head. She was visibly fighting back tears, and Richard felt a blackguard as he watched her struggle. He offered her his handkerchief, but she shook her head again and half turned away, her shoulders shaking with suppressed emotion.

Richard, standing there helpless watching her, was overwhelmed by another wave of anger. His anger was all for himself this time. In a moment he had ruined all the edifice of trust and respect he had been working so hard to build during the last two months. How could he have been so foolish as to succumb to a momentary urge? And at such a time, too—right after she had been assaulted by Sir Maximilian, and right after he had insulted her by implying the assault was her own fault. No wonder she wanted nothing to do with him!

"I'm sorry," he said again. "Forgive me, Miss DiMarco. I thought— But it doesn't matter what I thought. It shall not happen again, I promise you."

As he was speaking, a party of guests came down the corridor on their way to the refreshment room. They looked curiously at Richard and Alexandra as they passed. Alexandra said nothing until they were out of sight. When they had gone beyond sight and earshot, she addressed Richard in a voice that was cold as ice.

"I shall trust you to keep your promise, my lord. Indeed, I can remain at Brentwood under no other condition." Her voice wavered slightly as she added, "It is a fortunate thing that my stay here is nearly over. In the meantime, perhaps it would be better if we pretended this had never happened. I will endeavor to do so, at any rate." She glanced down the corridor, where another party of guests could be seen approaching. "For now, I think it would be better if we went back to the party, my lord. You need not trouble to escort me."

Turning on her heel, she walked swiftly back along the corridor, leaving Richard standing by himself.

FIFTEEN

The rest of that evening was a nightmare to Richard.

He had experienced unhappy moments in his life before, of course. Indeed, such moments had been frequent during his marriage to the late Countess of Brentwood. And even after that lady's death, he had continued to experience repercussions in the form of futile regrets, staggering debts, and a daughter whose temperament bade fair to take after her mother's.

But painful as all these things had been to him, they seemed nothing compared to the misery of the present moment. Richard felt as though he had never truly suffered until that evening. It was torment to have to smile and make conversation with his guests, all the while knowing that he had lost Alexandra: lost her forever through his own ill-judged conduct. It was that which was most painful to bear. His mood sank lower and lower as the evening wore on, until he was wallowing in a perfect morass of guilt, misery, and self-reproach.

Alexandra was luckier. When she returned to the ballroom, she found Lady Margaret just coming off the floor after her dance with Mr. Tallistand.

"Ah, here you are, ma'am," said that gentleman, saluting Alexandra with a beaming smile. "I've brought her ladyship back to you, safe and sound and none the worse for wear, as you can see. Nay, 'tis I who's showing the wear. Her ladyship came near to dancing my legs off!''

Lady Margaret laughed, highly pleased with this praise. Soon after Mr. Tallistand had gone off, however, she began to complain of being tired. "I think I wouldn't mind going upstairs now, even if it isn't quite midnight," she told Alexandra, with the air of one making a great concession. "All that dancing made me sleepy."

Alexandra seized on this statement gratefully and lost no time bundling her pupil and herself up to the nursery.

Having changed Lady Margaret into her nightgown, listened to her say her prayers, and tucked her into her bed, Alexandra was then able to give free vent to her grief and misery in a way denied to the unfortunate Richard.

Like Richard, a large part of Alexandra's misery was rooted in self-reproach. She felt her conduct must have been dreadfully wrong if it could have inspired her employer to behave as he had done toward her. On further reflection, she decided that it was not just her conduct but she herself who must have been wrong. Any decent woman would have shrunk from the embrace of a man whom she knew was merely trifling with her. Any decent woman would have done so—but she had not. Instead of shrinking from Richard's embrace, she had positively reveled in it until recalled at last by a belated sense of self-respect.

Alexandra could not deny it. Try as she might to be angry at Richard, she could manage nothing stronger than a halfhearted resentment—and this resentment was rooted more in the fact that his advances had been made without serious intent than in proper indignation over the advances themselves.

Alexandra felt her own lack of moral fiber very keenly. She, who had been bred up to practice discipline and self-control, had fallen to such depths as these! Whatever would her great-aunt and -uncle say? Alexandra made up her mind that they must never know the extent of her depravity. She would have to confess some part of her recent activities, of course, when she returned home to Mannington, but regarding the subject of Richard and her relations with him, it would be best to maintain a complete and irrevocable silence.

Indeed, it was time she was thinking of returning to Mannington. Alexandra reached this conclusion during the small hours of the night, lying sleepless in bed as she lived and relived that encounter in the corridor with Richard.

In the morning additional proofs were forthcoming. Alexandra received a letter from Miss Harcourt, postmarked a few days previously.

My dear Miss DiMarco,

I apologize for not writing during this last week or two, but you will understand this has been an anxious time for us here. Although Mother survived her operation, there was some question as to whether she might not succumb to infection following the surgery. We have all been waiting anxiously to see what the outcome would be.

Now, however, I am happy to report that she is definitely on the mend. The surgeon gives a good report of her condition and tells me he thinks it quite likely now that she will make a full recovery. That being the case, I see no reason why I should impose on your generosity and good nature any longer. I am fully conscious that I have done so much longer than is at all conscionable. But oh, what a boon your friendship has been to me! I am convinced Mother's recovery is due as much to your efforts as to the surgeon's.

I can take the stage and be at Wanworth as early as next Monday. I trust this will be acceptable to Lord Brentwood—and to you, too, for you have been so

kind that I would not put you out in any particular.
I am sure, however, that you must be eager to return
to your own home and family. Dear Miss DiMarco, I
am looking forward to tendering my thanks to you
in person, as well as to making the acquaintance of
my pupil, Lady Margaret, who is doubtless as grateful
as I for your unsparing efforts on her behalf.

> Yours with gratitude,
> Laetitia Harcourt

Alexandra read through this letter twice, then folded it
away and stared unseeing into space. At last her summons
had come—the summons she had been alternately dread-
ing and hoping for these last two months. Even now she
was not sure which emotion was uppermost. Eager as she
was to leave Brentwood—eager to quit the scene of her
disgrace and disillusionment and begin the process of for-
getting Richard and all he had meant to her—she still felt
a wistful, almost jealous sadness when she thought of going
away and leaving Miss Harcourt in her place.

Alexandra told herself that it was on Lady Margaret's
account that she felt so reluctant to leave. And indeed,
she did feel a very definite pang of jealousy at the thought
of abandoning that young lady to another's care. Those
words of Miss Harcourt's, "my pupil, Lady Margaret,"
struck her as being disagreeably proprietary. Of course it
had been a foregone conclusion that Miss Harcourt must
someday take her place at Brentwood. Equally, of course,
Alexandra had no wish to remain there as governess all
her life. This truth struck her suddenly as she sat reflecting
on the matter, looking out at Brentwood's snow-covered
gardens. Much as she loved Lady Margaret, much as she
had enjoyed her new freedom and the pleasure of order-
ing her life without interference from her relatives, she
had found herself in the end hardly less dissatisfied at
Brentwood than when she had been living at Mannington.

I suppose I was not meant to be happy, Alexandra told herself. *I must be like Aunt Emily—someone who is impossible to please.* Yet this explanation did not satisfy her. She *had* been happy at Brentwood—happy to be of use to others, and happy to be working out what she felt to be her own destiny. It was only when her happiness had begun to be bound up in Richard that the issue had become more complicated.

Never mind, Alexandra told herself firmly. *It's almost over now. When I am back home, I daresay I shall soon recover my peace of mind. It's only being here where I cannot avoid him that makes the situation so difficult. But I can certainly bear it until next Monday. New Year's Day, that would be, and it's less than a week away now. Yes, I can certainly bear it until then. I am thankful Miss Harcourt gives me this much warning. I'll put the time to good use and work on reconciling Lady Margaret to the idea of my leaving.*

The six days allotted proved none too short for this endeavor. Lady Margaret's first reaction, when she learned Alexandra was leaving, was flat denial. "No, no, no," she cried, covering her ears. "I won't listen—I won't, I won't. I won't listen, Miss DiMarco. You may as well stop talking about it, because I won't hear of your leaving."

Alexandra patiently explained that she had no choice in the matter: that she had only been allowed to come to Brentwood in the first place as a substitute for Miss Harcourt, and that it had been agreed from the beginning that her stay there would only be temporary. She described Miss Harcourt in glowing terms: her sweet appearance, quiet, ladylike manners, and brilliant academic accomplishments. When these descriptions failed to stir Lady Margaret to enthusiasm, she changed tactics and described how much Miss Harcourt needed her position. As Alexandra had expected, Lady Margaret could not help betraying sympathy when she heard about Miss Harcourt's recent difficulties, but her sympathy did not take exactly the form Alexandra had hoped for.

"If she really needs a job so badly, then I suppose I do not mind her teaching me. But I do not see why you must go away, Miss DiMarco, just because she is coming to Brentwood. After all, you told me once you had lots of different teachers when you were growing up. Why can I not have two governesses? I don't think Papa would mind. He is rich enough to afford it, I'm sure, and I know he likes you very much. I'll go ask him this minute."

"No!" said Alexandra, so sharply that Lady Margaret looked at her in bewilderment. "I don't think that would be a good idea, Lady Margaret," said Alexandra, moderating her voice but speaking no less decisively than before. "Your papa has concerns enough without disturbing him over this business. I *must* leave Brentwood this Monday. It is already arranged that I should leave when Miss Harcourt arrives. And though I shall miss you and Brentwood very much, I have no doubt that you will get on very well with Miss Harcourt."

Lady Margaret's response to this speech was to burst into tears. Alexandra's heart contracted painfully at the sight of the small sobbing figure. Stooping, she put her arms around Lady Margaret. "Don't cry, my dear—oh, don't cry," she begged. "If you cry, I shall cry, too, and that will never do."

Even as she spoke, however, Alexandra felt her eyes filling with tears. Lady Margaret stopped crying and looked with some curiosity at her face.

"You *are* crying," she said. "Why are you crying, Miss DiMarco? Don't you want to go?"

"No," admitted Alexandra, sniffling dolefully and fumbling about her person in futile search of her handkerchief. "No, I don't want to go. But I must go, and so there's

o use talking about it. Oh dear, what a wet-goose I am. I
an't think what I have done with my handkerchief."

Lady Margaret fetched her a fresh handkerchief from
er room. As she watched Alexandra blow her nose and
ipe her eyes, her small face wore a thoughtful expression.
I suppose it is like when I did not want to do my geog-
aphy lesson," she suggested. "And you said I ought to
ecause it was the right thing to do. It's a case of self-dis-
ipline, like you are always talking about."

"Yes, exactly that," agreed Alexandra, energetically
lowing her nose. Lady Margaret pondered this idea a mo-
nent longer.

"Well, then, if you really don't want to go, then I don't
nind so much that you have to," she told Alexandra with
catch in her voice. "I still don't like it, mind you. But at
east I know you're not leaving because you think I'm a
uisance and—and because you just don't want to bother
vith me anymore."

"Oh, my dear!" said Alexandra, enfolding her pupil in
er arms once more. Lady Margaret returned her embrace
iercely, tears streaming down her face.

"Will you come visit me, Miss DiMarco?" she demanded
n a whisper. "If I thought you would come and see me
iow and then, I wouldn't feel so sad about your going
way."

"Oh, Lady Margaret, I wish that were possible," said
Alexandra sadly. "But after I leave here, I doubt I shall be
ble to visit you again. At the very least it would not be
intil you are a great deal older than you are now."

Lady Margaret was still a moment. "If you cannot visit
ne, could you at least write to me?" she said in a woeful
oice. "If you wrote to me, it would be something—not so
ood as having you here, but not so bad as nothing at all."

"Yes, of course I will write you," said Alexandra warmly.
I will write you nice long letters, telling you everything I
m doing back at Mannington. And you can write me in

return and tell me about things at Brentwood and how
your studies are going."

Lady Margaret's face had brightened a little at this
speech. "That sounds nice," she said. "Will you write me
often, Miss DiMarco? Every day?"

"Every day," promised Alexandra recklessly.

This pledge seemed to cheer Lady Margaret. If she did
not straightway become her former happy self, she did at
least consent to study her lessons that afternoon, and by
evening she was in something resembling her usual spirit.
Alexandra had hopes that by the time Miss Harcourt arrived, she would have resigned herself to the change that
was so soon to take place.

The days that followed seemed odd, indeterminate days
to Alexandra. The house continued in its Christmas trap-
pings, but something of the holiday spirit seemed lost or
at least suspended. The Christmas tree had been brought
back up to the nursery, where it stood as a silent reminder
to Alexandra of her tarnished hopes and dreams.

She could not help wondering now and then about the
present Richard was to have given her Christmas Day. Had
there ever been a present, or had he been speaking meta-
phorically of the kiss he had bestowed upon her that evening? Alexandra could not satisfy herself as to whether
that kiss had been a spur-of-the-moment inspiration or part
of a long-thought-out plot of seduction. She had certainly
read of such plots—*Pamela* once more came to mind, as
did its sister work *Clarissa*—but Alexandra could not somehow see Richard in Lovelace's role. It seemed more likely
that he had simply succumbed to the temptation of the
moment. And that was a weakness Alexandra could hardly
hold against him, seeing that she had been similarly weak.

Indeed, she found herself unable to resent Richard's
behavior as she knew she ought. She could force herself

o avoid his company; she could force herself to greet him
:oolly on the few occasions when she could not avoid meet-
ng him; she could force herself to keep her words to him
orief and formal. But she could not force herself to despise
him, or to feel other than desolate at the idea of never
eeing him again. It was a shameful admission, but there
t was.

*My only comfort is that he will never know how much I care
or him*, Alexandra told herself. *At least I am spared the hu-
miliation of being seen to love a man who doesn't love me.* She
miled wryly when she recalled Lady Margaret's innocent
emark: "I know Papa likes you very much." That might
oe true, but liking was not loving, and neither was simple
ust. She herself knew better than to believe Richard had
erious or lasting feelings for her, but Lady Margaret's in-
istence to the contrary was—she could not deny it—very
gratifying.

Likewise very gratifying, albeit in a rather painful way,
were Lady Margaret's continued lamentations about her
ast-approaching departure. She presented Alexandra with
everal dilapidated but treasured possessions by way of
oarting gifts, clung close to her day and night, and spoke
:onfidently of the future happy time when Alexandra
would come back and visit her.

Alexandra could not think it right to encourage these
nopes, but at the same time she hesitated to destroy what
eemed to be Lady Margaret's chief source of comfort at
he moment. She consoled herself with the reflection that
Lady Margaret was a child, and children were notably re-
ilient in their feelings. By the time she had been gone
rom Brentwood a month or two, she trusted that Lady
Margaret would have forgotten her and become attached
o her new governess.

For herself, she had no such optimistic hopes. She was
not a child like Lady Margaret, but rather a young lady of
one and twenty, and young ladies of one and twenty clearly

lacked the resilient feelings of children. Alexandra could only trust that peace and resignation would come to her at some future time, for both commodities seemed to be denied her at present. She lived the days between Christmas and New Year's in a state of turbulent emotion and looked forward to the date of Miss Harcourt's arrival with all the zeal of a prisoner anticipating her day of execution.

SIXTEEN

Like Alexandra, Richard was prey to some uncomfortable reflections during the days between Christmas and New Year's.

Like her, he had passed a restless night in the aftermath of the Christmas Ball. But he had arisen the next morning feeling, if not much more rested, at least insensibly more hopeful than when he had gone to bed the night before. He had made a misstep, to be sure, but missteps were not necessarily fatal or irreversible. Alexandra might be offended with him now, but given enough time it was possible that he might regain her trust. He might even inspire her to return his feelings if he were careful and did not attempt to go too fast. It was a well-known proverb that good things came to those who were willing to wait for them.

Richard recited this proverb to himself numerous times during the course of that day. It was Boxing Day, the day after Christmas and the day on which gifts were traditionally presented to tenants and tradespeople. Richard forced himself to go about this business as he had in former years, though he would rather have postponed it and sought out Alexandra first thing. But he told himself that he must not alarm her by approaching her suddenly, at a time when she was not expecting him. Now more than ever, it was crucial that he show her he was a dependable, sober, well-conducted person.

The proper time to approach her, in Richard's estimation, was the hour after dinner, the time of his usual evening visit to the nursery. Alexandra would be expecting him then, and he would have to make no explanation for his presence. Of course Lady Margaret would be on hand and would be expecting a share of his attention, but doubtless there would be some private moment when he could take Alexandra aside and make her a formal apology for his behavior the evening before. And if she were receptive, he might even reveal to her the feelings that had prompted his behavior.

In truth, Richard felt he might be rushing things a little if he attempted this last. Yet he was eager to declare himself and get his feelings out in the open. After all, there was nothing dishonorable about loving a woman and wanting to marry her, even if one were a widower with a less-than-successful matrimonial record behind one. And surely no young woman could be really offended to know she had inspired a man with an undying passion!

So Richard told himself, and he looked forward to that evening even more eagerly than he had looked forward to the ball the evening before. This was the more so because he had not managed to catch a single glimpse of Alexandra throughout that day. She and Lady Margaret had absented themselves from the dinner table, and though it was not uncommon for her to take meals in the nursery most days, Richard felt for her to do so now was probably due to him and his behavior the evening before.

Never mind, he told himself. *I will explain it all tonight. Tonight I will lay my cards on the table, and see what response I get.*

He could not go upstairs immediately after dinner, for courtesy obliged him to spend time in the drawing room drinking port with his male guests. But as soon as the greater part of the gentlemen had drifted into the drawing room, he excused himself to the remainder and mounted the stairs to the nursery. He was nervous as he approached the door, but he forgot his nervousness a moment later, as the sound of voices came drifting out to him in the hall. One of the voices was Alexandra's, but the other was male, and it sounded remarkably like Sir Maximilian Savage's.

Richard's brows drew together. Not bothering to knock, he pushed open the door of the nursery.

The visitor was indeed Sir Maximilian, as Richard ascertained at a glance. And it was a Sir Maximilian in an unwonted mood of humility, if one were to judge from his posture. He knelt before Alexandra in the classic pose of remorse and adoration, clasping her hand in his and gazing up at her imploringly. Alexandra, looking flushed and embarrassed, was seeking to disengage her hand, even as Sir Maximilian sought to draw it to his heart. Lady Margaret was perched nearby on a low table, surveying the tableau with an interested but critical gaze.

"You must forgive me," Sir Maximilian was saying, as Richard came into the room. "I forgot myself last night. I have cursed myself a thousand times since for my bestial behavior. Only say you forgive me, Miss DiMarco. Just one word of forgiveness: that is all I ask. If you deny me that, I shall have no choice but to fling myself off the battlements."

"Don't be foolish, Sir Maximilian," said Alexandra in a voice of exasperation. "Of course I will forgive you, but only if you promise to go away this minute. I really cannot have you causing scenes in the nursery in this ridiculous manner."

"Yes, Max, you a have a curious taste in venues for your lovemaking," said Richard. Both Sir Maximilian and Alexandra jumped at the sound of his voice. Lady Margaret leaped off the table and came running to him, a beaming smile on her face.

"Oh, Papa, we have been having such fun!" she said. "That man over there has been asking Miss DiMarco to marry him. Only she says she doesn't want to marry him, and so he says he will jump off the battlements!" There was laughter in her voice, but an instant later her expression became worried. "He won't really jump off the battlements, will he?" she said, looking at Richard appealingly. "Not really?"

"No, not really. But if he keeps harassing young ladies, someone may well push him out a window," said Richard, looking significantly at Sir Maximilian. That gentleman, taking the hint, rose to his feet and addressed Alexandra with an air of much-tried dignity.

"It seems I must go, Miss DiMarco. I hope you will accept my apologies for last night—and for this evening also, if I have disturbed you. Good evening to you, and I hope you will think well about the proposal I have made you before you decline it absolutely." He bowed formally and left the room, shooting Richard a resentful look as he passed out the door.

When he was gone, Alexandra sighed wearily. Lady Margaret went skipping over to join her. "That man is silly, isn't he?" she said brightly. "Nobody would jump off the battlements only because somebody wouldn't marry them, would they?"

Alexandra merely shook her head. Her eyes flickered to Richard. Richard felt he ought to say something, but for the life of him, he could not think what. The situation was an impossible one. Coming after Sir Maximilian's grandiose pleas for mercy, his own straightforward apology could only look flat or foolish. It was still more impossible to declare his feelings, now that Sir Maximilian had muddied the waters.

Just as Richard was wondering whether he ought to leave without saying a word, the situation was unexpectedly eased by Lady Margaret. She had been dancing about, giggling over Sir Maximilian's foolishness; now, in an abrupt change of mood, her face crumpled. "Miss DiMarco is going away," she told Richard in a voice like a wail. "She says she must go on New Year's Day. And she says I shall like Miss Harcourt as much as I like her—but I know I won't. I wish she didn't have to go."

"You are leaving?" said Richard in a voice of shock. His eyes sought Alexandra's, but she turned away, pretending to be adjusting the screen around the nursery fire.

"Yes, Miss Harcourt writes that her mother is nearly recovered now. She can be here on New Year's Day if that is satisfactory to you, my lord. Someone would have to drive to Wanworth to meet her, of course, but if I was leaving at the same time, the carriage would only have to make one trip."

There was a long silence. "I see," said Richard at last. "Yes, I suppose that would be the most sensible plan. You may write Miss Harcourt and tell her that that arrangement will be quite satisfactory."

He spoke calmly, but inwardly he was feeling anything but calm. This, then, was the end of his hopes! He would have no time or opportunity now to rebuild Alexandra's good opinion of him. She would be leaving in only a matter of days, and he felt in his bones that there would be no further chances to declare himself. The cool way she had spoken about leaving just now told him clearly enough that she would be glad to escape.

For a moment hot rebellion swept over Richard. He knew an urge to seize Alexandra in his arms, crush her close, and tell her forcefully that she could not, must not go. He stared at Alexandra. She continued to avoid his gaze, however, and gradually his rebellion drained away, leaving him in the grip of a cold fatalism.

It would be madness to kiss Alexandra now, of course. She had been angry enough at his kissing her on Christmas Night. If he attempted any such high-handed maneuver as he had been contemplating, it would only make her angrier than she already was. It might even provoke her to leave immediately rather than waiting till New Year's Day.

In the silence that hung between them, Alexandra spoke. "Was there anything else, my lord? Anything that you wished to talk to me about?"

"No, nothing," said Richard, and left the nursery without another word.

He felt as though with this scene, the seal had been set on his disappointment. There was nothing for him to do now but try to forget Alexandra and his shattered hopes. Accordingly, Richard set himself to forget. He was fortunate in having picked a time so conducive to that exercise.

The days between Christmas and New Year's were a time of gaiety and dissipation in the neighborhood of Brentwood, and there were parties of one sort or another every evening—sometimes several parties in an evening. Richard, together with his houseguests, made a point of attending as many of these as possible. Neighbors who had not seen him in years marveled at his sudden, reckless appetite for society. Others shook their heads and said he had grown profligate since his wife's death.

Miss McBride put it more succinctly. "Daftness, pure and simple. Not that there's anything amiss with that, my lord, assuming it's a purely seasonal phenomenon," she told Richard kindly. "In Scotland, you ken, they call all the days between Christmas and New Year's 'the daft days.' When I was living at home, we all used to amuse ourselves verra much with pranks and mischief-making during that time. You must have a drop of Scots blood in you, my lord, to make you kick up your heels in sich a fashion at this particular time of year."

Richard laughed recklessly. "Possibly," he said.

Miss Spence, who was standing nearby, smiled in a condescending way. "I'm sure Lord Brentwood is an Englishman through and through," she told Miss McBride. "He would never do anything as childish as playing pranks." She smiled sweetly at Richard, who straightway resolved to prove her wrong before the day was out. He did it, too, by serving her a wineglass full of vinegar at dinner that evening, igniting a wave of pranks and practical jokes that swept like wildfire among the houseguests. Apple-pie beds abounded; sugar found its way into salt-cellars; and Lady Rosalie complained that her dressing maid had given notice because she had received a deluge of cold water from a bucket suspended over her mistress's door.

"I would not mind if it had been me who got wet," said Lady Rosalie, looking appealingly pretty and self-deprecating as she spoke. "After all, it was only water in the bucket—although rather cold water, from what I have been given to understand. But Louise takes it as a personal insult, even though I have explained that the trick was undoubtedly meant for me. I cannot think who could have done such a thing." Her eyes wandered innocently to a pair of ladies who had been heard occasionally to murmur about the airs Lady Rosalie chose to give herself.

The two ladies in question looked uncomfortable, and Richard said diplomatically that he would speak to the injured maidservant. A generous tip was effective in soothing Louise's offended feelings, and after this the pranks tended to take a less serious turn. But they continued more or less unabated right up until New Year's Eve.

Richard tried hard to be as hilarious as everyone else, but he was aware all the while that his hilarity did not ring true. He did not feel hilarious, but rather deeply depressed. It was only a mixture of pride and determination that kept him pretending otherwise. As soon as Alexandra was gone, he feared his pretense would come crashing down in the most disastrous way.

To the others, however, he appeared the most jovial and lighthearted of hosts. He appeared that way to Alexandra, too, and she wondered at it. It was not that she expected him to mourn her departure. He had shown clearly enough that her leaving was a matter of indifference to him, but this mood of reckless gaiety seemed out of character. She reminded herself that she had never thought him a libertine, either; yet he had felt free to kiss her Christmas evening merely because he had seen another man do so. There were clearly unsuspected depths to his character. Alexandra told herself that it was a fortunate thing she was leaving now, before she discovered them all and perhaps glimpsed something even more shocking to her feelings.

She took no part in the orgy of practical-joking that was going on among the houseguests. She might well have done so, for after that first evening—the evening of Boxing Day, when Richard had come to her in the nursery—she had been forced to dine downstairs. Her personal preference would have been to take dinner in the nursery, but Lady Margaret had known her rights and been vocal about demanding them.

"Papa said I might eat with the guests, Miss DiMarco. You know he did say that I might, as long as it is Christmastime, and Christmastime won't be over till Twelfth Night. I didn't mind eating upstairs last night because I was rather tired, and it was fun for a change. But tonight I want to eat downstairs with the grown-ups. Can Méchante and I wear our pink dresses again?"

Alexandra had vetoed the pink dresses, but she had been unable to veto dining downstairs. Lady Margaret had accordingly dined with the company every night thereafter, and the jokes and pranks of the other guests had made a deep impression on her.

"What's an apple-pie bed, Miss DiMarco?" she demanded one evening. "That man with the whiskers said someone had made him an apple-pie bed last night. Did someone really put an apple pie in his bed?"

Alexandra explained that no apple pies were involved in making an apple-pie bed. "It is merely a way of arranging the bedclothes so as to prevent anyone from getting between the sheets," she told Lady Margaret. "It is a prank—a kind of joke or trick. Someone was playing a trick on that man."

"Like when that lady got a raw fish instead of a cooked one at dinner," said Lady Margaret, laughing in reminiscent delight. "I thought that was very funny. Can we play a trick like that on someone, Miss DiMarco? I like to play tricks, too. I once put some caterpillars in mam'selle's washing-jug, back when she was my governess instead of you. She screamed and screamed!"

"Presumably she did not enjoy finding caterpillars in her washing-jug," suggested Alexandra.

Lady Margaret's face grew pensive. "No, I don't think she did. She was very afraid of caterpillars. She left right after I did it, even though Papa made me apologize to her." Lady Margaret pondered a moment, then looked at Alexandra apologetically. "I suppose I ought not to have played a trick like that on mam'selle. But I was younger then and didn't know any better. I won't ever put caterpillars in anybody's washing-jug again. But I don't see why I couldn't play a different kind of trick. An apple-pie bed wouldn't frighten anybody, and it sounds very funny."

Alexandra smiled a little at her pupil's pleading expression. "Who did you want to make an apple-pie bed for?" she said. "Me?"

"Oh no, not you. I would never play a trick on *you*, Miss DiMarco." Lady Margaret lowered her voice to a conspiratorial whisper. "I thought we might make one for Papa. He doesn't smile so much nowadays when he comes to the nursery. If we played a trick on him—a little trick like

an apple-pie bed, not a bad one—it might make him laugh
and joke like he did before.''

"Your father's bed?'' said Alexandra, drawing back in
horror. "Oh, I don't think that would be a good idea, Lady
Margaret!''

"Papa won't mind,'' said Lady Margaret confidently.
"He has a very good sense of humor. He even laughed
about the caterpillars, but he still said I had to apologize
to mam'selle.'' Taking Alexandra's hand, she tried to pull
her toward the door. "Come, let's go and do it, Miss Di-
Marco. Let's make Papa an apple-pie bed!''

Alexandra stood firm, however, and refused to accompany her pupil on this errand. "No, I really couldn't, Lady
Margaret,'' she said. "Your father is my employer and I—
Well, I wouldn't be comfortable touching his things.'' The
very idea of setting foot in Richard's room, let alone tam-
pering with his bed, made Alexandra blush rosy pink.

"But you won't have to touch anything,'' argued Lady
Margaret. "I'll do it all, every bit of it. I only need you to
tell me what to do.''

Despite Alexandra's continued refusals, Lady Margaret
went on begging and pleading for her assistance in making
her father an apple-pie bed. Alexandra sought to remain
firm, but looking down at her pupil's wistful face, she
found a certain ambivalence creeping into her refusals.

The prank was certainly a harmless one, and her role
in it could probably be executed without inconvenience
or embarrassment to herself. In a way, she felt she owed
it to Lady Margaret to support her effort to lighten her
father's mood. Hilarious as Richard might be among his
guests, it was a fact that he had smiled and spoken very
little during his last few visits to the nursery. Nor had his
visits to that region been as frequent and long-lasting as
had been the case before what Alexandra mentally termed
"the evening of disaster.''

Lady Margaret could not know that this was her govern-

ess's fault and not her own. But she, Alexandra, knew, and
she felt it incumbent on her now to make it up to Lady
Margaret as best she could. After all, she reasoned, there
could be no impropriety in her entering Richard's room
as long as his daughter accompanied her.

"Very well," said Alexandra aloud. "I will go with you,
Lady Margaret, but you must make up the bed all by yourself. And mind you tell your father it was all your idea
when he taxes you with it."

Lady Margaret laughed delightedly. "I will," she promised. "I will tell him it was all my own idea. Come on, let's
go this very minute, Miss DiMarco. Papa is out hunting
this afternoon, so he shouldn't be back for hours and
hours yet."

Reassured by this intelligence, Alexandra consented to
accompany her pupil down the stairs to Richard's rooms.
She waited nervously outside in the hall as Lady Margaret
slipped inside to make sure the coast was clear. "It's all
right," she hissed, reappearing in the doorway. "Nobody's
here, and the maids have already made up the bed for the
night. All we need to do is remake it—you know!" She
laughed.

Reluctantly, yet with a certain curiosity, Alexandra
stepped inside the room, closing the door carefully behind
her.

The apartment in which she was standing appeared to
be Richard's study, with his bedchamber and dressing
room beyond it. The furnishings of all three rooms were
neither new nor fashionable, but they radiated an aura of
solid comfort and masculine dignity that Alexandra
thought consonant with their owner's personality. Looking
about her at the deep-green hangings at bed and windows
and the heraldic carvings on the heavy oak furniture, she
could imagine, all too well, Richard going about his intimate daily activities—activities such as sleeping and bath-
ing and dressing, for instance. Overcome by the images

such ideas suggested, Alexandra blushed and went hastily
into the bedroom, where Lady Margaret was already busy
at Richard's bedside.

It soon became clear to Alexandra that she would have
to relinquish her "advisor-only" status. Lady Margaret
tucked and tugged and folded with all her might, but her
six-year-old hands could not manage to make up the bed
in anything resembling a proper order. Alexandra, keeping a nervous eye on her watch, saw she would have to
take a hand in things if they were not to be there until
dinnertime. Already it was less than an hour till the dress-
ing-bell was due to ring, and the hunting party might be
expected back at any time. Accordingly, Alexandra took
hold of the counterpane and began to fold it back, pre-
paratory to straightening the sheets. At that moment, the
door to the bedchamber swung open and Richard stepped
into the room.

"It's Papa," shrieked Lady Margaret. "It's Papa, Miss
DiMarco! Run!" Suiting action to words, she took to her
heels, basely abandoning her coconspirator, who was left
alone to face the wrath of her victim.

At the moment, he looked more confused than wrathful.
"Miss DiMarco?" he said in a stunned voice. "What on
earth are you doing here?" Looking about him in a blank
manner, he added, "Was that my daughter's voice I
heard?"

Alexandra nodded. At the moment, words were quite
beyond her. Richard continued to survey her with puzzlement. "Why did Margaret run away?" he said. "And what
was she doing in my room in the first place? And what are
you doing?" he added, observing for the first time the
counterpane still grasped in Alexandra's hands.

Alexandra lifted her chin. "I am making you an apple-
pie bed, my lord," she said.

A brief silence followed this announcement. Richard
continued to gaze at Alexandra wordlessly. Alexandra

spoke again in a defensive voice. "It was Lady Margaret's idea, my lord. I was only here as her aide-de-camp. But you see she has run off and left me to face the full punishment for her misdeed."

Laughter sprung into Richard's eyes. "Is that so?" he said. "I had thought rather you were here as an answer to my prayers, Miss DiMarco."

Another silence followed these words, but it was a different silence than before. To Alexandra, it was a silence pregnant with meaning. She began to edge toward the door. "I must apologize to you for my part in this business, my lord," she said, speaking rapidly and rather breathlessly. "I ought not to have allowed your daughter to play you such a trick, I know, but I could not resist her pleading. You may be sure it shall not happen again while I— Oh!"

She finished the speech on a breathless gasp, as Richard swiftly moved to cut off her escape. "My lord, you must not," she squeaked, as he caught her in his arms. Richard's response was to lower his lips to hers and kiss her.

It was almost the same maneuver Sir Maximilian had practiced on her a few days before, yet what a difference! Alexandra was appalled to find herself responding with enthusiasm to Richard's embrace. Her arms seemed to twine themselves around his neck of their own accord, and her lips returned his kiss as naturally as breathing. She made a halfhearted effort to break free from Richard's grasp. "Indeed, my lord, you must not," she said again, weakly.

"Why not?" he said, as he bent to kiss her again. "Why must I not, Miss DiMarco?"

Alexandra tried to think why he must not and found her reason curiously clouded. "Because it is wrong," was all she could think to say. It struck her as a lame excuse, and it seemed to strike Richard the same way. He paused, frowning down at her.

"Why is it wrong?" he demanded. "Why should I not

kiss you? You must know by now that I love you, Miss Di-Marco. Indeed, I love you with all my heart and soul."

Alexandra gazed at him openmouthed. He went on, his voice growing more impassioned with every word. "I didn't mean to tell you this way. I meant to wait and win your trust. But now you are going away, and it doesn't matter anymore. What have I to lose by kissing you?" He gazed defiantly down at Alexandra. "I love you, damn it!"

Alexandra felt the world spinning wildly out of orbit. Regardless of sanity and prudence and decorum, conscious only of the amazing coincidence of feeling Richard had just revealed to her, she opened her mouth and spoke. "Oh, my lord," she gasped. "I love you, too!"

The effect of these words on Richard was quite magical. His eyes seemed to kindle, and a look of incredulous joy replaced the defiant expression he had worn a moment before. He did not speak, but lowered his lips to Alexandra's once more in a purposeful manner. She submitted without a murmur to his embrace, but a moment later sanity reasserted itself.

"No, my lord! Indeed, you must not. I ought not to have spoken as I did."

"Why not?" said Richard, pausing in his assault upon her lips. Alexandra found this question as hard to answer as his last. She could not say, *Because you intend to seduce me, and I cannot resist you if you do.* Fortunately, however, Richard went on without waiting for an answer.

"I am glad beyond measure that you did speak as you did. It gives me the courage to go ahead and give you—the present I meant to give you Christmas Day."

He released Alexandra as he spoke and went into his study. She stood, waiting and watching with breathless interest as he rummaged about in one of his desk drawers. A moment later he returned, carrying something in his hand. Silently he handed it to Alexandra, who gazed blankly at the object now resting in her own hand. It was a magnificent sapphire-and-diamond ring.

"Why . . . why are you giving me this?" she faltered.

A faint smile touched Richard's lips. "It is customary to give one's betrothed wife some sort of a ring as a token," he said. "I know diamonds by themselves are a more traditional choice, but somehow this looked more like you. Your eyes, you know. You've got the bluest eyes I've ever seen. Bluer than sapphires and twice as beautiful."

Alexandra was silent, looking down at the ring in her hand. Richard cleared his throat, a trifle nervously. "And now, tradition demands that I make a fool of myself and emulate our old friend Sir Maximilian." Going down upon one knee, he took Alexandra's hand in his. "Miss DiMarco, will you do me the honor of becoming my wife?" he said, looking steadily into her eyes.

SEVENTEEN

Alexandra gazed at Richard openmouthed. Never had she expected him to propose to her. Never had she expected him to declare he loved her with all his heart and soul! It was like seeing her most extravagant fantasies suddenly made real, or like seeing the gates of heaven open and the wonders of paradise revealed to her dazzled eyes.

For a moment a flood of happiness threatened to overwhelm her. Now she might accept Richard's proposal, marry him, and live happily ever after like a storybook heroine. Now she might remain with Lady Margaret forever, and never be forced to give her over to the care of another woman.

It was only for a moment that Alexandra indulged in these roseate fantasies. Almost at once, reality raised its ugly head. Richard might love her, and he had certainly proposed to her, but he did not know who it was he was really proposing to. She was not plain Miss DiMarco, a young woman capable of both earning her own living and determining her own destiny. She was Alexandra Elizabeth Manning DiMarco, and her destiny had been determined from the moment of her birth. Richard could not know, in asking her to marry him, what he was getting himself into. And Alexandra felt herself incapable of telling him. How could she blithely inform him that she had been deceiving him all along—that she was not really a governess, but rather a young woman with a crushing weight of family obligations and expectations upon her?

"Oh, my lord, you do me the greatest honor," she said, in a voice which held a hint of tears. "I would give anything if I might become your wife. But I cannot, my lord. You must believe me when I say it is impossible."

In novels, gentlemen whose proposals were rebuffed in this manner accepted their rebuffs quietly and went away without asking any further questions. Richard did neither. "Why is it impossible?" he demanded, looking at her keenly. "You know I love you, and you say you love me. If you were telling the truth just now—"

"I *was* telling the truth!" said Alexandra indignantly. "But the fact remains that I cannot marry you, my lord. There are reasons—private reasons—why it is impossible."

Richard continued to regard her keenly. "It's not Margaret, is it?" he said. "I realize it is asking a great deal to expect a young woman like you to take on the upbringing of another woman's child. But I had hoped you had become fond of Margaret over these last few months. She has certainly become fond of you."

Alexandra, even more indignantly than before, refuted the suggestion that she was not fond of Lady Margaret. "I love her as much as if she had been my own child," she said, her voice breaking slightly. "And let me tell you, my lord, that I regret refusing your proposal almost as much on her account as on yours. But the fact remains that I must refuse it—not because I do not love you and Lady Margaret, but because I love you both too much to cause you embarrassment or unhappiness. There are circumstances connected with my family and background that would do both, I fear."

"So that's the trouble," said Richard, his brow clearing. "You need not worry your head over any of that, Miss DiMarco." He paused a moment, then went on, choosing his words with care. "I know, of course, that up till now you have deliberately refrained from telling me much about your family and background. No doubt you have perfectly good reasons for doing so—or what you imagine to be perfectly good reasons. But I can assure you, Miss DiMarco, that whatever your family and background may prove to be, I am still willing to marry you."

"You cannot know that," said Alexandra, looking at him doubtfully.

A smile curved Richard's lips. "But I do, Miss DiMarco. In my own mind, you see, I am convinced I already know everything of importance about you. Remember that I have lived on close terms with you for more than two months. I have seen you in conditions of stress, faced by situations that would perplex the strongest and wisest of men." He looked into Alexandra's eyes. "And never have I seen you behave other than I would wish my wife to behave. I know you for a beautiful, intelligent, accomplished woman, with principles such as must command the highest admiration. That is what you are—what you yourself are, Miss DiMarco. As far as I am concerned, your family and background are immaterial."

A sigh escaped Alexandra. "I doubt you would say that if you knew more about them," she said ruefully.

"Then try me," urged Richard. He looked anxious but resolute as he got to his feet, taking Alexandra's hand in his. "At least let me have the option of deciding for myself, Miss DiMarco. What is there about your family and background that you are convinced is so damning?"

Alexandra opened her mouth to speak. At that moment, a low tapping sounded on Richard's study door. Before either she or Richard could gather their wits, Lady Eleanor thrust her head around the door. "Richard, are you busy?" she called. "I wondered if you—"

At that moment she caught sight of Richard and Alexandra standing together in the bedchamber beyond. She checked herself, looking almost comically dismayed. "I beg your pardon," she said. "I did not mean to interrupt, Richard. Indeed, I can come back another time, if you are busy."

It was a situation worthy of a farce, although it did not strike Alexandra as particularly funny. She felt convinced that Lady Eleanor was thinking the worst of her. This conviction impelled her to speak aloud in a calm, clear voice. "No, don't go, Lady Eleanor. I assure you that you are not interrupting. His lordship and I were merely discussing a matter concerning Lady Margaret. We are quite through now." She made a small curtsy to Richard, another to Lady Eleanor, then turned and hurried out of the room.

Lady Eleanor watched her go, then turned to look at her brother. Richard reddened slightly under her gaze. "It wasn't what you think, Eleanor," he said. "I assure you that Miss DiMarco's being here was entirely accidental."

"Was it?" said Lady Eleanor. Coming further into the room, she shut the door behind her.

"Yes, it was," said Richard defiantly.

Lady Eleanor continued to survey him without speaking. At last she spoke, in a voice of detachment: "What you say may be true, Richard, but Miss DiMarco struck me as a trifle distraught just now," she said. "I hope you have not been making a fool of yourself."

Richard started to reply angrily, then suddenly smiled. "That depends what you mean by making a fool of myself, Eleanor," he said. "The fact is that I have just been asking Miss DiMarco to marry me."

He regarded his sister with a look of defiance. Lady Eleanor's brows rose, but she only said quietly, "I see."

"Of course, I do not expect you to approve my conduct," continued Richard in an aggressive voice. "But I have fully made up my mind to take this step. I hope that you will support me, Eleanor—and I hope also that, whatever your personal feelings may be, you will make Miss

DiMarco welcome as my wife. Assuming I can convince her to become my wife, that is."

"Has she shown herself unwilling, then?" inquired Lady Eleanor with interest. Richard nodded reluctantly.

"Yes, she imagines that—well, that her marrying me would involve me in difficulties." He met his sister's gaze with an air half defiant, half embarrassed. "I gather there is some mystery connected with Miss DiMarco's family or upbringing—some mystery which she imagines will make me unwilling to marry her."

"A mystery?" repeated Lady Eleanor with interest. "What mystery could there be?"

Richard looked more embarrassed than ever. "I don't know. Obviously she has been raised in genteel circumstances. I rather fancied that perhaps the mystery had to do with her birth—that perhaps she was born, as the saying goes, on the wrong side of the blanket."

"And such a possibility does not deter you from wishing to make her your wife?" said Lady Eleanor. Her voice was expressive of nothing more than polite interest, but Richard responded hotly.

"No, it does not! What does birth matter, anyway? Half the members of the *ton* have blots on their escutcheon of some sort or other—blots much worse than the innocent victim of a parent's indiscretion could ever boast. I am willing to marry Alexandra no matter what her birth or parentage may prove to be. And I tell you plainly, Eleanor, that no argument of yours will serve to dissuade me. I have quite made up my mind in this regard."

"Then I suppose there is no point in my arguing the matter further," said Lady Eleanor in a regretful voice.

"None whatever," said Richard firmly.

He was surprised when his sister laughed. Even more surprising was her next speech. "I am not very wise, Richard, but I have learned a few things in the past ten years," she told him. "Whom you marry is your own business, and

I am heartily glad you realize that fact. And if you succeed in convincing Miss DiMarco to marry you, you will find that I shall endure the attendant blot upon our escutcheon with a pretty good grace." Still laughing, she went away, leaving Richard puzzled but a good deal relieved.

One obstacle was out of the way, at least. He had hopes that the largest obstacle of all would shortly be removed: namely, Alexandra's own inexplicable qualms about accepting his proposal. It was irritating that his sister had interrupted them just as Alexandra was going to confess the exact nature of her qualms. She had gone away with her confession still unmade—but she had taken the diamond-and-sapphire engagement ring with her. This Richard regarded as a hopeful sign. It was too late to pursue her now, for the hour for dinner was fast approaching, and he was obliged to attend to the exigencies of his toilette. But he resolved that, whatever might come of it, he would find a private moment with Alexandra sometime that evening and get to the bottom of the mystery.

Alexandra, in the nursery, was a good deal less collected in her thoughts. She made her and Lady Margaret's toilette for the evening in a state of mental agitation scarcely inferior to that which had afflicted her after the Christmas ball. Richard had asked her to be his wife. He had said he wanted to marry her, regardless of who or what her background might be. He had given her a ring as a token of his love—the most beautiful ring in the world, Alexandra thought, stealing surreptitious peeps at it as she went about the business of dressing. She felt she could not bear to give it back now she had held it in her hand, yet at the same time, she could not see her way clear to keeping it. When she was finally dressed, she tucked it in the bosom of her gown and went downstairs in a most unsettled state of mind.

In spite of her mental turmoil, she had taken pains to dress herself with as much elegance as her wardrobe could provide. Her gown of sapphire-blue silk was less formal than the one she had worn for the Christmas ball, but quite as flattering, she hoped. Lady Margaret was wearing her pink satin dress once again that evening, as she had successfully campaigned to do, and she was in high gig, dancing about and swinging Méchante wildly in her arms. "Will there be dancing at the party tonight, Miss Di-Marco?" she asked. "I would like to dance again. I liked it very much last time when I got to dance with Mr. Tallis-tand."

"I don't know whether there is to be dancing or not this evening," said Alexandra. "I do know that it is not to be so large or formal a party as at Christmas. But there might be some impromptu country dances later on, per-haps, if everyone is so minded."

"I hope they are so minded," said Lady Margaret wist-fully. She came over and took Alexandra's hand. "Tonight is your last night at Brentwood," she said, looking up at her. "You will be leaving tomorrow."

"Yes," assented Alexandra. She found the idea did not depress her as much as it had done previously. Exploring her feelings curiously, she discovered she was no longer depressed about leaving Brentwood because, in her heart of hearts, she no longer believed she would be leaving. Try as she might to convince herself that her departure was still as necessary as before, her inner self refused to be convinced.

Her interview with Richard that afternoon no doubt had had something to do with it. He had seemed very deter-mined to marry her, no matter how disadvantageous her circumstances. If he persisted in his determination, Alex-andra suspected she must eventually give way to his wishes. Just how the matter could be thrashed out between them, she could not imagine, but she had a strong respect for her lover's capabilities, based on two and a half months of intimate daily dealings.

"Somehow, some way, it shall all work out," she vowed. "I love him, and miraculously he loves me, too. It is inconceivable that we should let these other things stand in our way when there is so much drawing us together. Somehow, some way, we will find a way to resolve the situation."

The thought filled her with a sudden, soaring happiness. To cover her emotion, she bent down and hugged Lady Margaret. "Yes, I am to go tomorrow," she said. "But we must try not to let that spoil our good time tonight. I have a strong feeling"—again she stooped and kissed Lady Margaret—"that everything will work out for the best."

Lady Margaret looked dubious, but summoned up a wan smile. By the time they got downstairs, she had forgotten her momentary sadness and was ready to make the most of the evening's festivities.

In the drawing room, Alexandra was a little embarrassed to be hailed by Lady Eleanor, who was standing apart with Miss McBride and several other guests. Lady Eleanor's manner was perfectly friendly, however, and so Alexandra supposed that her feeble excuse for being in Richard's bedchamber must have passed muster. She joined the group and listened with interest to Miss McBride, who was expounding on the festivities attached to the Scottish New Year.

"We call it Hogmanay in the auld country," she was telling the group. "And it's a bigger day than Christmas Day there. We dinna make such a show of Christmas as you Southrons do, you ken. All the eve of New Year's and the day itself are given up to paying calls, drinking healths, and all manner of like gaieties."

"Don't you have a good many quaint customs associated with the holiday, too?" inquired one of the gentlemen who was listening to her. "I was once in Scotland over New Year's, and I recall there being a great to-do in the household over who was to come through the door the first time in the New Year."

"Aye, the First Footing," said Miss McBride with a reminiscent smile. " 'Tis a grand old custom, and there's nae doubt that it remains a serious matter in a great many Scottish households—aye, even in this day and age. I have known families who hired a dark-haired man to come and call on them the minute the clock struck twelve on Hogmanay, so as to ensure there being good luck all the coming year."

"A dark-haired man?" asked one of the ladies curiously. "Is that supposed to be good luck?"

"Aye, a dark-haired man first through the door in the New Year means the best kind of luck. A fair or red-haired man is nae sae good, and a woman of any sort means naught but ill in the coming year. I have often thought," said Miss McBride, looking around the group with a mischievous smile, "that an unprincipled lady might make a fair sum at Hogmanay, merely by promising *not* to call upon her neighbors that evening!"

Her listeners all laughed and agreed that the Scottish seemed vulnerable to that particular brand of blackmail. Alexandra's attention was distracted at this point, for Richard had just come into the room. With a mixture of eagerness and anxiety she watched him greet several people who were standing near the door. At last he turned and looked around him. His eyes met Alexandra's, and a glowing smile instantly lit up his face. Somehow that smile satisfied all Alexandra's anxieties. Her eagerness was obliged to go unchecked for the moment, however, for Miss Spence, dazzling in spangled muslin, came swooping down on him just then, forcing him to give her his attention. Still, he managed first to give Alexandra another smile and a bow replete with playful formality. Alexandra shyly returned the gestures, and a few minutes later they all went into dinner.

The cook served up a dinner of uncommon splendor that evening. There were two soups, thick and clear; fried whiting and turbot with lobster sauce; roast beef, venison, and raised mutton pie; pigeons and roast turkey for the second course, with plum pudding and mince pie. Alexandra hardly noticed what she ate, however. Soup and fish; roast and entrées; fowl and entremets; dessert in all its manifold splendors—all were alike to her distracted palate. She divined Richard meant to resume their interrupted interview sometime during the evening, and she looked forward to that moment with an impatience she could scarcely conceal.

Alas, the moment showed no signs of arriving anytime soon. The dinner itself took more than two hours, and the gentlemen spent nearly an hour more afterward, sitting over their port with what Alexandra felt to be unforgivable torpor. When they finally did join the ladies in the drawing room, and Alexandra was waiting breathlessly for the summons she felt soon must come, someone suggested dancing. "But we have no orchestra," responded one lady, looking about the assemblage rather doubtfully. "I suppose we could move the pianoforte in here from the music room, but who would play?"

"Let the governess play," said Miss Spence. Her gaze rested coldly on Alexandra as she went on, addressing the rest of the party. "Even if she is only a children's governess, she ought to be able to play a simple country dance. And it will do her good to make herself useful for a change."

Some of the other ladies looked shocked by this speech, and one or two cast apologetic glances at Alexandra. "Miss DiMarco is not—" began Lady Eleanor, but she was drowned out by Lady Rosalie. That lady, elegant in a toilette of white lace and seed pearls, turned to Alexandra with a look simultaneously eager and beseeching.

"Do say you will play for us, Miss DiMarco," she said in her sweet, childlike drawl. "I am sure you must play divinely. If it isn't too much trouble, we would appreciate your playing for us for just a little while. Nothing fancy, mind you: just any little dancing tunes you might happen to know."

Alexandra, who would have had no hesitation declining Miss Spence's haughty demand, found it hard to refuse a request such as this. With an inward sigh but an outward smile, she went to take her place at the pianoforte, which several gentlemen obligingly moved over from the adjoining music room.

Lady Margaret came over and joined Alexandra on the pianoforte bench. She watched admiringly as Alexandra's fingers flew over the keys, invoking the lilting strains of a country dance. "That's lovely, Miss DiMarco," she said, wriggling in ecstasy upon the bench. "Such lovely dancy music! It makes my feet move all by themselves!"

Alexandra laughed, but her exasperation softened a little under the balm of her pupil's ingenuous praise. She found also, as she went on, that the act of music-making gradually began to exert its familiar magic over her. Soon she had entirely forgotten that she was playing under duress. It came as a surprise to her when, at the conclusion of the piece, the drawing room erupted into cheers, applause, and cries of approbation.

"Miss DiMarco, that was perfectly splendid," cried Lady Rosalie, sweeping down upon Alexandra with Mr. Taft, her late partner, in tow. "I knew you must play divinely. Do you know *'Le pouvoir de la beauté'*?"

Alexandra did know it and smilingly played it through for the delighted Lady Rosalie. Other requests followed, and soon quite a large group was gathered about the pianoforte, listening and occasionally joining their voices to the melody of some popular song.

Miss Spence, scorning her rival's pretensions, carried

on a loud-voiced conversation with Mrs. Renfrew while the music-making was going on. But these two were almost the only dissidents. The majority of the guests hung about the pianoforte, praising Alexandra's abilities in extravagant terms and receiving her every effort with applause and cries of "Just one more! Oh, please, just one more song, Miss DiMarco."

Soon it was nearly midnight. Alexandra observed this fact and sighed ruefully at her continued servitude. She glanced at Richard, wondering if he were as impatient as she was to resume their interrupted interview. Thus far he had been content to hover on the fringes of the group about the pianoforte, watching and listening but taking no active part in the music-making.

Richard seemed to feel her eyes upon him. He turned to look at her, and once again Alexandra felt the almost magical sense of reassurance his presence always communicated to her. She also felt a breathless certainty that the moment she had been waiting for all evening was not far off. As if her look had been a prearranged signal, Richard began to move toward her, through the crowd that were crying for "Nancy Dawson," "The Battle of Prague," and other songs. Alexandra's heartbeat began to quicken.

At that moment, Richard's butler approached him and said something to him in a low voice. Alexandra could not hear the butler's words, but she heard Richard's surprised response. "A visitor? I am expecting no visitors this evening, certainly none who would be arriving at this hour. Why, it's almost midnight!"

One of the ladies who was standing nearby also overheard him. "A First Footer," she cried. "It's a First Footer, Lord Brentwood! You must find out if he is a dark man first before you let him in the house. Hattie was telling us all about it before dinner."

There was a murmur of agreement from the other guests, and several announced their intention of accompanying Richard to the door to interview the unknown guest. Alexandra, watching them go, felt a faint premonitory tingle down her spine. This was soon lost in a wave of irritation, however.

Goodness knows how long this visitor will keep Richard at the door, she told herself with disgust. *The whole world seems to be in a conspiracy to separate us tonight.* Then, more cheerfully, she reflected that even the efforts of all the world united were well known to be insufficient to keep two determined hearts apart. And with that reflection to console her, she turned back to the pianoforte.

EIGHTEEN

As Richard followed his butler to the door, he suffered no premonitions of doom or disaster. His mood was tranquil enough, though not precisely euphoric. He was curious as to whom the late-arriving visitor might be, and irritated that he, or she, had interrupted him at such an untimely moment. He was also a trifle irritated at those guests who had chosen to accompany him to the door and who swarmed around him now, chattering in a silly way.

"You mustn't let anyone in, Brentwood, unless they happen to be a dark man," instructed one gentleman with a waggish smile. "That's the rule, and we intend to see you enforce it."

"Yes, for Hattie says that if you want luck in the coming year, it's got to be a dark man who first crosses your threshold in the New Year," chimed in another.

"It's not the New Year yet," pointed out Richard.

"Aye, but it soon will be. My watch says midnight now, Brentwood. I believe your clocks must be slow."

"There! There, I hear it striking midnight now," cried another guest excitedly. They all paused to listen as a distant clock somewhere in the house struck twelve in slow, mournful tones. As soon as it was done, two of the gentleman guests seized Richard by the arms. "Come, Brentwood! Let us see what the fates have in store for you in the New Year!"

Richard shook them off irritably and walked toward the door. His butler accompanied him, addressing him in a confidential undertone. "The . . . er . . . person who wishes to speak with you is waiting outside, my lord," he said. "I thought it better not to admit him to the house until your lordship had seen and spoken to him. He seems . . . er . . . slightly disturbed."

The guests raised a joyful cry at this speech. "It's a man, then! The First Footer is a man!" cried one.

"That's so much to the good anyway, Brentwood," said another. "Now to see if he's dark or fair."

"I'll lay you ten to one that he's a redhead," offered a third gentleman.

Richard ignored them all and stepped forward to the door. His butler opened it, bowing. "This is his lordship, the Earl of Brentwood," he said, addressing a shadowy figure who stood on the steps outside.

The figure came forward, and Richard found himself face-to-face with an elderly gentleman. A glance showed him that the gentleman had salt-and-pepper hair, a tall, spare figure, and a pair of vivid blue eyes that struck a vague chord of remembrance in Richard's mind. A second glance showed him that his butler had not erred in describing the visitor's mood as "disturbed." His face was red with choler, and when he spoke there was a throb of suppressed fury in his voice. "My lord, I have come to demand the return of my niece!" he said.

Richard looked at him, wondering if he had heard him aright. The gentleman spoke like a character in a play or a bad novel. "Your niece?" he repeated.

The gentleman surveyed him more fiercely than before. "Let us not quibble over technicalities, my lord," he spat. "Miss Manning is my grandniece, but she is to me like a daughter—like a daughter, I say!" He glared at Richard from beneath bristling salt-and-pepper brows. "And I demand that you restore her to me instantly."

Richard felt more than ever as if he were taking part in a singularly incoherent play. This impression was heightened by his guests, who came crowding up at that moment to see the unknown visitor.

"Dark or fair? Dark or fair?" chanted one, peering at the gentleman on the steps. "Here's a poseur, to be sure! Neither dark nor fair, but salt-and-pepper! Now, how are we to interpret that?"

"He looks to have been dark-haired to begin with," pointed out another. "I say he counts as dark."

"He ain't red-haired at any rate," said a third, surveying the gentleman with satisfaction. "You owe me a pony, Cartwright."

One young matron, who was among the party of guests, addressed the elderly gentleman with an air of pretty deference. "Would you consider yourself fair or dark, sir?" she asked.

Richard, observing the elderly gentleman's expression, feared an explosion was imminent. He spoke up hastily. "Never mind that now," he told the young matron. "I have business with this gentleman—private business. I expect it will take us some little time to thrash it out. You had all better go on back to the party and make my apologies to the other guests."

When the guests had finally taken themselves off, the elderly gentleman turned again to Richard. "What manner of nonsense is this?" he demanded in ringing tones. "I come here in search of my niece and find myself insulted—yes, insulted, I say!"

"Yes, but you see I do not know your niece," said Richard apologetically. "Miss Manning was the name you mentioned, was it not? I am not acquainted with a Miss Manning."

"You lie, my lord!" declared the elderly gentleman, glaring at Richard. "I have proof positive that you lie. I know my niece is here!"

Before he could adduce his proofs, however, another interruption occurred. A frail-looking elderly lady enveloped
in a fur-lined cloak came hurrying up the front steps and
joined the elderly gentleman where he stood. "Frederick,
you have been an age," she said plaintively. "I could not
stay in the coach all night." She turned to survey Richard.
"Is this Lord Brentwood? What is his explanation for this
business?"

"He claims he has not seen Alexandra," said the elderly
gentleman, in the contemptuous voice of one repeating
some singularly dubious piece of testimony.

At the name, Richard stiffened. He surveyed the gentleman and lady with astonishment and dawning comprehension. No wonder those vivid blue eyes looked familiar!
"Alexandra," he said in a stunned voice. "You are Alexandra's great-aunt and -uncle!"

"Ah, so you *do* admit you know her," charged the elderly
gentleman, surveying Richard with an air of mingled contempt and satisfaction.

"Yes, but not under the name of Manning," said Richard. "This is a very complicated and delicate business. I
think you had both better come inside so we can discuss
it in privacy."

Ushering the elderly couple into the house, he led them
to an unoccupied parlor just off the entrance hall. Shutting the door carefully behind him, he turned to face them
once more. "I think we had better begin again," he said.
"We both appear to have been operating under a misap-
prehension. I am Richard Brentwood. And you are . . . ?"

"Frederick Manning," the elderly gentleman said
grudgingly, as though reluctant to relinquish his original
belligerent attitude. "And this is my wife, Mrs. Manning."

Richard bowed, impressed in spite of himself. The name
of Manning was known to him, indeed, as it was to all of
England. Fabulously wealthy, unassailably genteel, and ex-
clusive to the point of reclusiveness—that was the Man-

nings. If Alexandra were connected to them, even through a so-called left-handed issue, then hers was no mean pedigree.

Mrs. Manning acknowledged Richard's greeting with a gracious smile and a sweet-voiced, "How do you do, my lord?" As soon as these formalities were complete, however, her husband took up the conversation again, with the air of being only half convinced by Richard's words.

"You say you are acquainted with my niece, but not under the name of Manning. What exactly do you mean by that, my lord?"

"Exactly what I say," said Richard coolly. "Your niece introduced herself to me as Miss Alexandra DiMarco."

A faint gasp escaped Mrs. Manning. Mr. Manning drew himself to his full height. "That may be Alexandra's legal name, my lord, but she has never used it," he said in an awful voice. "She has always been known among us as Miss Manning."

"I do not doubt you, sir. I can only say that on this occasion she apparently chose to do otherwise," said Richard.

The Mannings exchanged glances. When at last they spoke, it was Mrs. Manning who addressed Richard. "The matter of Alexandra's parentage is a very painful one," she told him. "Her mother was Elizabeth Manning, the daughter of Frederick's younger brother. Both he and his wife passed away when Elizabeth was but a child. Since Frederick and I had no children of our own, we were glad to take her into our home and raise her as if she were our own daughter. We became very attached to Elizabeth— very attached indeed. She was a most beautiful and lovable girl. Alexandra bears some resemblance to her, although I fear she will never hold a candle to her mother where beauty is concerned."

"If that is the case, then her mother must have been beautiful indeed," said Richard in amazement.

"She was, my lord: she was," Mr. Manning said gruffly. He took out his handkerchief and blew his nose, while his wife took up her narrative once more.

"As I said, we loved Elizabeth dearly and would have been only too happy to keep her with us forever. Unfortunately . . ." Here Mrs. Manning hesitated, looking at her husband.

"Unfortunately, my lord, a damned scoundrel came and stole her away from us," finished Mr. Manning, with something like a groan. "Would that we had kept Elizabeth safe at home!"

"She was set on having a Season in London," said Mrs. Manning, her voice pleading as if she were seeking Richard's forgiveness. "You will understand that we could not like to deny her anything, my lord. And indeed, there seemed no harm in her having a Season. But while we were staying in London, our niece made the acquaintance of the late Conte DiMarco—and that was her undoing."

"Conte DiMarco was a scoundrel, my lord! A damned scoundrel," Mr. Manning said fiercely.

"I see," said Richard. Both Mr. and Mrs. Manning looked at him as though they expected him to say something more. "I suppose that Alexandra is the—er—fruit of the union between your niece and the Conte?" he inquired delicately.

Mrs. Manning nodded sadly. "We did all we could to dissuade my niece from her unhappy attachment," she told Richard. "As soon as we became aware of the danger, we determined to take her back to Mannington, where the Conte could not communicate with her. But we were too late. On the eve of our departure from London, Elizabeth eloped with the Conte. Such a shocking thing it was! They were actually married over the anvil at Gretna Green."

"Were *married!*" exclaimed Richard. "You mean Alexandra is the *legitimate* daughter of your niece and an Italian *conte?*"

Both Mannings looked shocked by this speech. "To be sure, she is legitimate, my lord," Mr. Manning said severely. "Alexandra was born a year to the day after my niece's unfortunate marriage!"

"Sadly, Elizabeth did not survive her lying-in," added Mrs. Manning with a sigh. "The Conte had already passed away some months earlier, which was a blessing in a way, but it meant that Alexandra was actually born an orphan, poor child. Frederick and I knew our duty, however, and we did not let the circumstance of her paternity influence us in any way. We took her in and raised her as our own, just as we had done with her mother before her."

"Good God," said Richard faintly. A great many things that had puzzled him about Alexandra had suddenly been made clear to him. Her reticence in speaking about her past; her ignorance concerning money; her naive delight in simple things like choosing ribbon or a trip to the village pastrycook's—all were easy to understand in a young lady escaped from such a rarefied atmosphere as the Mannings'. And though it might seem odd that a girl from such a privileged background should choose to earn her living as a governess for several months, Richard thought he could understand that, too. The only thing he could not understand was how Alexandra had managed to escape from the net of chaperonage that was evidently drawn tight about her. It was evident from Mrs. Manning's next speech that this point was puzzling her, too.

"I do not understand why Alexandra came here in the first place, my lord," she said plaintively. "You must understand that my husband and I were under the impression she was staying with my sister Emily in Tunbridge Wells. We were both ill, you see, and she had to be sent away to avoid risk of infection. She has been very delicate all her life, as was her mother before her."

"Indeed," said Richard, a trifle incredulously. It was hard to associate Alexandra, glowing with health and spir-

its, with Mrs. Manning's descriptions of a feeble near in-
valid. "And so you thought your niece was staying at Tunbridge all these weeks?" he asked.

"At first, my lord. Later we received a letter from her
saying that Emily was away from home, so she was staying
with you and your family here instead. You must understand that her letter distinctly implied that Emily was *also*
staying here as your guest."

"Indeed," said Richard, stifling a smile. The last piece
of the puzzle had fallen into place. In a solemn voice he
added, "It is true I have a number of guests staying here
at present, but I do not believe your sister is among them,
ma'am."

"We know she is not, my lord," said Mr. Manning,
brusquely breaking in upon this dialogue. "We received a
letter from Emily at Christmas, saying she was staying with
friends in Devon and making no mention of Alexandra at
all! So what we wish to know is why Alexandra is here—and
what means you have been using to keep her here for
these last two and a half months."

Both he and Mrs. Manning looked at Richard, the one
belligerently, the other expectantly. Richard regarded
them both a moment, then shook his head. "I think it
would be better if Alexandra herself explained that," he
said. "If you will both wait here a moment, I will bring her
to you."

Alexandra, back in the drawing room, was pleased to
see Richard reenter the room. In his absence she had continued to play songs for the company, but her spirit chafed
at her continued servitude. As time went on, her initial
mood of cheerful optimism began to be eroded by anxieties both rational and irrational. What if Richard did not
return to the party that evening? What if he postponed
speaking to her until tomorrow? Or, even worse, what if

he postponed speaking to her altogether, and she was forced to leave Brentwood on the morrow as she had originally planned?

And then suddenly there he was, and Alexandra's fears vanished in a flood of pleasure and relief. She expected that Richard would approach her presently, perhaps maneuvering his way up to the pianoforte in a roundabout fashion under the pretense of requesting a song. But to her surprise, he came directly up to her and addressed her quite openly. "I wonder if you will do me the favor of accompanying me outside for a few minutes, Miss DiMarco," he said with a bow.

Alexandra's surprise grew greater at this speech. It was spoken in the tone of a demand rather than a request. "I cannot leave just this minute, my lord," she said, regarding Richard with astonishment. "As you can see, I am still playing for the guests."

"Someone else can no doubt fill your place. My sister would be happy to, I'm sure. Eleanor," he said, raising his voice. Lady Eleanor, who was standing not far away, came over to join them, a look of inquiry on her face. "Eleanor, I wish you would take over for Miss DiMarco at the pianoforte," Richard told her. "She is obliged to accompany me out of the room for a moment.

"Certainly, Richard," said Lady Eleanor. Her voice was warmly acquiescent, but her eyes held a hint of speculation as she looked from her brother to Alexandra.

Alexandra made way for Lady Eleanor at the pianoforte bench reluctantly. "Of course I will accompany you, my lord, but you must remember that I am here tonight as your daughter's governess," she told Richard. "I cannot leave Lady Margaret by herself—"

"Eleanor can attend to that, too," said Richard, cutting short her objections. Addressing his daughter, he continued: "Margaret, you stay here with your aunt and be a good girl. Miss DiMarco and I are obliged to leave the party for a few minutes."

"All right, Papa," said Lady Margaret. Her tone was docile, but like Lady Eleanor her eyes held a speculative gleam as she looked from her father to Alexandra. Nor were hers the only ones. The guests around the pianoforte naturally had been privy to the whole exchange, and they were regarding Richard and Alexandra with intense interest. Alexandra felt as though every eye in the room was upon her as she rose and accompanied Richard out of the drawing room.

"What is all this about, my lord?" she asked, as soon as they were in the hallway. Richard turned to face her, taking both her hands in his and looking down at her with an expression of gravity.

"Miss DiMarco, I must throw myself upon your mercy," he said. "I find myself in a position of gravest extremity, and if you will not take pity on me, there will be nothing for it but for me to flee the country."

Alexandra gazed at him, astonished and dismayed by these words. Then, as she observed the twinkle in Richard's eye and the faint irrepressible curve of his lip, her dismay gave way to exasperated relief. "Oh, I thought something was seriously the matter, my lord! You ought not to scare me like that."

"Something seriously *is* the matter," said Richard, skillfully recapturing the hands she had been trying to withdraw. "Your great-aunt and -uncle are in the parlor down the hall. Yes, you may well stare," he added, as Alexandra gazed at him speechlessly. "They have discovered you have not been with Aunt Emily in Tunbridge all these weeks, but rather have been spending your time with me, whom they half suspect of being a dangerous and disreputable character. Unless I can provide an unimpeachable excuse for your presence here at Brentwood—in the shape of a betrothal, for instance—I am afraid your great-uncle means to call me out. And so I am throwing myself on your mercy and asking you to marry me, this time for the ignoble purpose of saving my own skin."

"Uncle Frederick and Aunt Elizabeth here!" exclaimed Alexandra. "Whatever made them come to Brentwood? I had thought—" She threw Richard a guilty look. "The fact is that I had written them more or less implying that you were friends of Aunt Emily's, and that I was staying here under her auspices."

"So they informed me. But it appears that Aunt Emily very disobligingly let the cat out of the bag. She wrote them from wherever she was truly staying—Devon, was it?—and made no mention of you. Naturally this made them suspicious, and so they came here to discover what was really going on."

Alexandra flushed. "You must think very ill of me, my lord," she said in a small voice. "Indeed, I did not set out to deceive my aunt and uncle. It was not until I reached Wanworth that I discovered Aunt Emily was from home. And then I met Miss Harcourt—and she needed help so badly, and there was no one else to help her, and really I had nothing better to do. And so I came here—and then, once I was here, I met Lady Margaret . . . and you, too, my lord. And once I had become attached to you both, it seemed as though I could not bear to let you go. Especially since Miss Harcourt still needed me—"

"You need not explain," said Richard, smiling down at her. "I flatter myself that I have pieced together the story tolerably well on my own. Your behavior was completely understandable—and I might add, quite commendable as well. There are not many young women in your circumstances who would choose to work as a governess for two and a half months."

Alexandra threw him a frightened look. "What do you know of my circumstances? Oh—!" The word came out a long sigh. "I suppose Uncle Frederick and Aunt Elizabeth

told you. Indeed, I did not mean to deceive you, my lord."
She looked at Richard pleadingly. "And I did not know
when I first came here that a hundred pounds a year was
a tremendous salary for a governess. I felt badly once I
did know and tried to be very conscientious about doing
my duty by Lady Margaret. And I would be glad to give
back what money you have given me if you like—"

"Only if you will take a betrothal ring in exchange for
it," said Richard, smiling down at her. "Do you still have
the ring I gave you?"

Slowly Alexandra drew the ring out of her bosom. Richard took it, holding it in his hand and looking deep into
her eyes. "Miss DiMarco, I have asked you twice before to
marry me and got no response worth the having," he said.
"Now I know all your guilty secrets—at least, I think I do—
and I assure you that I am still eager to marry you. Will
you do me the honor of becoming my wife?"

Alexandra looked at the ring, then at him. "Oh, my
lord, I wish I might," she said. "But I hardly know what I
ought to do."

"Just say yes," said Richard encouragingly. "Say, 'Yes,
my lord'—or, better yet, say, 'Yes, Richard.' It is high time
you dropped this 'my lord' business and started calling me
by my Christian name."

He smiled at her as he spoke, and Alexandra could not
help smiling back. "Of course I will call you by your Christian name if you want me to, Richard," she said. "But as
for the rest of what you ask—that's a good deal more complicated."

"It doesn't seem complicated to me," said Richard. "I
love you, and you love me. What could be more natural
than that we should wish to marry? Besides, I consider that
you've an obligation to marry me now, if only to protect
me from your uncle's wrath. The odds of his calling me
out would be considerably reduced if I could present myself to him as your affianced husband."

Alexandra laughed shakily. "That shows how little you know him, Richard! Nothing would be more likely to make him call you out than to tell him you mean to marry me. I daresay that seems very strange to you, but if you knew a little about my family history—"

"Oh, yes," said Richard, with sudden comprehension. "Your aunt and uncle did tell me something about your mother's marriage, Alexandra. Naturally they would be opposed to your marrying, too, for fear it might have a similarly disastrous outcome."

"Exactly," said Alexandra with a sigh. "They have spent the last twenty-one years trying to save me from my mother's fate. If I tell them now I mean to marry you, it would make them very unhappy. Yet if I do not—"

"It will make *me* very unhappy," finished Richard.

"And me, too," said Alexandra. Lifting her chin, she looked at Richard with determination. "I love my great-aunt and -uncle, Richard. They have been so good to me that I would be the most ungrateful soul imaginable if I did *not* love them. But I refuse to let us both be made unhappy for what is, after all, only an irrational prejudice. If worse comes to worst, I can marry without my great-aunt and -uncle's consent. I am of age, and not penniless—at least, I suppose I am not penniless. But it may be that my aunt and uncle will choose to deny me a marriage portion if I marry without their consent." She looked doubtfully at Richard.

"I don't care about that," said Richard, with a smile. "Remember, my dear, that until an hour ago the only money I knew for certain that you possessed was the salary I myself had paid you!"

"That is true." Alexandra smiled at him. "You are obviously disinterested where money is concerned. But Richard, there is bound to be a fearful scene when I tell my aunt and uncle I mean to marry you. Are you sure I am worth the bother?"

"Quite sure," said Richard. "I was never more sure of anything in my life." Slipping the ring on her finger, he raised her hand to his lips and kissed it.

"Then I will marry you," said Alexandra, smiling tremulously up at him. "I love you, Richard—and I love your daughter, too. From now, it shall be the study of my life to make both of you happy."

"And I have no doubt you will succeed as brilliantly at that as in all your other studies," said Richard, drawing her into his arms. Alexandra very willingly returned his embrace. But so well developed were her habits of discipline and self-control that it was a mere half hour later when she recalled there was business still to be transacted that evening.

"Much as I enjoy kissing you, Richard, I think I would enjoy kissing you more if we had this business settled," she told him with a smile. "We had better go see Uncle Frederick and Aunt Elizabeth and get the worst over with."

NINETEEN

Alexandra was not wrong in supposing that her great-aunt and -uncle would raise an outcry when they learned of her engagement.

The Mannings' outcry was both loud and prolonged. The newly engaged pair stood firm in their resolution, however, and eventually, once the Mannings' first shock was past, they began to grow calmer and to accept the fact that their grandniece really did intend to marry the Earl of Brentwood and Barstock.

"You do not plan to marry immediately, do you?" said Mrs. Manning, looking tearfully at her niece. "At least wait until spring, so we may accustom ourselves to the idea that you are to leave us. We have just found you, and now we learn we are to lose you again—" With a stifled sob, she applied her handkerchief to her eyes.

Alexandra looked at Richard. They had not discussed wedding dates as yet. Their engagement was too recent for that, but in both their hearts was a desire to be soon united and a secret dismay at the prospect of waiting till spring. "If only you could return with us to Mannington for a few months," continued Mrs. Manning, still dabbing at her eyes. "We cannot force you to do so, of course, but both your uncle and I would regard it as a great favor. You must understand that you are like our own child, Alexandra. We cannot learn to do without you all at once. Can we, Frederick?"

Mr. Manning did not reply directly to this question. Instead he said gruffly, "It would mean a great deal to your aunt and I if you could return home with us for the present, Alexandra. I trust Lord Brentwood would allow you to spend a few months with your relations, seeing that he means to permanently deprive us of your company."

"Of course, I can see you and Aunt Elizabeth's viewpoint, Uncle Frederick," said Alexandra, as diplomatically as she could. "And of course Lord Brentwood and I could stand to be apart from each other for a month or two if necessary. But there is another person to be considered." Both Mannings looked at her inquiringly. "I am speaking of Lady Margaret," explained Alexandra. "She has come to depend on me, and I would rather not go away and leave her just at present."

"Lady Margaret? Oh, yes, Lord Brentwood's daughter that you wrote about." Mrs. Manning looked doubtfully at Richard. "You hardly look old enough to have a grown-up daughter, my lord."

Alexandra laughed guiltily. "But you see, she is not grown-up! I may have given that impression in my letters, but the fact is that Lady Margaret is really a child of six years old. And she and I have grown very close these last few months. I have been acting as her governess, you see."

This statement produced a second outcry from both Mannings. "You, working as a governess!" said Mr. Manning in a voice of stern disapproval. "Whatever does this mean, Alexandra?"

Alexandra endeavored to explain the circumstances that had led her to become governess to Lady Margaret. Watching her great-aunt and -uncle's faces, she was cheered to see that her explanations were not without effect. Mrs. Manning clucked her tongue sympathetically at the story of Miss Harcourt's difficulties, and even Mr. Manning acknowledged that Alexandra's behavior had been well intentioned.

"But you would have done better to have hired some qualified person to take this Miss Harcourt's place, rather than doing so yourself," he told Alexandra. "Not that there is anything really *disreputable* about working as a governess. I know a great many gently bred girls do so, and I recognize that there may be no alternative for young women in reduced circumstances. But for you, a Manning, to undertake a position of that sort! It seems a very eccentric action, to say no worse of it."

"I can see, of course, that you would not want to leave the little girl you have become so attached to," Mrs. Manning added kindly. "The thing you must remember, Alexandra, is that you are *our* little girl. And we are very attached to *you.*" She looked appealingly at Richard. "I quite understand that you and your daughter would not wish to part with Alexandra, my lord, but surely you can understand the feelings of those who have stood in the place of Alexandra's parents? Frederick and I would like her to come home for a short visit at least, before she leaves to make her home with you."

It was at this moment that Richard had what he later termed his great inspiration. "To be sure, I can understand your feelings, ma'am," he told Mrs. Manning. "Your request is an eminently reasonable one, and I would have no objection to Alexandra's paying you a visit, either now or later on. But it occurs to me that a somewhat different arrangement might suit all of us better than the one you propose. If, for instance, you were willing to stay on here at Brentwood for a few weeks, then both Alexandra and I might afterward visit you at your home—as husband and wife. It could be part of our wedding trip. And we could make you another, longer visit later in the year, perhaps sometime during the summer."

Richard paused, looking rather anxiously at the Mannings to see their reaction to this proposal. They looked taken aback, but it was clear they were both interested. Richard went on, smiling at them as he spoke. "In fact, I would not mind our making an annual visit to Mannington if you so desired," he said. "My affection for Alexandra is of recent date compared to yours, but even so I feel as though I could not bear to be parted from her for a single day. I am sure it must be a hundred times worse for you, who have known her from a child. This change must necessarily be a difficult and painful one for you, but perhaps the arrangement I describe would make it a little easier. At least it would give you a little time in which to become accustomed to the idea of Alexandra leaving you, before you are called on to actually be parted from her."

The Mannings exchanged glances. "Why, I don't know," Mrs. Manning said slowly. "What you propose sounds a fair compromise to me, my lord. What do you think, Frederick?"

Mr. Manning surveyed Richard for a moment in silence. At last he spoke, in a voice from which his customary note of belligerence was missing. "You are obviously a man of tact and sensitivity, my lord," he said. "I think I speak for both my wife and I when I say that we mind losing Alexandra less, seeing what manner of man she is marrying." Clearing his throat, he added, "We accept your offer with gratitude, my lord. My wife and I look forward to entertaining you and Alexandra as guests in our home."

Mrs. Manning endorsed this statement, but in a rather perfunctory way. Her thoughts had obviously moved on to what she considered more important issues. "And so you plan to be married immediately," she said, surveying Richard and Alexandra with interest. "My, what a lot of work we will have to do in these next few weeks, getting ready for the wedding. And your brideclothes, Alexandra! I am sure every stitch you have must need replacing. It's been an age since you've had any new clothes."

Alexandra looked at Richard and laughed. There was triumph in her laugh, and her eyes were alight with glowing happiness. Richard smiled back at her, conscious of the same two emotions. The Mannings obviously had accepted defeat and were preparing to make the best of the situation. "The first thing to be done, even before new clothes, is to formally announce the engagement," he said. "And that may well prove to be the most challenging part of this whole business. My family and friends know Alexandra only as my daughter's governess, you see. Even if I tell them who she is and why she is here in her current position, I cannot expect them to immediately accept her with open arms. There will inevitably be a certain amount of gossip and speculation when we announce we mean to marry. For Alexandra's sake I would rather it be kept to an absolute minimum. We must think of how best to smooth the situation over."

"You may safely leave all that to me, Richard," said a voice behind him.

Richard turned in surprise. Lady Eleanor was standing in the doorway, regarding them all with a broad smile. "I take it you have done what you threatened and induced Miss DiMarco to accept you, Richard. Well, then, let me be the first to congratulate you. You have chosen a very pretty bride, and I doubt you shall have any call to be ashamed of her antecedents." With a droll look at Alexandra, she added, "There are, of course, people who discount all foreign titles, and so her being the daughter of Conte DiMarco may not always carry the weight it ought. But it is a relief to know that the name of Manning cannot fail be respected."

Richard gazed at his sister in astonishment. "You knew?" he said. "Eleanor, is it possible you have known all this time who Alexandra really is? Or have you merely been listening at the door this last hour?"

"Certainly not. I have only been listening these last five

minutes." Lady Eleanor made this shameless announcement with perfect aplomb. She went on, addressing her brother with a superior air. "Of course I knew who Alexandra was, Richard, right from the beginning. Anyone who knew her father and mother could not fail to guess who she is. Hattie has guessed, too. And though I have encouraged her to spread the word among the others, she is so good-natured that one cannot depend on her to spread gossip reliably. We shall have to take a more drastic approach—and I flatter myself that I have thought of just the one."

The Mannings were staring at Lady Eleanor as though they thought she might possibly be some species of escaped lunatic. Richard thought it well to make formal introductions. "Mr. and Mrs. Manning, this is my sister, Lady Eleanor Taft. Eleanor, allow me to introduce to you Mr. and Mrs. Manning, Alexandra's great-aunt and -uncle."

"I am very pleased to meet you both," said Lady Eleanor, extending her hand to the Mannings with her most winning smile. "You must know that Alexandra's mother was a great friend of mine. I was delighted to discover her daughter staying here at Brentwood. Elizabeth was a charming girl—a very charming girl indeed. And Alexandra is just the image of her."

"Not quite the image," said Mr. Manning. He spoke reprovingly but looked pleased nonetheless by Lady Eleanor's words. "Although Alexandra is certainly a pretty girl, I am afraid she cannot hold a candle to her mother's beauty. But you are kind to praise her, ma'am. And I am pleased to make the acquaintance of one who was a friend to my late niece."

"And I, too," said Mrs. Manning, curtsying as she touched Lady Eleanor's hand.

Having placated both the Mannings in this manner, Lady Eleanor turned again to her brother. "Now as to what

I was saying before, Richard. I think the best way to smooth this business over is to treat it all as a joke."

"A joke?" repeated Richard dubiously.

"A joke!" exclaimed Mr. Manning. "I fail to see how my niece's engagement to Lord Brentwood could be considered as a joke!"

Lady Eleanor turned an indulgent smile on him. "Ah, but that is because you have just arrived at Brentwood, sir," she told him. "If you had been staying here during this last week, you would know that we have been playing all manner of pranks and practical jokes on each other. And if we claim that Alexandra has been my brother's fiancée all along, and that we thought it might be amusing to have her pretend to be Lady Margaret's governess and see if she could fool the other guests—well, it will merely seem the biggest joke of all."

Richard and Alexandra looked at each other. "It *might* work," said Richard. "I must say, however, that I cannot really approve my own conduct in this joke. It seems to me a rather caddish trick, to make my fiancée work as a governess all these weeks."

"Yes, but you did *not* make her, Richard. It was she and I who came up with the idea, and you only went along with it reluctantly."

"And the servants?" said Richard. "How are they to be convinced that this is a long-standing practical joke? Remember that they were here when Alexandra arrived in October. They must know something of the true circumstances of her arrival here."

Lady Eleanor laughed. "They may know the true circumstances, Richard, but that doesn't mean they believe them! They have all along been convinced there is something odd about Alexandra's presence here. That is what my maid tells me, at any rate, and I have no doubt she is voicing the common opinion in the servants' hall. Servants have an amazing way of smelling out the true quality of a person. A penniless governess trying to pass herself off as a fine lady could never hope to impose on them, and I believe the reverse is true, too. You'll see, Richard. When we announce that Alexandra is really your fiancée, they will nod and say among themselves, 'Ah, I never thought she was a real governess! The pranks young ladies play nowadays do go beyond anything!' "

Both Richard and Alexandra laughed at Lady Eleanor's droll imitation of a gossiping servant, but Alexandra also looked a bit indignant. "But I *am* a real governess, Lady Eleanor," she said. "I have worked very hard teaching Lady Margaret all this autumn. And indeed, she has made considerable progress under my tuition."

"We don't doubt you have taught her a great deal, my love," said Lady Eleanor, smiling at her. "But you know it is not only governesses who teach things. Have you never heard the expression, 'I learnt it at my mother's knee'? I assure you that when we announce your engagement to Richard, no one will wonder that you chose to spend so much time with your future stepdaughter!"

"I believe it might pass," said Richard, his eyes kindling as he considered his sister's words. "Certainly I can think of no better plan. Very well, Eleanor: we will leave the matter all in your hands. You may announce Alexandra's true status and take credit for imposing on my guests and servants all these weeks. I will remain an apologetic figure in the background—except, of course, when I am receiving my guests' congratulations on my impending marriage!" He smiled down at Alexandra, and she smiled back, tucking her hand in his.

Mr. Manning's response was less enthusiastic. "But what part have we to play in this charade, my lady?" he demanded of Lady Eleanor. "My wife and I can understand the circumstances which prompted my niece to work as Lord Brentwood's governess, but that does not mean we approve of her conduct. Indeed, you cannot expect us to give our countenance to such a thing, even as a practical joke."

"Certainly not, and I would not expect you to," returned Lady Eleanor promptly. "You and your wife may disapprove as much as you like, Mr. Manning. In fact, I hope you will do so a great deal during your stay here, as that will add verisimilitude to the story we are trying to put about. You must know that several of the guests witnessed your arrival tonight. They observed that you seemed rather—ahem!—put out, and they have been speculating ever since about what brought you here. We can say you got wind of Alexandra's activities and came to put a stop to them. And that, of course, forced us to come out in the open and announce her and Richard's engagement now, instead of waiting till the end of the house party!"

Mr. Manning looked mollified by this speech and, with a good deal of ponderous rhetoric, agreed that he and his wife could fulfill the role Lady Eleanor had outlined.

"Then I think it is time we all rejoined the party," said Richard, moving toward the door with Alexandra's hand still in his. "I will leave you to make the announcement of our engagement, Eleanor, and also to introduce the Mannings to the other guests. And Alexandra and I will stand in the background and look modestly happy."

This program went off without a hitch. As soon as they were back in the drawing room, Lady Eleanor called for the guests' attention. In a short and witty speech in which truth mingled artfully with half-truth, she revealed the circumstances of Alexandra's imposture, her true position as Richard's fiancée, and the role she herself had played in concealing these facts. She ended by begging the guests' pardon for the joke which had been played on them.

Stunned silence followed Lady Eleanor's announcement. It was Miss McBride who first broke the silence. "I must say that I have suspected something of the kind all along," she said cheerfully. "You havena deceived us so completely as you suppose, Eleanor. A great many of us have observed Lord Brentwood's fondness for his governess's company."

There were laughs and murmurs of agreement from the other guests. Sir Maximilian was observed looking rather red-faced, and Miss Spence's expression was distinctly chagrined. But the majority of the guests, once their first surprise was worn off, were disposed to be delighted with the joke.

"You pulled the wool over our eyes this time, Brentwood," said one gentleman. "It's the best joke of the season."

"Indeed it is," agreed another. "But I intend to revenge myself on him by kissing his fiancée, by Jove." And he proceeded to put this threat into action.

What followed was a perfect frenzy of kissing and congratulation. An astonishing number of people told Alexandra that they had suspected all along that she was not a real governess. "Much too soignée," stated one matron with lofty conviction.

"Much too pretty," added her husband sotto voce, inspecting Alexandra with an admiring eye.

"Oh, I knew you could not be a governess, Miss Di-Marco," cried Lady Rosalie, enveloping Alexandra in a perfumed hug. "You are too clever by half—and too stylish, too. I have never seen a governess with a particle of style. You must come and be presented in London this spring after you and Lord Brentwood are married. I'm sure you would make a great sensation."

There was one person whose congratulations were more fervent than all the rest. Lady Margaret, who had been sitting with Miss McBride during Lady Eleanor's absence from the drawing room, had listened in uncomprehending silence to the announcement of her father's engagement. Observing her expression, Richard made his way quietly to her side as soon as he was able and begged her pardon for not informing her first of his plans.

"You ought really to have been informed before the others. I hope you will forgive me, Margaret, and not let my conduct prejudice you against Miss DiMarco. I know you have been happy having her as your governess. Now I hope you will be equally happy with her as your new mother."

Lady Margaret made no response to this speech. Her eyes were fixed over Richard's shoulder, where Alexandra stood in the midst of a bevy of laughing and congratulatory guests. Presently Alexandra disengaged herself and came over to join Richard and Lady Margaret.

"Papa says you're going to marry him," said Lady Margaret, coming directly to the point. "Is that true?"

Alexandra stooped down, so that her eyes were on a level with Lady Margaret's. "Yes, it is quite true that your papa and I mean to marry," she said. "I hope that does not displease you, Lady Margaret?"

Lady Margaret shook her head vigorously. "No, for it means you don't need to leave Brentwood now. You can stay here with me and Papa, and we can all be happy together." In a satisfied voice, she added, "I am glad you are marrying Papa rather than that other man. Papa will be a much better husband for you. That other man was very silly."

Alexandra laughed, nodded, and embraced Lady Margaret. Lady Margaret returned the embrace fervently. At that moment, the voice of Mr. Manning rang out in shocked disapproval.

"What's this, what's this? A child—and still up at this hour? Why, it is nearly two o'clock in the morning!"

Both Richard and Alexandra looked guiltily at the clock. "It *is* rather late," said Richard. "But you know it is New Year's Eve, sir. I see no harm in her staying up late just once in the year."

"This is Lady Margaret, Uncle," said Alexandra in an explanatory aside. "She is Lord Brentwood's daughter that I was telling you about."

"So you are Lady Margaret, eh?" Mr. Manning surveyed the child with interest. "I am very pleased to make your acquaintance, my dear. You know my niece here is to be your new stepmother, so we are soon to be relations."

Lady Margaret looked interested. "Are we?" she said. "You are related to Miss DiMarco?"

A faint spasm crossed Mr. Manning's face. But he replied, quite mildly, "Yes, only we know her as Miss Manning. I am Mr. Manning, her great-uncle."

"Oh, yes, she has talked about you," said Lady Margaret in an enlightened voice. "You're the one who says, 'Discipline and self-control are the cornerstones of all success and happiness in life.' And also, 'He that would be healthy, happy, and wise, let him rise early.' "

Mr. Manning looked both surprised and pleased. "Why, yes, I do. So Alexandra has mentioned me, has she?"

"Hundreds of times," Lady Margaret assured him solemnly.

Mrs. Manning joined her husband at that moment. She, too, looked with interest at Lady Margaret. "Is this Lord Brentwood's little girl? What a charming child!"

"Yes, this is Lady Margaret," said Mr. Manning. "I have been telling Alexandra and Lord Brentwood that she ought to have been in bed hours ago."

Mrs. Manning was all concern at once. "Dear me, yes! It is fearfully late, isn't it?" Holding out a hand to Lady Margaret, she said persuasively, "I am sure you must be very tired, my dear. Why don't you take me up to your nursery, and I will help you get ready for bed?"

Lady Margaret solemnly surveyed her a moment, then put her hand in Mrs. Manning's. "All right," she said. Hand in hand, the two went out of the drawing room.

Mr. Manning watched them go with an approving smile.

"Late hours are very bad for children," he told Richard and Alexandra. "And irregular hours are almost as bad as late ones. It would be better if your daughter were on a strict regimen, my lord, with an appointed hour for every activity. Children thrive on regimentation, I have found. Alexandra was raised on a strict regimen, were you not, my dear? And I flatter myself that she has turned out tolerably well."

"I certainly would not quarrel with that statement," said Richard, smiling at Alexandra. "Indeed, sir, if it is your regimen that is responsible for Alexandra's being what she is, then I can only say that its results are wholly admirable."

Mr. Manning, expanding under this flattery, went on to give Richard and Alexandra a great many more pointers on the rearing of children. They both listened politely, but were relieved when he stated that it was time he was seeking his bed. "For it is not only children who thrive on regimentation, you know," he said, waving an admonitory finger at them both. "I myself am extremely regular in my hours of rising and retiring. *'Sanat, Sanctificat, et ditat, surgere mane,'* you know: 'He that would be healthy, wealthy, and wise, let him rise early.' I consider that maxim to be the foundation of good health."

"We know, Uncle Frederick, we know," said Alexandra, laughing. "And Lady Margaret knows it, too. You have already seen for yourself!"

Mr. Manning acknowledged this fact complacently. "Your daughter seems a most intelligent child, my lord," he told Richard. "I was quite impressed by the maturity of her speech. Obviously you have taken pains with the development of her mind. Now we shall only have to see that her physical well-being is tended to with the same degree of care, and then there will be nothing to wish for."

"To be sure," said Richard in a pacifying voice. He waited until Mr. Manning had taken ceremonious leave of the gathering, then turned to Alexandra. "Well, we weathered the storm pretty well, considering," he said. "But I feel badly in need of some fresh air. It's rather cold outside, I know, but not offensively so. If I sent for your cloak, would you object to taking a turn or two in the shrubbery with me?"

"Not at all," said Alexandra. Her cloak was duly sent for, and soon she and Richard were strolling arm in arm down the shadowy length of the shrubbery.

It was a beautiful night, cold and clear, with a sprinkling of stars strewn across a sky of deepest blue. The ground was still snow-covered from the fall on Christmas Eve, but the shrubbery path had been cleared, and Alexandra had no difficulty treading its graveled surface even in her thin evening slippers.

As she walked arm in arm with Richard, she cast glances at the stone bulk of Brentwood looming above her. Frost glittered on its battlemented roof, and its lighted windows cast ruddy patches on the snow-covered ground. Alexandra scanned the house's facade, trying to pick out which was the window of the nursery. Then she laughed aloud. In one of the upper windows a series of tiny lights were appearing, one by one, until at last a tree-shaped silhouette glowing with candles stood revealed against the frosty glass.

"Look, Richard!" she said, pointing upward. "My aunt is lighting the Christmas tree!"

"She is?" said Richard, pausing and turning to look upward also. "Why would she do that?"

"Because your daughter has asked her to," said Alexandra, choking with laughter. "Ever since we put up the tree, Lady Margaret has insisted that the candles be lit for at least a few minutes before going to bed. The plain fact is that neither my uncle nor my aunt, dear souls, can enforce their own excellent rules. They can scold us for letting Lady Margaret sit up late, you observe, but then they themselves let her sit up even later because they cannot deny her a single indulgence!"

Together Alexandra and Richard watched until, one by one, the lights of the tree were finally extinguished and the nursery window was dark once more. "It's easy to see Uncle Frederick and Aunt Elizabeth were very much taken with your daughter," said Alexandra. "If we are not careful, they will shoulder us aside and take charge of her upbringing themselves. And then we may look to see her spoiled completely."

Richard smiled. "I have been very impressed with their previous efforts at child-rearing," he said. "I doubt they would go much astray, even if they did take charge of Margaret's upbringing."

Alexandra shook her head at him. "I have worked too long and hard on your daughter to see my work undone by well-meaning indulgence," she said severely. "You do not know my aunt and uncle as I do, Richard. They mean well, but there are many points where their system of child-rearing needs improvement. You see, I have developed a few theories of my own on the subject over the years."

"I see that you have," said Richard. "I hope your theories do not require that fathers as well as well-meaning steprelatives be excluded from the nursery? I have greatly enjoyed the privilege of taking part in Margaret's day-to-day activities these last few weeks."

Alexandra gave his arm an affectionate squeeze. "Of course not, Richard. Margaret is your daughter, and I would not dream of excluding you from her upbringing. Nor do I mean to wholly exclude Uncle Frederick and Aunt Elizabeth if they truly wish to lend their assistance. I only want to curb their worst excesses until Margaret is past the age of being spoiled." In a thoughtful voice, she added, "Naturally I shall continue to supervise Margaret's education and upbringing, but it did occur to me, Richard, that after we are married, I might find my time a bit too full to act as her full-time governess."

"Much too full," said Richard with emphasis. "It's a lowering admission, but I have been most dreadfully jealous of my own daughter these last ten or twelve weeks. After we are married, I intend that you should give me, if not all your time and attention, at least a good half of it."

"Exactly what I thought," said Alexandra with a satisfied nod. "And that means I will need someone to help me with teaching Margaret. And I had thought—well, you know Miss Harcourt has been expecting all these weeks to take up her position here. It seems rather hard lines on her to tell her now, suddenly, that her services are not needed. Would it be all right if she went ahead and came here as we originally planned? She really does seem to be a most superior girl, and if I am there to smooth the transition I think she and Margaret should work very well together."

"As to that, I am willing to be guided by you," said Richard, smiling. "You know more about governesses and teaching than I do!"

Alexandra acknowledged this statement quite seriously. "I do know about governesses," she said. "And I must say, Richard, that it would be a nice gesture if you paid Miss Harcourt the salary you are paying me now. Being a governess is hard work, and one hundred pounds a year is not any too much to pay the woman who is responsible for the education and upbringing of your children. Besides, if Miss Harcourt had a hundred pounds a year, she might rent a cottage for her mother somewhere near here, and hire a good servant to take care of her. Then she could go and visit her mother on her half-days and holidays and make sure all was going well. It stands to reason that she could do better work if she was not worrying about her mother all the while."

"My dear, it shall be just as you say," said Richard, looking down at his betrothed with tender amusement. "I will pay Miss Harcourt a hundred pounds a quarter if you say so!"

Alexandra laughed, but shook her head. "No, I have a better idea of what a hundred pounds will buy now, and I do not mean to be extravagant. Oh, Richard, how can I make more demands on you when you have been so generous already? To have promised my great-aunt and -uncle to make them an annual visit, and to visit them on our honeymoon, too! Not many men would make such a sacrifice."

"Ah, but my sacrifice was small compared to theirs," said Richard seriously. "I had nothing to begin with, you know, and so to have you to myself any length of time is an improvement on what I had before. But to them, who are accustomed to having you completely to themselves, it must have seemed a hollow bargain at best."

"Rather like what Demeter must have felt, when her daughter was obliged to spend six months of the year in the underworld," said Alexandra mischievously. "You see you stand in the role of Hades, Richard!"

Richard tried to give her a reproving look, failed, and laughed instead. "No, for I have negotiated a much better bargain than Hades did! I am not called on to give up my wife entirely for any length of time, but only to share her attention with others now and then. And that is a bargain I am willing to live with."

Although Richard had been smiling during the first part of this speech, he made the last in a tone of sober simplicity. With equal simplicity, Alexandra answered, "I am glad, Richard." They continued walking down the shrubbery, looking up now and then at the lighted windows of the house above them. There were fewer lighted windows now, and Alexandra pointed this out to Richard in a regretful voice. "I suppose it is time we went inside," she said with a sigh. "But how I hate to see the evening end. What an evening it has been!"

"Never mind," said Richard, patting her arm. "We have

a whole new year ahead of us, in which we can 'live together and be happy,' as my daughter says."

"Yes," said Alexandra, smiling up at him. "A whole new year. And the auspices, on the whole, look very favorable!"

"The First Footing, you mean?" returned Richard with a grin. "With all due respect to the Scottish, I cannot quite bring myself to believe in that sort of superstition. I would rather put my dependence on the good old English tradition of, 'Begin the New Year as you mean to go on.' "

Alexandra shook her head. "I don't think I'm acquainted with that particular tradition, Richard," she said. "How is it practiced?"

"Well, if you are a farmer, you plow a token furrow or two," said Richard, slipping an arm about Alexandra's waist. "If you are a housewife, you do a bit of baking or sewing. And if you are a gentleman who intends to marry, you make sure to kiss your bride-to-be."

"I see," said Alexandra in a voice of enlightenment. She had no time to say more, for the next instant Richard had bent to kiss her. Alexandra returned his kiss with enthusiasm, but when it had gone on for some minutes, she could not resist murmuring mischievously, "I thought you said it was to be a *token* gesture, Richard?"

"This *is* a token gesture," he assured her solemnly. "I intend to be doing a great deal of this in the New Year."

"Then carry on, by all means," said Alexandra, and raised her lips to his once more.

ABOUT THE AUTHOR

Joy Reed lives with her family in the Detroit area. She is the author of six Zebra Regency romances: *An Inconvenient Engagement, Twelfth Night, The Seduction of Lady Carroll, Midsummer Moon, Lord Wyland Takes a Wife,* and *The Duke and Miss Denny.* Joy's newest Regency romance, *Lord Caldwell and The Cat,* will be published in October, 1999. Joy loves to hear from her readers, and you may write to her c/o Zebra Books. Please include a self-addressed stamped envelope if you wish a response.

ROMANCE FROM JO BEVERLY

DANGEROUS JOY   (0-8217-5129-8, $5.99)

FORBIDDEN   (0-8217-4488-7, $4.99)

THE SHATTERED ROSE   (0-8217-5310-X, $5.99)

TEMPTING FORTUNE   (0-8217-4858-0, $4.99)

ROMANCE FROM FERN MICHAELS

DEAR EMILY   (0-8217-4952-8, $5.99)

WISH LIST   (0-8217-5228-6, $6.99)

AND IN HARDCOVER:

VEGAS RICH   (1-57566-057-1, $25.00)

LOOK FOR THESE REGENCY ROMANCES

SCANDAL'S DAUGHTER   (0-8217-5273-1, $4.50)
by Carola Dunn

A DANGEROUS AFFAIR   (0-8217-5294-4, $4.50)
by Mona Gedney

A SUMMER COURTSHIP   (0-8217-5358-4, $4.50)
by Valerie King

TIME'S TAPESTRY   (0-8217-5381-9, $4.99)
by Joan Overfield

LADY STEPHANIE   (0-8217-5341-X, $4.50)
by Jeanne Savery